THE GUNSLINGER'S WIDOW

A. M. VERGARA

The Gunslinger's Widow

By A.M. Vergara

Published by Damocles' Blade Press.

A NOTE ON CONTENT

Some scenes in this book may be upsetting for some readers. A non-exhaustive list of potentially upsetting content may be reviewed at my website for those so inclined: https://www.amvergara.com

For Troy

*"To lose the earth you know for greater knowing;
to lose the life you have, for greater life; to leave
the friends you loved, for greater loving; to find a
land more kind than home, more large than
earth."*

Thomas Wolfe
You Can't Go Home Again

1

My name is Flaka Garcia Hasani Kedar, and it's my fault my husband is dead.

Sure, folks say it weren't my fault, they say it was his own damn fault, but I know better. They tell me that just so as I feel better about that empty spot on the bed next to me, and so as I don't get crushed by that overwhelming guilt when I wake up to an empty house, on top of all the other struggles of running our little patch of land in this godforsaken stretch of desert all by my lonesome. But I ain't stupid. Oliver Kedar would still be alive today if it weren't for me.

Oliver was a good man. I felt that the first time I laid eyes on him—the moment I saw those little crinkles in the corners of his eyelids and knew he was smiling at me from behind that bandana. He was a good man and he liked me. No. He loved me. Oliver loved me. I think he loved me the very first second he looked at me, that broiling hot day in August of 1880, when he rode onto my family's little *hacienda*, scattering chickens in his wake, yelling out for help in a piss-poor mix of Spanish and English.

He pulled up by the house, clouds of dust rising around him as he hauled his big, sweaty bay to a halt. I had been on the porch, husking corn, and I didn't stir. Perhaps I should have. Out here, you never know what's coming when you see that rolling cloud in the distance, but something made me hold still. It were something about the way he rode that horse, like he was born up there, with that lazy, confident grace of his. I could see it from a mile away, long before he galloped into my parents' yard.

He just stared at me for a minute, and I saw that smile in the corners of his eyes, as if he had plum forgotten whatever he had been yelling about a minute before. Then he seemed to remember and glanced over his shoulder, far off into the distance. He jumped down from his horse, tossed the reins over the hitching rail, and came dashing up the steps, stomping with his boots, his spurs jingling. I ain't never forgot the sound of his boots thudding and that jingling, like the bells in that old "One Horse Open Sleigh" song. He came at me holding his arms out wide, as if he were going to herd me back into the house and wanted to stop me from getting past him. I didn't feel afraid then. Somehow I felt safe with Oliver, right from the start. He walked just the same way he rode, with that same lazy easiness.

"Spreckenzie inglés?" he asked.

I laughed at that and then said, "I spreckenzie English, I reckon."

"Oh." His brows knitted across his forehead, just the way I grew to love so much months later, showing his confusion. He didn't know he was mixing Spanish and German, I thought. I suppose he had as much a chance of finding a German speaker on that porch as a Spanish speaker, so perhaps he meant to say it that way. Still, I don't think I've got the look of a German, with my tan skin, my brown eyes, and my wavy black hair. I noticed his voice was low and husky, the kind of quiet voice that sounds like it might break if it's raised any higher. I think that voice of his was the first thing I really loved about him, the first thing that set butterflies fluttering around in my stomach, anyhow. It was so soft and even, like the gentle hiss of golden red embers in a fireplace on a chill winter's night. For a second, just a second, I found myself remembering some tale my older sister Martha had read me years ago at bedtime, about a man in shining armor that had rescued a fair lady from a dragon or some such monster.

"We've got to get inside the house," he was saying. "They're coming. Not a mile behind me."

I stared at him, my mouth dropping open and filling with dust, as will happen in this parched land. I snapped my *boca* shut then, remembering myself, and asked, "Who's coming?"

"The bandits!" he exclaimed, as if I ought to have known. "Are your folks inside?"

"No—" Then I stopped and clamped my mouth shut once more.

I oughtn't to have been speaking like that, telling some strange man that I was alone. My ma had done told me what happened to Mexican girls when a white man found them unprotected. I weren't Mexican, but I sure enough looked it.

"Yes, they're both inside," I finished. 'Twere a bold-faced lie.

The stranger raised one eyebrow and behind the drawn bandana I saw his mouth opening to speak. Then his gaze darted toward the distant mountains, dark and gray against the desert world around them, and I saw a plume of dust coming over the plains, the dust of men riding hard toward us. A lot of men.

The stranger drew his revolver and turned from me to the door of our *casa*, reaching for the cast-iron doorknob.

I jumped right up then, corn husks scattering around me as I lunged forward, blocking him from entering my parents' home.

"You best get outta here," I said. "My pa'll shoot you if you open that door. If those men are coming for you, we don't want no part of that trouble. Best move along afore you get into a world of hurt, mister."

Again those tawny eyebrows shot up. "I don't think your pa is home, *señorita*. And if I leave you here alone those men are liable to 'get *you* into a world of hurt,' as you say. So just let me go inside and barricade the door. You have guns?"

This time I laughed, still putting on a fierce confidence that I didn't feel at all, my gaze darting between the tall, dirt-covered cowboy on my family's porch and the distant riders quickly eating up the distance betwixt us. "We live in the middle of nowhere in Texas, mister. We got a lotta guns and you'll be finding out about what kind of shot we've got in a minute if you don't light outta here real quick, like I done told you to."

He gently pushed me aside and entered the house. I followed him inside, against my better judgment, still scolding him as I walked. I shot one last glance outside. The riders were less than a quarter mile away. The stranger slid the rusty bolt closed and began shoving Ma's big cabinet over to block the entryway. As he hefted his shoulder into the heavy oak, pots and pans toppled from the shelves, and a beautiful red vase my ma had brought up from Chihuahua a few years back fell and shattered into a thousand pieces.

"Now look what you've gone and done!" I cried. "My ma'll skin you alive for that, mister."

"She'll have to skin me dead if we don't block the door," he snapped back and kept shoving the cabinet. After a moment, I heard the clatter of horse hooves in the yard, and a loud voice calling out, and then the crack of a pistol shot and the thunk of a bullet striking the door frame outside. Suddenly I thought better of my reservations and joined the stranger in his labors. At last, combining our strength together, we hefted that enormous oak structure in the way of the door.

The stranger then turned and dashed into the parlor. I

followed, just in time to stop him from breaking out one of the fine glass panes in the window. It had cost Pa a fortune to buy the glass for our windows and I'd be damned if I let some gunslinger from who-the-hell-knows-where come running into our home and bust them out.

"It takes three more seconds just to lift the damn window open!" I hissed at him.

He had been holding one of his pistols by the barrel, about to use the butt of it to break the glass. When I chided him and grabbed his hand, he reluctantly flipped the revolver around to how it should be. I lifted the window and propped a stick from the floor onto the sill to keep it open. Then all the glass exploded, spraying around us as a gunshot rang out from the yard. I let out a little yelping scream as I slammed myself against the wall. Another flurry of shots buried themselves dully in the wood around us. One bullet whistled through the glassless window and struck a painting of some fruits and vegetables. It were one that my oldest sister Rachel had made many years ago, before she'd went off and married Mr. Young and moved all the way up to Denver. Ma was going to be mad as a hornet when she saw this mess.

This stranger, who I had by then decided was either a lawman, like a marshal or some such, or a gunslinger, had let his bandana fall down and I could see his grin. It were a gleeful, impish expression, and aggravating as hell. I glowered back at him, but he didn't seem to mind none. He slid down beside the window and pushed his hat back, showing all that thick tousled hair that gleamed like gold in the afternoon sunshine. Then he popped his head up from below the sill and fired a few shots. I heard a scream of pain somewhere in the yard. The stranger dropped to the floor again and waited as another wave of crackling gunshots sounded outside.

"You said you have guns?" he asked. "Or were you lying about that too, like you lied about your folks being home?"

"Mayhap I ain't got no folks and this is all just my ranch that I keep all by my lonesome," I retorted sharply.

"Then you wouldn't have threatened me with your mama's taxidermy skills." He popped his head up again and fired a few more bullets into the yard.

It was a fair point, I had done exposed myself, despite my best attempts at a clean lie. My older brother and sisters had always done told me that I weren't much good at lying. Keeping low to the floor, I left the parlor and scurried through the hall, across the kitchen, and into my parents' bedroom, where the gun closet stood tall and imposing against the inner wall. The room was nearly pitch dark with the curtains pulled over the windows.

I could still hear the gunfire outside, and there was a dreadful feeling teeming in my gut, the feeling that I was going to die in my own home with this stranger, at the hand of some unknown bandits outside. I opened the closet door and scanned Pa's armory. I hadn't never hunted humans, nor shot them at all in the past, so I weren't sure which would be best agin 'em, but I figured the bigger the better, so I grabbed the Remington, the big ol' coach gun, and the Colt pistol too, leaving the carbine behind, and turned back toward the parlor. Then I thought better of it and grabbed the carbine too. I tried to carry the pile like a heap of wood across my arms, but I couldn't keep them balanced, and they kept slipping and sliding around, like they had come to life and were just bent on aggravating me. I almost dropped the coach gun but managed to get all the weapons back to the stranger, letting them all tumble into a heap beside him as I lost my grasp.

He let out a low whistle, pausing in his firing to survey the weapons.

"I think you weren't lying about how many guns you had here. You have bullets?"

"Damn it!" I cursed, flushed and annoyed that I had done gone and forgot to bring the bullets.

"I'll be right back," I said and turned again to scramble across the wooden floor back to the gun closet in the master bedroom. Before I could leave though, the gunslinger grabbed my arm. My whole body tensed when his strong fingers wrapped around my forearm. Perhaps he did mean to do me harm, just like Ma had warned me. I yanked myself away, my neck and shoulders stiff. Looking back now, it were a foolish notion to have at that moment. There were a whole passel of men firing upon us, hardly the time to be ravishing any woman, no matter how pretty she might be.

"Here," he said simply and placed one of his two pistols in my hand.

He took another careful shot out the window, dropping down just before a bullet flew past us and lodged in the back wall of the parlor. I checked the pistol to make sure it was loaded.

"Why come they chasin' you anyhow?" I asked. If I might get kilt on my way back across the house, I felt I ought to know the reason for it.

"Slept with their leader's wife," he replied, and I frowned. Seeing my face become cross he laughed, took another shot out the window and said, "Alright, that's not the story, but the real story is a bit too long and complicated to divulge while we're under fire. Let's just say that I saw them robbing a stagecoach, recognized a few of them, and I think they'd like to kill me so there's no witnesses to their crime."

I curled my lip. Sure I didn't know what *divulge* meant, but I weren't no fool. There was more to this man's tale than what he was telling. But the gunmen were still shooting at us, so I let the story stay at that and crept back across the floor, through the kitchen and into my parents' room. I clenched the pistol in one hand, holding it close against my side. I had to stand on tiptoes to reach anywhere close to the crate with the bullets that sat atop the gun closet. The loud, heart-stopping cracks of gunshots still filled the air and I was sweating—and not just from the sweltering heat of an August afternoon in southern Texas. I stretched even taller, on my tiptoes, biting my lip, my fingertips still just barely grazing the side of the crate. Behind me, the window glass shattered and I dropped to the ground and waited, breathless and perfectly still.

"Everything okay over there?" called the handsome stranger from the parlor.

"Just fine!" I hollered back and stood up again. This time I left the pistol behind me on the floor so I could use both hands and began jumping up and down, crouching low and then leaping high, grasping for that damned crate and cursing my pa for putting it up so high and my ma for making me so confounded short, and myself for hating buttermilk as a child. My distaste for the stuff was surely why I hadn't grown as tall as my older sisters and my brother.

I coiled my body low on the ground, stretching my right hand up, bracing myself for a final, hopeless leap. I heard the sound of someone behind me, the sound of scraping against the windowpane and a man's voice cursing about something. My heart in my throat and my guts playing some kind of circus contortionist trick, I jumped one more time, putting my everything into that last despairing leap.

My hand struck the side of the crate and knocked it off the top of the closet. Down it came, bullets jingling as they struck the ground all around. It was almost like a musical symphony, I reckon, the pretty metal dings of those bullets striking the wood and each other. I fell back and landed in a sprawling heap on my butt, staring up at the closet, and then around at the mess.

"Well, what do we have here?" I heard a man say from behind me. It was not the gunslinger in our parlor this time. It was someone else, with a rich, clear voice, articulating mighty fine, like a proper, edjicated man. I swiveled around on the floor and froze.

Three men with bandanas over their faces had come

through the shattered glass window behind me while I was trying to get the bullets. They each had a few bleeding scrapes on their hands from wrestling with the broken windowpanes. One was stout and short, so much so I wondered how he had gotten through the window at all; another was wiry and small, but the third, the third was a specimen indeed. He was tall, with sandy red hair that poked out from under his wide-brimmed hat and pale blue eyes that looked somehow familiar. He was broad-shouldered, with muscles that bulged beneath his dusty shirt. A right looker, I fancied, though I couldn't see the lower half of his face. It was he who had spoken, and as I pushed myself backward against the closet, he started toward me. I could feel the pistol on the ground, pressing against my right leg, and as he drew nearer I wrenched it out from under my skirts and pointed it at him.

The redhead paused and raised his hands, one still holding his own revolver, and I could tell he was smiling behind his bandana. His eyebrows lifted up, as if in mock terror, a gleam of laughter in his eyes. I rankled at his amusement and cocked the pistol.

"Now, now, lady, we're not here to hurt you. We're looking for a dangerous gunslinger you've got holed up in your house. You wouldn't want to obstruct an officer of the law, would you?"

I shook my head, my mind racing. A dangerous gunslinger? Could that handsome young fellow in the parlor be lying to me after all? Could he be running from the law, rather than from stagecoach robbers? My instinct had told me he was being honest, but Ma always told me I was too damn trusting.

"I don't see no badge," I said, keeping my gun pointed directly at the redhead's chest, annoyed that he didn't seem more afraid of my menacing him with that gun.

"Oh, well, we had to chase that man right out of Fort

Davis. I didn't have time to grab my badge from my desk, I'm afraid."

"What'd he do?" I pressed.

"Why, he raped and killed a girl just about your age, and about your size. Left her dead, bloody body for her mama to find."

I took in a breath sharply and slowly breathed it out, reeling from this revelation. I think my hand wavered with that pistol and the redhead took another step toward me. I inhaled a slow, deep breath, steadying my hand, and he stopped.

"Why should I believe you?" I asked.

"Why would I lie?" he replied, and he was again grinning behind that bandana.

"So I don't kill you," I snarled back. Stupid question.

"You wouldn't kill me, don't you know who I am?" asked the redhead, and I saw the masked men behind him were grinning as well, the lines around their eyes crinkling. "Now, come on, why don't you be reasonable and put that gun down, and then let's just go and kill that bad man you've let in your house before he hurts you."

"Kill him? What about arrestin' him? Ain't that what an officer of the law should be doin'?"

Out of the corner of my eye I thought I saw a movement in the kitchen. The gunslinger, or rapist and murderer, depending on who you believed, must've been coming to help me. He must've removed his spurs because he didn't make a sound.

"Of course we'll arrest him, but he raped and murdered a young woman, you really think he's fit to stand trial? A scumbag that would do a thing like that?" asked the redhead. His voice had become soothing, like he was talking to a little child, and still he kept easing forward, reaching slowly toward my hand.

I darted a glance toward the kitchen, where I saw another

flash of movement. Then the redhead jolted forward, lunging toward me, his hand snatching at my pistol. I pulled that trigger as fast as I've ever done anything in my whole life and the revolver jerked in my hand as it fired. I think, for a second, there was a look of surprise on what I could see of the redhead's face, and then he crumpled into a bloody heap on my skirt.

The stranger who had started this entire mess burst into the room, his gun barrel barking flames with how damn fast he was firin'. The two men behind the fallen redhead both darted out the window. I think the gunslinger wounded one of them, but they both made it out of the house alive. I shoved the redhead's body off me and followed the stranger to the door. In the yard, the remaining bandits were throwing themselves into their saddles and lighting off, just as fast as they'd come.

"Damn," I said softly. I was still holding the pistol and my skirt was still covered in blood. I must've looked a real sight. When the gunslinger turned back to me I pointed that weapon directly at him. "That man I kilt told me you done raped and murdered a young'un, a girl my age, back in Fort Davis. He said he was chasin' you for the crime. Said he was a lawman."

"He was lying," replied the gunslinger coolly and holstered his pistol, raising his hands. "But I'm not sure there's anything I can say that will prove that to you. So, if you believe him, you can go ahead and shoot me, or take me prisoner and take me to a real lawman in Fort Davis, if you like. They'll tell you it's a lie."

"I'll . . ." My mind was racing. I didn't know who to believe, or if I should believe anyone. If the man I'd kilt was right, then I had gone and murdered a lawman—in self-defense, yes, but a lawman nevertheless, and one who'd identified himself to me as such before I went and shot him. Furthermore, I couldn't have a rapist and a murderer on my hands, alone out here with just me. Ma and Pa would be home soon, of that I was sure. They had left early yesterday for Fort Stockton, where my pa often went to preach on his itinerant circuit. But Ma and Pa weren't home yet, and I had to make up my own mind what to do with this man, and whether or not to trust him. I straightened my shoulders and puffed my chest out. "There's a shed in the back. It's for chickens, but they're out for now, scrapin' in the yard. I'm gonna put you in there till my pa gets home. He'll know what to do. But I need you to drop that gun belt, mister, and any other weapons you got on you."

He slowly undid the gunbelt and let it fall, then lifted his hands again. "I don't have any other weapons, ma'am."

"Don't 'ma'am' me," I retorted. "Turn around and walk nice and easy, and keep your hands where I can see them."

He turned around, and then I saw the dark maroon stain on the back of his shirt. I hadn't noticed it before, and I think I took in a breath real sharp. He had only taken a few steps but he stopped at the sound.

"What's wrong?"

"You been hit," I replied.

He shrugged. "It's nothing. Barely feel it."

I frowned at him, my conscience churning with indecision. Ma and Pa wouldn't want me to lock an injured man in the chicken coop. Pa was a preacher, for God's sake, and helping the injured was something I'd done heard him preach about a time or twelve. Something about some Samaritan or other . . . goats and sheep too . . . least of these. It was all a muddle in my mind, but I knew what Pa thought about helping the hurt. Ma was all kindness too, with any injured creature, animal or human. Then I remembered what the redheaded man had told me, and I swallowed hard and clenched my jaw.

"Good. We can look at it later, when Ma and Pa get home," I said, pulling my shoulders back, trying to be firm and fierce. "Walk on now, toward that chicken coop over yonder. No funny business."

I made him crawl in through the *pollo*-sized door into the coop, scraping his body through the narrow entry, slithering in the dirt like a snake. He did gasp, just a tiny bit, when his left side, where the injury was, rubbed against the frame. There was a streak of blood on the chipped white paint of the chicken house when he finally disappeared inside. He scared a few hens out, and I closed up the door and latched it on the outside. I couldn't imagine how hot it was in there, but I forced myself not to feel guilty about it. I didn't know if I could trust him. I couldn't afford to take any risks. I didn't know who he was. That redhead I had gone and kilt told me he was a murderer and, worse than that, a ravisher of women. If the redhead had been right, then my prisoner was the worst kind of monster you could find—even out here in our lawless world. Raping and killing young women, that just wouldn't do at all. So I had to lock him in there. Ma and Pa would know what the best thing to do was when they got home.

I turned to survey our farm with a sigh. The yard was a disaster. Looked as if a cyclone had struck our little spread. The gunslinger's horse still stood in front of the porch. She had caught her breath from her mad run, but she was still in a hot lather, her head hanging low. The hoofprints all around her showed how nervous she'd been when caught in the crossfire between the bandits and my prisoner. There were four bodies laid out, scattered around in the yard—the work of the gunslinger now imprisoned in the chicken coop. I made my way among them, checking for any signs of life, but they were all dead as doornails. Just like the man I'd kilt. I couldn't quite bring myself to go back inside and look at that particular corpse.

The idea that I'd gone and kilt the wrong man was tearing me up inside. I didn't want to look at his face under that bandana or check him for any identifying papers in his pockets, or, heaven forbid, the portrait of his sweetheart that might be crumpled up in there. I didn't want to know who he was before. Now, thanks to me and my itchy trigger finger, he weren't nothin' more than a corpse.

No, I sure as hell didn't feel good about having shot a man. I'd never done it before, and it didn't sit easy with me. Like locking a wounded man up in a chicken coop didn't sit easy with me. But I didn't have much of a choice in all this. It weren't my fault that bastard rode onto our farm that day pursued by bandits. None of this were my fault.

I didn't know what else to do in that big old mess, so I went out to the family plot about a hundred yards from the house, the place where we had buried my grandma and two of my sisters that didn't make it past infancy, and I started digging. I was going to need five man-sized holes and that was going to take a long while and a lot of work. Pa would probably want to ride in to get Sheriff Oversby before we buried the men, but either way, we were going to need five man-sized holes at some point.

Digging in the dirt with the old shovel was doing something, and simply doing something, anything, kept me from reliving in my head that conversation I had with the redhead before I shot him. It distracted me from that terrible feeling of knowing I had done kilt a man. It was s'posed to be easy when it were done in self-defense, just kill or be kilt, no choice in the matter. That young gunslinger had sure made killing look easy. I didn't fancy he was lying over there in that chicken coop being eaten alive with guilt, but here I was, just diggin' and diggin' and diggin', and trying to bury the memories of that wild, horrific afternoon in the steadily growing heap of dirt next to the grave I was making.

II

I HAD DUG ONE *TUMBA* BIG ENOUGH FOR A MAN AND WAS working on the second when Ma and Pa finally got home. I was so dad-blamed focused on the work I was doing and on avoiding thinking about the redhead that I didn't even hear them ride in on the wagon. Our old ranch dog, Blossom, had up and died in March, after eleven years of dragging dead animals onto the farm and barking to alert us when folks approached, and I think Ma was so heartbroken over the loss of that flea-bitten old animal that she couldn't bring herself to ask any of our neighbors for a new pup. But we needed a dog, or at least a burro, some animal to warn us before gunslingers like the man in the chicken coop came galloping onto the ranch. Without Blossom, or any other watchdog or burro to give an alarm, I didn't know Pa was home until I heard his voice, shrill with worry, calling my name from the porch.

"Flaka! Flaka! Where are you? Flaka!"

I straightened up, feeling the fierce ache in my back, shoulders, and neck, my every muscle begging me to put up that darn shovel and stop working altogether. There was another soreness I could feel, somewhere deep in my chest, more of a throbbing weight than the tearing, overworked pain of the other muscles. I pressed against the ribs to try to soften the ache, but it did nothing. I clambered out of the hole I was digging—about three feet deep at that point—and scurried across the yard.

"Pa! I'm over here, Pa!" I hollered.

Pa was sweaty and his round, serious face was bright scarlet from screaming for me. When he saw me, I swear he relaxed from his shiny bald pate to the soles of his feet, deflating the way a cow's udder wilts when she's milked. He ran at me and gathered me up in his arms like I was a little girl again, squeezing so tight I couldn't hardly breathe. The pressure of his arms around me made that ache in my chest ease a little. Finally he gripped my shoulders and held me at arm's length, his eyes running over me, looking for any injuries. His high forehead was all creased with wrinkles as he studied me. I think in the time he had been looking for me in that yard full of bodies, he had aged a dozen years, at least. I heard Ma running toward us from the house too, calling my name.

My ma had come from Mexico, while my pa was a preacher, from someplace called the Balkans—so he said, anyway. I don't rightly know where nor what the Balkans are. Pa had migrated to this godforsaken land when he was a young'un and he'd been farming *la tierra muerta* and riding his preaching loop for as long as I could remember. In all those years, through all those struggles of working the land and preaching, I don't think I'd ever seen him look so worried in my whole life. Both Ma and Pa treated me like a little child still—like their baby—but I was coming up on one and twenty.

Pa relinquished me into Ma's arms when she reached us, and she squeezed me too, just as tight as Pa had before. But the instant she let go I felt that pain returning to my chest, that strange, heavy agony that I didn't understand.

"Tarnation, girl!" exclaimed Pa. He had an accent from his youth in those Balkan mountains he was always talking about, though sometimes I thought he had lost a lot of the language of his childhood, living in Texas so long and not using it. Still, when he was upset, sometimes little snatches of that tongue would burst out of him, words I didn't understand. "*Roftsh sa malet*! Scared the living daylights out of me, you did! Place is full of dead men and you nowhere to be found. I thought someone had gone and taken you away, I did. Scared me to death, I'm telling you, girl."

"I'm sorry, Pa, I was digging to bury them over there." I jerked my head toward the family plot.

"*Obobo!* You meant to bury these men in the family plot, did you?" Pa scoffed, then his face softened as he studied me again. "It's alright, it's alright now," he whispered and wrapped his arms around me again, kissing my temple hard. "You just scared me is all, my Flaka girl, you scared me. I'm so glad you're not hurt. What even happened here?"

"Gunslinger done came ridin' in from the north, and behind him a bunch of bandits. We fought them off together. I didn't kill these ones out here, the gunslinger did, but I—" I swallowed hard. "I kilt one of 'em, the one inside the house."

Ma's tan face paled. "I saw him," she whispered. "Did he hurt you?"

They were both looking at the stain of dark brown blood on my skirt, but I shook my head fiercely. "Not a hair on my head, Ma, I promise. I ain't hurt. This ain't my blood."

"I swear I'll never be leaving you alone out here again. *Me frikove*! I swear it," proclaimed Pa, and the way he clung to me, I thought he meant not only to never leave me alone again but perhaps to never let go of me again neither. Pa continued babbling as he squeezed me tight. "Just a month back the Hasletts lost their boy Clement to a group of blasted marauders. We shouldn't have gone off and left you here alone, Flaka. *A e merr vesh c'të thom?* We shouldn't be doing that, not ever. We've got to be getting ourselves a hired hand. Someone to keep this place safe whenever I'm out there preaching. Either that or we'll just have to be locking up, take Flaka with us, and be leaving the place untended when I'm going out on the circuit."

"We don't have money for a hired hand," replied Ma, her eyes weary. If Pa looked like he'd aged a dozen years in the last hour, Ma looked as though she had aged a hundred since I'd last seen her. Her dark eyes were careworn, her face drawn, her cheeks hollow, all the wrinkles on her beautiful *cara* standing out, and perhaps even a few more white hairs had appeared, mixed in with the sleek black on her head.

"I'll be earning money for it, I will!" cried Pa.

"Then you'll have to leave to earn that money," returned Ma, her face still serious as hell.

"I'll talk to Ian Marcus about this. I'll tell him everything, I will. He could spare me a hand for a few weeks, I'm sure of it, on credit, for our friendship's sake, really. He'd do that for me. He would. I'll be spreading my circuit, going into Mexico, even as far as the Arizona Territory, I tell you, whatever I have to do. You can translate for me down in Mexico, Rosa. I'll be earning enough, I swear I will. *A e merr vesh c'të thom?* We'll get a hired hand. This won't be happening again, not ever. Not as long as I'm drawing breath, you hear me? Never again."

Ian Marcus was our mayor, the mayor of Acantilados, the loose alliance of ranches, both big and small, that we considered to be our town, some dozen miles south of Fort Davis. Marcus was a big man with red hair, always friendly when I had met him. I think he and Pa came out west on the same train and the same coaches many years back. Long before Pa met Ma, and afore any of us were born. The two of them, Pa and Marcus, had always been particular friends, though Marcus was much too busy the last few years to come visiting. He still made time for Pa whenever he could. I don't think I'd seen him since I was maybe ten or eleven, but Pa met with him at the little saloon up the way now and again. Pa wasn't one to ask favors of Marcus—or anyone really, but especially not of his well-to-do mayor friend. My pa had always been too proud to ask for help, even when we desperately needed it. He really was worried as hell about me.

Pa was still reeling from the horror of what had happened on our little ranch in the middle of nowhere. I could see him calculating in his head how long it would take to ride in for the sheriff and whether or not he should do it now or wait until tomorrow. Someone would need to know about this— that we'd been attacked by bandits and five of them were dead on our property. It would need an official report of some sort, else we might find ourselves in a wagonload of trouble, 'specially if'n the families of these robbers came by looking for them. I weren't too worried about that, though; robbers didn't usually have much for families. Still, Pa was a respectable preacher in this region, and he would need to be honest and open about what had happened, just to maintain his preaching circuit and stop rumors before they got started.

"Bless me," whispered Pa, his eyes wide, studying the dead men in the dust. "*Përse s'je martuar akoma?* I wish I had gone ahead and married you off to that Miller boy that came asking. I wish that so much."

"You know I hated that boy," I replied and almost laughed. Not a cheerful laugh, I just felt like I needed to laugh, like if I didn't laugh or cry or something then my heart was liable to burst right out of my chest. My whole body was a kettle, fixin' to boil over at any second. I didn't laugh properly, though, I just let out a strangled, coarse sound. The boiling water inside me still roiled; that half-guffaw was just a little steam escaping.

"I know. Still, at least then you'd be safe and away with a husband somewhere else, not here. There's been a lot of trouble in the last few months around Fort Davis and Acantilados, you know. I'm hearing stories about bandits and killers everytime that I'm going into town, and then there's that business with the Clement boy getting murdered. It's . . . it's a bit late to try to ride in for Sheriff Oversby right now, isn't it? But I can head out first thing tomorrow, *në dritën e parë*—at first light. Maybe we can pile these bodies up, over by the grave plot, and cover them with tarps. Hopefully that would be keeping the coyotes off of them, just for tonight. Then we can show the sheriff tomorrow afternoon, before we bury them. That would work, I'm thinking."

"We could load 'em up in the wagon and take 'em into town," suggested Ma. "That might be the best thing. Let the sheriff sort it out with the bodies. I think I'd rather that than to put 'em in the ground next to our own kin."

I wanted to protest because I'd spent about three hours digging by that point, and didn't want all my *trabajo duro* to go for nothing, but Pa nodded after a moment's thought.

"Aye, I reckon that'd be the best thing," he said, wiping a hand over his shiny, sweaty forehead. "We'll be piling them in the wagon and I'll be taking all five of them in tomorrow and talking to the sheriff. Why don't you and Flaka go and drag the one from inside out here and I'll try to get these ones loaded up on the wagon while you're bringing him out?"

Me and Ma went inside. It was my first time seeing the man since I'd done gone and kilt him. Ma rolled him over, his listless eyes staring all sightless-like up at our ceiling, the bandana still fixed around his face. It felt like a rattlesnake was coiled in my belly, its body vibrating and tail shaking like mad. For a moment I just stared at the man before reaching down to grab his arm, struggling alongside Ma to drag his hardening body. The snake in my belly struck then, and I lurched to the window and chucked out into the yard, just next to the porch. As I kept heaving until there was nothing left, I felt Ma rubbing my back, just below my shoulder blades, and whispering gently in Spanish.

"Está bien, mi amor. Todo está bien."

I shuddered and turned back from the window, wiping my cotton sleeve over my mouth, yellow and orange vomit smearing across the faded green of the fabric. I was a sight, I knew that, covered in blood and now vomit. My black hair looked like a dust devil had done rolled across my head, leaving my already wavy and unruly hair in a terrible disarray. Worse than normal. I had unmanageable waves of hair, always difficult to control, always unkempt, unlike my mother's perfect, smooth hair, so shiny and beautiful.

"Todo no está bien," I replied and shook my head. I spoke pretty poor Spanish for the daughter of a Mexican, like a child, but enough to get by. We spoke English in the house, because Pa had come from the mountains of Europe and Ma from just south of Chihuahua and neither spoke the other's native tongue. I was the youngest, as well, so Ma's energy to teach her children her language had about dried up by the time I came along. "I kilt a man, Ma. I kilt him dead."

"I know," she crooned and took my thick, manlike hand in her smaller, dainty one, clenching me tight with her worn fingers. "But he would've killed you, Flaka, or worse. I'm glad you killed him. I'm so glad."

A little of the tightness in my stomach eased, and that rattler finally began to uncoil. I went back to the body, trying hard not to look at those staring eyes that I had made sightless. I took one of his pale, bluing hands, and together we dragged him out into the yard. I had to stop after the thunks of his body going down the steps of the porch. I retched again, but there weren't nothin' left inside to throw up by then. Once I'd recovered, we dragged him the rest of the way to the wagon. Pa was strong, but he was a short, potbellied man, a preacher, not a cowhand, and he had only managed to get the smallest of the men into the wagon. He turned to us, and I thought for a second he was going to faint. His beet-red face turned pale as a ghost, his eyes growing again wide and round and frightened.

"Hold on," he said before Ma and I could attempt to lift the man into the wagon. He reached down, his hands trembling, and pulled that bandana off the dead redhead's face. "Goddamn it," he whispered through clenched teeth, and rubbed his eyes and shook his head. "God fucking damn it!" he exclaimed again.

"Jozef," my ma said, her voice low and scolding, but also apprehensive. I had never heard Pa swear before, not once, and going off Ma's face, she hadn't neither.

"I'm sorry, Rosa, but God fucking damn it all to hell," he replied, shaking his head. "That's Grant Marcus."

"Grant Marcus?" I asked, not liking having to learn the name of the man I'd kilt.

"Ian's son. This is Ian Marcus' only son—*i shtrenjti i tij i vogël*," replied Pa, and in the two minutes since he'd seen the body, I thought he had grown ancient, like Methusaleh in them old stories from Genesis. "My God. You killed the mayor's son, Flaka. What will we be doing about this? Did anyone see you shoot this man?"

"Two of them that was with him saw it, then they ran," I said. "They got clean away."

"They'll tell Marcus you did it," said Pa, his voice strained and quiet, a whisper I could barely hear. He seemed to sag, reaching out to hold the wagon for support. "They'll tell Marcus you've gone and killed his boy."

"In self-defense!" cried Ma. "It'll be hard, but I'm sure Marcus will understand, eventually."

Pa was just shaking his head. "*Kjo është marrëzi!* He won't be understanding this, Rosa. My God, Rosa, he'll kill Flaka. He'll kill her. For sure he will. Nothing has ever been so sure."

"How could he? She's barely more than a girl. She was just defending herself."

"He'll be killing her," replied Pa gravely. "Just as soon as he finds out he'll be heading here to kill her, sure as the sun shines. You don't know Marcus like I do. He'll not be resting till Flaka's dead, Rosa. I promise you. *Është tmerr*! He would travel all the way to hell and back to kill anyone that touched his son. And you say two men got away that saw you did it? Christ. He'll be heading this way before midnight, as soon as those men reach him. What'll we do? There's nowhere here we can be hiding her from him. There's nowhere we can be getting her to tonight that would be a safe distance from here."

I stared in horror at the body of that man I'd kilt, that man who had been living a few hours ago, that man called Grant Marcus. I stared at his face, his mouth slightly agape, his tongue blackening already in that sweltering Texas heat, flies buzzing around his eyes. I didn't know what horrified me more, knowing the name of the man I'd put to death or the knowledge of the danger I was in now. I knew Marcus was a ruthless man. I knew it from the stories I'd heard in the valley over the years. Yes, he was a particular friend of Pa's, and yes, he was nice enough in person to his friends and their families, but I knew he hunted down and kilt the men that crossed him. He was a powerful man, as powerful as anyone could be out here in the wild deserts, and Pa was right, he would not rest as long as his only son's killer was alive. I had made myself the target of the most powerful, most ruthless man for hundreds of miles, and there couldn't be no escaping from his avenging hand.

"I'll leave. I'll head south. I'll go down to Chihuahua maybe and find Ma's people, our kin down there."

"You barely speak a lick of Spanish. What are you going to do in Mexico?" replied Ma. I could see she had not yet come to terms with the inescapable consequences of my actions. The sun was getting low on the horizon, sending long orange beams across the land, making the shadows stand up tall all around us, and darkening the lines in my mother's craggy, sun-worn face. "Surely if we just talk to Marcus, if we make him understand that it was self-defense, he won't do anything. In a trial they would let her off for sure."

"Ian Marcus owns this valley, he owns the sheriff, he owns the deputies, he owns the banks, he owns the churches, he owns every person that lives here, Rosa. Every person for more than a hundred miles is afeared—afeared to death, I tell you—of Ian Marcus. We can try to be convincing him that it was all self-defense, that Flaka was fearing for her life, but that's going to take weeks and if, in the meanwhile, he sees Flaka—*ai do ta bëjë veten për Zot*—he'll execute her himself. He won't bother waiting for a trial. Flaka has to be leaving here and she has to be somewhere far away before dawn comes. Long before dawn comes."

"Then I'll leave. I'll go to Chihuahua, like I said. I'll be just fine," I said, my voice sounding firmer and more sure than I felt. "I know how to survive out there. You done taught me everything I need to know to get by in the desert by myself."

"Fuck," whispered Pa, and Ma and I both flinched at another swear from the fussy, sweet little preacher man we'd never known to curse before.

"I can protect her," said another voice, a low, husky, smooth voice, seemingly coming from nowhere.

I leaped back, thinking for a second the voice had come from the corpse lying stiff on the ground. But the dead man kept staring sightlessly into the sky. Then I remembered, in another rush of mad guilt, the man I had locked away in the chicken coop, probably cooking alive as we talked and fretted outside.

"Who's that?" asked Pa, his eyes darting around the ranch yard. I thought if another thing startled Pa he would die from the tension.

"The gunslinger!" I cried. "That's the gunslinger who helped me when these men attacked. It's the man they were chasing. He's shut up in the coop."

Before either Ma or Pa could speak, I darted across the yard to the chicken coop and undid the latch, lifting the door wide and hooking it to a rusty eye in the wood above. Pa grabbed up the shotgun from the bench of the wagon and raised it, pointing at the little square of darkness from which my gunslinger emerged, slowly and painfully. He had taken his bandana off, and his shirt was half unbuttoned. The entire left side of his body was a mass of dried and damp blood. There was chicken scat smeared on his trousers and shirt, and feathers clinging to his hair. He looked a good deal paler than when I had first met him, like a ghost. Another twinge of guilt tore through my chest and I winced at the sight of the man as he gingerly stood to his feet, reaching out one hand to steady himself against the coop, lifting the other in acknowledgment of the gun my pa was pointing at him.

"And just who are you?" asked Pa gruffly.

"Nobody, sir, nobody in particular. But it was my fault your daughter was ever in any danger, and it was my fault she shot Grant Marcus. And I fancy her safety is my responsibility now. These men were chasing me and I rode onto your peaceful little spread here and brought all this upon you and your lovely family."

"Why were these men chasing you in the first place?" Pa demanded.

"I saw them robbing a stagecoach, about a dozen miles or so up the way. They meant to kill me, as I was the only witness. They were trying to destroy any evidence against themselves, I assume," the gunslinger replied calmly. He spoke in a polished way, with that soft, low voice, a voice that ignited a strange sensation in me, a warmth in my core and a yearning in my chest.

"And why would we trust you to look out for our daughter?" asked Ma.

"I haven't hurt her yet, have I?"

There was a moment of silence. It was not exactly a convincing promise of safety.

"You're going to have to do better than that, *a e merr vesh c'të thom?*" replied Pa. "Why should we be trusting you, a man we know nothing about, who came riding onto our property bringing trouble and death behind him? Why should we be trusting you, of all people, to be protecting our daughter? If you think I'll be sending my daughter away with some gunslinger we don't know who came riding up in a flurry with some half-baked story about being a witness to a robbery and then went and killed men on our ranch, then you must be having a real low opinion of our intelligence."

The gunslinger chuckled a little at that, and it appeared to take him a few minutes to make sense of my pa's peculiar way of speaking and accent. Finally the stranger's face hardened, becoming sad and thoughtful again, and he said, "I don't know that you have much of a choice, sir. And I say that with all due respect. You're not wrong about the kind of man Ian Marcus is. He will hunt your daughter down and he will kill her. But I can protect her, and I'm offering to do so."

The gunslinger looked as if he was about to faint, but his voice was convincing, gentle and firm. I found myself remembering again the look on his face when he reached the porch, how he stared at me in admiration, but not the leering sort of expression that the redhead's henchman had gaped at me with. Not the look of a man about to poke a prize whore he had bought. His look had been different. It had been respectful, and amused, but respectful, more than anything. It was intuition, and I knew I was too trusting. I knew my intuition might be wrong, but I had always been one to trust my gut.

"He's right," I said suddenly, and both my parents looked 'round at me in surprise. "What other choice do we have? I can either ride off alone or I can ride off with him, but I can't stay here, and you can't run away with me. I was defending myself, but Marcus ain't gonna believe that. What else can we do? I ain't afraid to ride off alone, but it would be better if I went with him. He can shoot, Pa. He can shoot real good, I saw him."

"*Ke humbur mendtë*! You must be crazy, girl. I can't be sending you off with this stranger. One defenseless young woman alone with this man in the wilds of Texas? Where will you be taking her?"

"I've got my sights set on a plot of land and a little house out in the Arizona Territory, about two weeks' ride from here. I finally have enough saved up to purchase it. That's where I was heading before I encountered these men. She'll be safe with me, and safe when we get there."

"I can't let you be going with this man, Flaka. I don't know anything about him, nothing at all," Pa insisted, still shaking his head. "There's got to be another way."

"Marry us," I said, still looking admiringly at the tall gunfighter, with his set jaw scattered with just a few sprigs of golden scrub, tawny blond hair carpeting his scalp, his striking blue eyes, and the tight creases of pain above his pale cheeks.

The jaws of everyone else present dropped open. It took a good few moments of silence before Pa tried to sputter something out, but he had reverted back to his old tongue in his shock and no one there knew what he said. I guess he hadn't forgotten the language of his childhood.

I interrupted him. "Think about it, Pa. You been dreamin' about marryin' me off for three years now. You've tried a time or ten and I ain't liked none of the boys you've tried to match me with. This man has a house and a plot of land in mind, and money saved up to buy it. You can't go lettin' your daughter wander in the desert with a stranger, it ain't right. It ain't moral. People would think I was a whore or something. But if we're married it ain't no thing for us to travel together. You're a preacher, Pa, just say the words and that's it."

Pa's mouth hung open for another minute, and when he

finally spoke it was just sputtering. *"Kjo s'bëhet* . . . but, what? I . . . I can't . . . I don't know . . . it wouldn't be . . . there isn't a way . . . *po më ikën mendtë* . . ."

"It's alright, Pa, trust me," I said, trying to sound soothing, trying to use that tone of voice you've got to keep when a horse gets tangled in a wire and you've got to make him calm to cut him out.

The gunslinger was leaning hard against the chicken coop by then, sagging, really, more than leaning. His face had become so white it might have been a cloud. He didn't look opposed to the idea of marrying me, his eyebrows rising, a faint smile on his pain-wrinkled face. He just seemed surprised by the proposition. He was looking less and less aware of the world around him. He weren't even sweating anymore by that point, and I reckoned that was my fault. I had done left him in that boiling hot coop, bleeding out of his side, without any water or bandages, for hours.

"She's right, I'll take care of her. Married or not, I'll keep her safe," he whispered, so soft I almost didn't hear him. Then the gunslinger fainted, his eyes rolling back in his head as he slumped to the ground outside the chicken coop. Ma and I both raced forward as his lashes fluttered and he came to again, but he still seemed barely conscious. His lips were dry and cracked, and he groaned faintly when I reached down to feel his side where the wound was.

"I'll get him some water," said Ma and darted away, returning a few seconds later with a cup of warm water that he guzzled greedily, like a man who hadn't tasted liquid in days.

I unbuttoned his shirt the rest of the way while Ma helped him with the cup. The wound had grazed the flesh along his left rib cage, under his arm, leaving a deep furrow. He had tried to wedge his bandana into it. The bullet hadn't gone in too deep, though I could see the white bone of one of his ribs, exposed where the flesh and muscle had been torn away. That rib had a little crack through it, I thought. It buckled a bit each time he breathed. Ma took the water away from his lips, though he reached weakly to stop her. She drizzled the little bit that was left over the wound, making bright red blood start to seep from it again as she washed away the clots. It had bled a lot, but it didn't look as if it would finish him, not a man like this, anyhow.

Pa was still standing over us with that look of blank disbelief on his face. "You can barely stay conscious, boy. You can barely stand. You think I'll be letting you escort my daughter across the desert, or let you be marrying her? You think I'm an idiot? How will you be protecting her?" he asked at last.

"Give me a gun," whispered the stranger with that silky, low voice of his. In his injured, fainting state, his voice was lower even than before. His brows were knitted tight, his lips pursed, as if working hard not to show us how much that wound hurt him.

Before Pa could stop me I ran across the yard and grabbed up the Mexican loop belt I had made the man drop, bringing it to him. There were only a few bullets left in the leather casings. It was an exceptionally nice belt, or it had been once —now it was worn, the leather soft in my hands. Pa tried to grab my arm, but I thrust the belt into the young man's hands. So fast I could hardly believe it, he plucked the gun from the holster and fired it, a resounding crack sounding through the air. As the puff of smoke rose above us, we all turned to follow the line of the barrel. One of our hens, about fifty paces away, was standing headless, not yet aware that she was dead. The gunslinger holstered the weapon as the chicken's body took a few more steps and then fell.

"Eat her for dinner tonight," said the gunslinger. "And while you eat, know that your daughter is going to be safer with me than she would be with anyone else in all of Texas."

Pa blinked, looking between the two of us in shock for a long moment and then back at the body of the hen. For a few moments he sputtered, then he drew his shoulders back, took a few deep breaths, and asked, "What's your name, boy?"

"Oliver Kedar," answered the young man, and I thought when I heard it that I'd never heard a more beautiful name in all my life.

"Repeat after me, then," said Pa. "I, Oliver Kedar, take you, Flaka Garcia Hasani, to be my lawful wedded wife."

"I, Oliver Kedar, take you, Flaka Garcia Hasani, to be my lawful wedded wife."

"To have and to hold . . ."

Within a few minutes we were married. I had Pa just add Kedar to my last names, which were getting to be quite a few now. Hopefully I didn't never have to marry again and add another. In Mexico the ma's name comes last I heard, but I guess Ma and Pa had thought the Pa's last name ought to come last in Texas. Once our vows were finished, Pa went inside to draw up an official paper for it, and Ma and I dressed my new husband's wound. Once Oliver was bandaged, and had drank more water, and had just a tiny bit more color in his cheeks, we packed for the journey right quick. We didn't need much else aside from some food, a little spare clothes, some cooking utensils, an old Colt Sidehammer that Pa insisted I carry, and my harmonica, though I didn't really think there would be time to play on the run. Most of the things we packed onto my plump pony Butterball as Oliver's saddlebags were already stuffed to bursting. Oliver—whose clothes were drenched in blood—and I both put on some old clothes that had belonged to my brother Ephraim. The pants, made for a man's narrow hips, hugged me tight around my butt and had to be rolled up at the bottom, but they would do alright, I reckoned, for a long, hard ride—better than a skirt anyway.

Pa insisted over and over that Oliver take care of me. He must have made him promise it a thousand times and swear it on everything that was holy, and Oliver obliged, without showing any qualms. Pa promised to work on Ian Marcus, getting him to accept that what I had done I had done only in self-defense. Pa insisted he didn't want the address we were goin' to, but just the nearest town. He told me he would send word as soon as it was safe for me to be seen again in this valley that had always been my home. Before the last shred of light had faded in the west, Oliver and I were riding away from the ranch where I had lived my whole life. The sun cast a deep red glow over the house, farmland, the yard, and the barn, giving it all a dreamlike quality. As I looked at that place, where I had spent all my life, a strange twisting sensation churned in my stomach, like the feeling you get after drinking sour milk.

I could hardly believe it. That morning when I had woken up I would never have imagined the day ending as it had, with me a wanted woman, riding away with my husband, a gunslinger from God knows where, as the bright orange star in the sky disappeared behind the mountains, throwing long shadows behind us as we rode west, into that setting sun. I remember glancing back over my shoulder at the ranch I loved, to see the comforting gleam of lamps in the windows, to catch that last scent of boiling chicken filling the air, and to hear the lonesome call of a coyote down by the crick, howling as my home faded from view. With that sick feeling of dread in my gut, I wondered if I would ever lay eyes on that place, or my parents, again.

███

WE RODE ALMOST ALL THAT NIGHT, NOT SPEAKING, EACH LOST IN our own thoughts. I expected to feel regret at what I'd done. It were utter foolishness. I remembered the words that Grant Marcus had spoken, the accusations he'd made against this man called Oliver, but I didn't believe it. I couldn't. I had judged Oliver the moment I laid eyes on him, and I had judged Grant Marcus the second I saw him too, and I ain't never been one to change my mind easy—not once I think I know who someone is. Ma used to quote the Bible about it— she would say, "Faith the size of a mustard seed can move a mountain, or so Jesus said, but I think it would take faith the size of a mountain to move Flaka Garcia Hasani." She was wrong. I don't know how much faith it would take to move me once I've gone and made up my mind, but I don't think a mountain would even be a drop in that ocean.

So I had gone and gotten myself married, after turning down every suitor for a hundred miles around Fort Davis. To be fair, I was too rough and coarse to be a proper wife, so there hadn't been all that many suitors. But I weren't unpleasant to look at, and I could do a hard day's work. I had rejected the boys that came one after another, until Pa had just given up on marrying me off. It weren't even that I didn't want to get married, it was just that all those boys were such terrible bores. They were just common farmhands, and I think somewhere inside I always knew I was going to marry some dashing knight that rode onto the farm and took me away like this, just like in those fine stories with all their fine words that my sisters used to read to me at bedtime. What would my sisters think of this predicament I had gotten myself into? Now there was a fancy word, *predicament*. But what else could I call this? I had kilt a man, and become a woman with a price on her head, and then I'd married a complete stranger only a couple hours after meetin' him. My sisters would have laughed and jeered at me and said it was exactly what they had expected would happen to me all along.

As the night wore on, I began to feel that my new . . . husband—it was powerful hard to think of him with that word—and I should be speaking. We ought to be having some sort of conversating. We didn't know each other, and we had just tied ourselves together for life. It only seemed right. But by the time I was convinced of this, it would have been a bit awkward. Neither of us had spoken in hours and it was well past *la medianoche*. I was also getting very tired, and I could tell he was as well, sagging in his saddle. It was a mite too dark to see how pale he was, but occasionally he appeared to sway a little, as if he might fall.

Finally I pulled Butterball up. The little pony was also nearly asleep. Oliver passed me and then halted his own horse and turned back, grinning. I could see the gleam of his teeth in the darkness.

"I think we should press on, Flaka," he said in that smooth, husky voice of his. "It is Flaka, right?"

I nodded. "Aye, it's Flaka, Oliver."

"Well Flaka, I firmly believe we should press on. I think we need to put as many miles between ourselves and Ian Marcus as we can from the outset of this journey. But, unfortunately, I do need a little rest. Just a little. I'm . . . well, I'm running low on strength."

"You talk real polished-like, you know. Like a bonafide dandy," I commented.

"Do I?"

I nodded again as I dismounted and set about untacking my pony. "You do, Oliver. I think you must've had some real edjicatin'."

"*Education*," he corrected, and then when he saw me flush he hastened to add, "Yes, I talk like I've been educated. You're not stupid, Flaka." Despite what he said, I thought he were laughin' at me. There were enough mirth in his voice, anyway, that I stayed mighty bristled.

"No, I ain't. And don't you forget that, Mr. Oliver."

With my pony tended to, I laid out my roll on the ground, putting my loaded Colt just under the head of it, and sat down with my legs crossed, feeling the tight sensation as the pants pulled at my stomach, wondering if I should take them trousers clean off for comfort or leave them on to be modest. I was tired enough by that point that I didn't care much either way. I was going to fall asleep, pants or no pants. I turned toward Oliver to find him standing over me, holding his own bedroll in hand. In a flash I remembered the warning Grant Marcus had given me, just before he died, and I yanked my pistol from beneath the blanket and trained the barrel on him.

Oliver raised his hands.

"Just because we're married don't mean you have any right to share my bedroll," I snapped.

"I would never presume such a thing. I just . . . thought perhaps a kiss goodnight might be in order, on our wedding eve."

"Well, you done thought wrong."

His face dropped, looking somewhat sad, and he nodded and began to turn away. A pang tore through me, the same shattering guilt I'd felt when I'd kilt Grant Marcus. "Wait," I said, and he looked back. I bent my neck, tilting the side of my face toward the sky above. "You may kiss my cheek."

He smiled then, and that smile sent a strange rippling sensation all through my whole body, as if I had never been alive before I saw that grin of his. He bent and pressed his lips gently against my cheek, and then he moved away, almost skipping with delight. It seemed as if my heart came alive with that kiss, and I lay down, gazing up at the stars above, warmth growing within my chest. I think I fell asleep that night with a big, stupid grin on my face.

The next morning I awoke to the cooing of doves in the tree branches above me. We had camped in a little grove of pine, about an acre of it, giving some relief to the flat, desolate land around us. There was a smell of fire, coffee, and something else—Lord, maybe pancakes, a-cookin'? It smelled so good I remembered how hungry I was, and my mouth started watering. I rolled over on my blanket, wiping some sweat from my brow, and found Oliver tending a set of little cakes that sizzled on a stone he had put in the fire.

"Someone's gonna see that firepit and know we was here, if'n they're following us," I observed.

"They are definitely following us," Oliver replied, using his knife blade and a finger to carefully flip the cakes. They were a perfect golden brown, their warm, heavenly scent filling the air around us. "But we still have half a day's ride on our pursuers. We only slept about four hours."

"No wonder I still feel so damn tired." I stretched and yawned, beginning to roll my blanket up. "That smells good as Ma's cookin'."

He flashed a grin. "The pancakes will give us strength for another long day of riding. There's a little creek about ten miles west of here where I intend to give Marcus some trouble with our tracks."

"You know this country mighty well. How come I ain't never seen you before?"

He shrugged. "I haven't been in this part of the country very long."

"How long?"

"A year, or thereabouts."

"And where'd you come from?"

"Back East."

"Back East like San Antonio or back East like Arkansas?"

"Back East like Boston. Born and raised and went to university there."

I whistled and took the cup of murky, blazing-hot coffee that he offered me. It tasted foul, like burning, and it was perhaps the chewiest coffee I'd ever had, but it woke me up like I'd been kicked in the back by a mule. My pa would've called it horseshoe coffee. Throw the pot on the fire and throw a horseshoe in it—once the horseshoe is standing up, the coffee's done. The pancakes Oliver handed me burned the skin off my fingertips, but I ate them ravenously. I hadn't eaten anything the night before, in our rush to be on the road as soon as we could.

"I ain't never met anyone that's been to Boston," I said through a mouthful of pancake. "I've heard tell it's a mighty fine place."

"It is, if you like crowds of people and tall stone buildings, cramped streets, the smell of smoke and tar so thick you can scarcely breathe and nights so full of light you can't see a single star."

I stuck my tongue out and shook my head. "That don't sound too nice. Is that why you came out here?"

He nodded, taking another slow draw of the coffee before dashing the last dregs from the cup on the ground. He stood up and began scattering the coals of the fire with his boots. "I think so. Boston was too cramped and crowded. There were too many rules. It was like living as a statue, not as a person.

Here you can breathe, you can stretch your legs out without getting into a world of trouble, bumping into someone and irritating them. Here you aren't constrained by endless rules. I think in Texas you can make your own rules, and be whatever you choose to be."

Finishing my last pancake and dusting the crumbs off my pants, I set to brushing my pony. Old Butterball had gotten plump in the last few months, sitting out in the pasture, munching the tumbleweed, dried grass, and the endless supply of oats he demanded. He hadn't been getting much proper exercise, but I fancied he'd lost a good twenty pounds in the fast ride the night before. By the time the two weeks it took to get to the Arizona Territory had passed he'd be in good shape.

Oliver had removed his shirt and was adjusting the bandage around his middle, over his wound. The rib was still visible, making the angry red gash look like a mouth on his side, white teeth leering at me with a hideous smile. I paused in my brushing to assess my new husband's lean, muscular frame, tan lines around his elbows where he habitually rolled up his sleeves, and a brown mark like an arrowhead down the center of his chest, where his shirt opened up to the Texas sun. I also took note of his scars. He had quite a collection, in fact, including one ugly mark on his left chest muscle, ribbons of hard, ropey tissue swirling like a dust devil up toward his shoulder, as if someone had tried to twist him open.

I had seen his scars before, while Ma and I were dressing the fresh wound, but it had been nearly dark then and I hadn't appreciated how brutal they were. There was a fresher wound on his abdomen, above the left hip, still red, but healing nicely. I wondered for a second if Grant Marcus had spoken the truth and perhaps he had kilt a girl, and perhaps that's where he got that mark. I shook my head. I couldn't believe that. I had married this man. To believe him a murderer and a misuser of women would break my very mind. I had to keep seeing him the way I did when he had walked up my porch steps the day before with that foolish, admiring grin on his face.

He was struggling with the bandage, so I offered him a hand, which he accepted gratefully, keeping his arms lifted as I worked to adjust and tighten the fabric around his ribs. He winced but didn't cry out as I yanked at it. I was trying not to be rough, but I weren't used to being tender and careful. There hadn't never been much place for gentleness in my world. Oliver was still pale, and thinking back to how much blood had saturated his garments before he'd changed into Ephraim's old clothes, I wondered at how he'd managed to push on so long overnight and get up again bright and early to cook for the two of us. He was stronger than he looked, stronger than you'd expect a dandy from Boston to be. Or perhaps dandies from back East weren't the fragile eggshells we'd been led to believe.

We rode out all day, keeping a steady pace, stopping for *agua* everywhere we could find it. We both kept quiet for the most part, our bandanas over our faces as the choking hot dust kicked up around us, parching us and our animals. After a while I could tell old Butterball was getting too hot and too tired. Oliver had promised a crick in about ten miles, but I was beginning to doubt that. It had to have been more than ten miles by then—the sun had already passed the middle of the sky.

"We're going to need to rest. Find some shade," I said. "You might not know this, but it ain't safe to ride in the middle of the day out here, not in August like this. You'll kill yourself and your animal if you push them in this heat."

"We stop now and Ian Marcus will catch up to us. We can rest tonight," replied Oliver, his voice calm and firm. He was pushing his bay mare up a narrow path between two enormous boulders. We had come to a rocky place, low mountains scattered with scrub that was yellowed and dried by the sun and crowded with dense, spiky cactuses. Enormous gray rocks jutted up all around us, cutting off our sight of the world west and north, where we were headed. Finding trails we could pass through with our horses and their packs was becoming a real chore, but this was a place where we might find shade, and—the good Lord willing—a touch of water and some grass that weren't burned to hell, for the horses to chew on.

I pulled Butterball up and glowered at Oliver's back, noting the dark spot at his side where his wound had been bleeding through his bandage and his shirt again. After a moment he realized I wasn't moving and the clop of Butterball's hooves had stopped. He turned back to face me from higher up the little draw we had entered, climbing one of the rocky *colinas*.

"Listen, mister," I said, jutting my jaw out a little. "You said you'd done lived out here a year. That ain't near time enough to know how to survive in these deserts. I been out here twenty-one years and I'm tellin' you we need to stop till this heat blows over a bit."

"I hear you, but there's a bloodthirsty man whose son you killed following us, and I'm telling you he isn't going to rest, even in this heat. Every hour we spend relaxing he's going to get closer."

"That's fine. We can make up time at night, or after we reach this crick you said we'd reach and hide our trail there. There is a crick, right? I'm beginnin' to doubt your word. It's been quite a bit more than ten miles and I ain't seen no water yet."

"We passed the creek already. It was dried up, I'm afraid," replied Oliver.

"And you're just now telling me this?"

"Lord, Flaka, we've been married less than a day, don't you think it's a little soon to be squabbling? Trust me, I know the way to get where we're going as safely and quickly as we can."

I harrumphed at that, entirely unconvinced. "You're wounded, don't forget that, and you're bleeding. You're liable to fall out again, like you did at the farm, pushing on so hard in this heat."

"I'm fine," he retorted and turned the mare, pushing her up the hill again.

"Where we goin' exactly, anyhow?" I asked, kicking Butterball's heaving flanks to follow.

"I already told you," said Oliver, turning his head as he spoke so I could hear him. "We're headed to a little parcel of land south of Tombstone that I've had my eyes on for about a year now."

"My brother lives up in Tombstone, you know."

"I did not know that."

"Well, he does. You'll get to meet him there, with any luck. But how we gonna get there?"

We had crested *la colina*. The pale blue sky became almost white in the distance where it mixed with the sand of the desert, a yellow-brown expanse that seemed to stretch on forever. Here Oliver paused, his face behind his bandana contorted a little with pain. He was trying to keep me from seeing it, but his hand was resting over his wound, and pressing hard, as if to give himself some relief by holding that cracked rib in place. He was sweating, a good sign, in a way: at least he weren't too dry. It was hotter than Hades atop that hill, no relief from the beating sun.

As I watched my husband, I wondered if I—a wife for less than a day—would be a widow before the week was out. A widow, especially a young widow, wasn't such a bad thing to be out here. Women were scarce enough that even a woman who'd been married could easily find another man, especially if'n she had any looks about her and didn't have a passel of children clinging to her skirts.

Oliver nodded into the distance, still grimacing. "We're going to cut through Mexico, just a bit. Outside of the jurisdiction of Ian Marcus, or any officer of the law in Texas. Good thing we've got a little señorita with us who can speak the language."

I laughed loudly at that, a cracked, dry laugh. I had run out of water from my canteen about two hours ago and my lips were parched. "I don't speak much Spanish, dummy. Not more than a toddler, anyhow."

"Is that so? Your mother looked about as Mexican as a woman can."

"Perhaps you shoulda married my ma, then, because she do speak Spanish. But I don't. I understand it pretty well, but the speaking . . . I ain't so good at that."

"*Por qué* not?" he asked.

"*Porque mi padre* came from some mountains in Europe and *mi madre* from Chihuahua and they didn't share a language 'cept English, so English is what we spoke at home and English is what I *hablo*, if you know what I mean."

He chuckled and shook his head. There was a pleasant shine in his eyes. "I don't suppose your pa would have taken too kindly to me marrying your ma. He didn't exactly fire off a twenty-one-gun salute when you proposed we wed. I suppose we'll have to make do with your toddler Spanish, then. I'm not inclined to speak to too many folks down there anyway, if I can avoid it."

"We passin' through Juarez?"

"I plan on it."

"One of my sisters lives somewhere in that city. Mayhap we could stop at her place for a day or two, rest the horses. Especially if we don't think Marcus will follow us into Mexico."

"I didn't say Marcus wouldn't follow us into Mexico."

"You said we were gettin' outside his jurisprudence."

"Out of his *jurisdiction*." Olivery gently corrected me, and then said in a soft but ominous tone, "But he'll still follow us."

"You seem to know what Marcus will do pretty well," I observed.

Oliver's eyebrows lifted and a gleam of fond amusement flashed in his eyes but was overwhelmed a second later by another twisting expression of pain. He turned in his saddle and looked east, back the way we had come. Then he reached out and grabbed my shoulder.

Instinctively I jerked away from him, still unsure that I should trust him, though I wanted to more than anything. But I saw that he weren't trying to hurt me—he was pointing with his other hand far to the east, miles and miles away, where a plume of dust rose from the desert, obscuring the riders that were kicking it up.

"That Marcus sure don't waste no time," I said and felt that dull, sick feeling in my chest again, the feeling I had when I looked at the dead face of young Grant Marcus. "You know of anymore cricks where we can wash our tracks out?"

"I know a few more," he said, his face becoming drawn and grim. "We could wait and take them down from way up here, shoot them down one by one from the high ground. An ambush."

"Killing one man was enough for me, mister, with all due respect," I replied firmly, feeling as if killing one man had actually been too much for me.

"Very well. Then we had best push on, and hard. You're welcome to call me Oliver, or even Olly, if you prefer. We're married, you can call me whatever you like." He gave me a pained but kind smile again, and then he turned his mare and set off down the steep hill, clattering along the rocks, pushing his horse toward the bottom of the draw and then onward, toward Mexico and away from our relentless pursuer, Ian Marcus.

IV

Oliver did find a few cricks, but it was August, and we were on the border between Mexico and Texas, a place hotter than tarnation. The cricks were barely trickles and I didn't figure riding in them for a mile or two would do much to hide our tracks from Marcus. We didn't catch sight of our pursuers again that day, and we kept pushing hard north and west. Late in the evening we passed into Mexico itself, I believe, though there weren't no fence or sign to tell where exactly we went from Texas into Mexico, nor any particular change in the sand, the scrub, or the cactuses. Having not eaten since early that morning, I was starting to think my stomach was gone, shrank up into nothing. We'd filled up on water in one of those little trickling cricks, but that muddy, foul liquid was near gone by the time Oliver finally let us rest.

Late *en la tarde* we reached a stand of high, smooth rocks, bigger than houses, and here Oliver finally pulled up. I dismounted, unsaddled Butterball and hobbled him, and then began digging in the bags for the food Ma had packed for us: salted pork, cornbread that had been smashed into a ball of yellow crumbs, and tooth-cracking hardtack. We had beans as well, but they were still dry, and it would take hours to soak and cook them. While I was considering our meager victuals, I heard a thump and turned to find Oliver lying in a heap beside his horse. The animal danced sideways away from him, skittish of her fallen master. By the time I reached his side, he had opened his eyes and was staring in confusion at the stars just coming out above us. Blinking, he focused on me and grinned.

"Guess I must have tripped," he said.

"Oliver"—it felt good to say his name instead of "mister" —"Oliver, you didn't trip. You done fell out. We've got to get you some food and some rest. That wound is liable to do you in, the way it keeps oozing. You can't have more than a quart of blood left in your whole body."

"I hope I've got more than that in me. I've got to get you to Tombstone, you know. I made a promise to your folks."

"I could sew you up," I suggested. "It'll hurt, but if I sew it tight it probly'll stop oozing like that."

Oliver shrugged as he sat up, wincing. "Worth a try, I suppose."

We saw to the horses first, and ate and relieved ourselves, then I set up a little fire. It weren't more than a flicker of flame, barely giving off as much light as a candle—nothing a rider in the distance could see, I hoped. Oliver took a small book out of his pack, then undid his shirt, taking his left arm out of the sleeve. He lay down on his right side by the fire, using that tiny patch of light to read the book while I inspected his wound.

His flesh around the bullet wound was swollen, red and ugly, and pulling the edges tight would take a lot of tension, but the horse mane hair that I'd borrowed from Butterball should do the trick. I found the little kit of sewing needles and scissors that Ma had made sure I packed and threaded the horsehair into the needle. After washing the wound a little with what small bit of water we could spare, I dabbed the angry edges dry and put my thumb and forefinger around the wound, pushing the edges together to cover the exposed bits of bone. His skin felt hot to my touch, but there was no pus around it. It was still oozing blood as I slid my needle through his skin and drew the two sides together. He took in a breath sharply and held it for a minute, blinking, but he stared hard at the book, and gradually his breathing eased.

"What're you readin' there?" I asked.

He held it up so I could see.

"I can't read," I said, annoyed.

"No schools around Fort Davis?"

"There was, but I only went two years and couldn't make heads nor tales of all them damn squiggles in them books. Anyway, Ma don't read and she ain't got no problems. Pa and my sisters and brother tried to teach me too, not just the schoolteacher, but they all said I was too dense."

"I don't think you're dense."

"You're just trying to get inside my pants."

Oliver laughed. "That's true, but it's also true that I don't think you're dumb, Flaka. Certainly not too dumb to learn how to read. You know your letters and numbers?"

"Course I do," I returned, rankling at the suggestion that I might not.

"Then you're already more than halfway to being able to read."

"Why do I even need to learn to read? What's the point of it? Like I said, my ma don't read neither, and she does just fine."

For a long moment Oliver didn't reply. I had to look up and check to see that he was still awake and hadn't passed out again. He was flipping through the pages of the little book. At last he cleared his throat and started to read aloud.

"What hope is here for modern rhyme
To him, who turns a musing eye

On songs, and deeds, and lives, that lie
Foreshorten'd in the tract of time?

"These mortal lullabies of pain
May bind a book, may line a box,
May serve to curl a maiden's locks;
Or when a thousand moons shall wane
A man upon a stall may find,
And, passing, turn the page that tells
A grief, then changed to something else,
Sung by a long-forgotten mind.
But what of that? My darken'd ways
Shall ring with music all the same;
To breathe my loss is more than fame,
To utter love more sweet than praise."

As I knitted his raw, swollen flesh back together, he kept reading, his breath catching every now and then in pain at my rough, yanking tugs. I don't rightly know what he was even saying—I think only about half the words meant something to me—but I couldn't help but listen, and as I listened I think my eyes turned misty. P'raps it was more the pretty pattern of the sounds, the beauty of the rhythm that the book contained, than anything in particular that he said, but when he finished I thought there was a sob locked up deep in my throat.

"Don't stop," I urged him, squeaking around that stifled sob. "I've got nigh on another inch of your skin to put back together again. You'd best keep reading."

"You like it, then?" he asked, and there was a note of pain crisp around the edges of his voice.

"Like it? I ain't never heard nothin' so beautiful in all my life."

He smiled and said, "Me neither, Flaka, me neither." Then he closed his eyes, resting his head on the crook of his elbow, and his breathing softened and slowed. I thought he'd fainted again, but he were just sleepin', plum wore out. His hand drifted to the ground, the book crunching into the sand by the fire. I finished sewing him, and, reaching down, I pulled the book from the dirt and dusted it off with a kind of reverence.

I sat back on my bedroll, holding the worn paperback, struggling to make any sense of the words, trying to remember the sound that each of those letters was supposed to make. But the lines swirled and squiggled before my eyes, almost dancing. I'll be damned if I could make a lick of sense out of it. Gradually, my head started to ache, and I let my eyes drift from the open book before me to the young man lying across from me, sleeping so peaceful-like, his left side open to the night air, woven back together by horsehair and my needlecraft. My husband. My beautiful husband. I fell asleep watching the rise and fall of his rib cage and hearing his voice reading those mysterious lines over and over in my head. "*A grief . . . then changed to something else . . . sung by a long-forgotten mind.*"

The sound of a gunshot jerked me awake and I rolled onto my belly, looking around without raising my head. My heart was thundering in my chest, but I was too bleary and exhausted to feel real fear. Honest, I wasn't even sure if I was dreaming or awake. The horses were stamping, tossing their heads. Another shot rang out and I heard someone scrambling toward me in the darkness. I yanked the Colt from under my bedroll and swung it toward the approacher. My hand was quivering like a leaf. I almost fired, but then I heard Oliver's voice.

"It's me, Flaka. Don't shoot. It's just me. Come on."

I leaped up, detangling myself from my bedroll. I heard another gunshot ring out, and then Oliver was herding me forward, toward the horses. Butterball squealed as if in pain as more bullets ricocheted off the rocks around us. The little pony reared with his hobbles, kicking and neighing. I realized as I drew near he had been struck on his bottom, but it didn't look deep, just a graze.

"They're trying to kill the horses so we can't get away," hissed Oliver in the dark. "You think you can get them both saddled behind that rock while I hold them off?"

I nodded, breathless, my heart still hammering harder than it ever had before. It felt like my pulse was in my neck and in the side of my head, and it thundered so strong it almost hurt. I grabbed each saddle in turn, tossing them onto the terrified animals' backs, still clutching my gun. Oliver swung his knife, and in two deft lashes, both animals were free of their hobbles. With the reins in one hand and dragging the heavy saddlebags in the other, I led the mare and Butterball away, the saddles still sliding and loose on their backs. We scurried behind a tall rock, where I worked to attach and tighten the girths and then bridle the spooked animals. I heard Oliver shooting, and answering gunshots, and then a dreadful silence fell. I worked faster, my fingers slick with sweat, the terror of how close we were to death was making me clumsy and terribly slow. The sun was nowhere near the horizon yet, but I was drenched, a strange, clammy, cold wetness all over my body, making my shirt cling to me.

Then I heard a voice call out, a strong, commanding voice, a voice I knew. "Give her up, Oliver, and no one will touch you. You'll ride out of here a free man if you give up the girl that killed Grant. If you don't, you'll die with her."

Oliver's response was to discharge one of his pistols. I heard the blast of his gun and I even thought I heard the ping of the bullet striking stone somewhere in the night. I winced, tightening his mare's girth one more time as she shifted uneasily beneath my touch and nipped at me from the tightness of the belly band.

"Thanks for the offer, old man," Oliver shouted back. "But that's not a deal I can make." He fired again to punctuate his rejection of the terms Marcus had offered.

"Oliver, Oliver, do be reasonable," said the same voice again, softer now, and closer. He was making his way along the rocks around us. Our safe camping place had become almost our tomb. When he next spoke, Marcus sounded like a wise teacher reprimanding an errant, stupid little student. It was the easy voice of a man accustomed to getting his own way. "What is she to you? Give her up."

"We're ready," I whispered, my voice hoarse in the darkness.

"You're right, old man, she's nothing to me, nothing at all. Just my wife," Oliver yelled and then fired three shots, and between the blasts I heard the tromping of his boots racing toward me, thudding in the sand and clattering among the rocks. In a moment he passed me and I heard him say, "Atta-girl," as he vaulted from the ground into his mare's saddle. Again something strange and new, a warm sensation, blossomed in my chest, my terror briefly replaced by joy at my husband's praise.

I scrambled aboard Butterball, kicking my feet into his round, protuberant flanks. The barrel-shaped little pony began running, as fast as his stubby little legs could carry him. All around us bullets zinged, one clipping a bit off the brim of my hat, so close to hitting my face that it took my breath away.

We kept ahead of them for about a mile, and then, quick as a rattler's strike, Oliver veered into a steep, empty riverbank and a moment later we were behind another enormous rock and under a huge stone outcropping, our horses panting from exertion but happy to be standing still. We waited there for what felt like an hour, listening to the clatter of our pursuers' hooves, hunting for us, and finally we heard them pushing on over the riverbed and then away into the distance. In all this, sitting under that slab of rock, barely daring to breathe for more than an hour, neither of us had said a word, but the whole time I kept my eyes trained on Oliver, studying him.

"How do you know Ian Marcus?" I asked at last, cutting into the perfect quiet that had fallen.

"What makes you think I know him?"

"He called you by name. He spoke to you like a man who knows the man he's talking to. I ain't stupid, Oliver. Even you said that. I know we're on the run and there ain't been much time for finding out about each other, but you've got to tell me how you know Ian Marcus and how you knew Grant."

Oliver opened his mouth and then clamped it shut, appearing to consider my request, like a man cooking up a lie. Finally he shrugged and said, "We had business dealings, over the last year, since I came out from Boston."

"What kind of business?" I kept insisting.

"Cattle business, what else can an able-bodied man do out here? I worked a couple cattle runs with Grant, for Ian. Anyway, we have to push on. We'll cut north and then west again. I want to put some more distance between us and them before the sun comes up and they turn back and try to find our tracks again."

I wasn't convinced, not even a little bit. Oliver was hiding things from me; he was hiding his true association with the Marcus family, for some reason I couldn't rightly understand. He wasn't lying, necessarily, maybe he had worked a couple cattle runs for Ian, but there was definitely more to the story. Perhaps he had a good reason for hiding it. Perhaps knowing would put me in danger. Perhaps I didn't want to know my new husband's past. Curiosity, my mama had told me as a child, had been known to kill cats, and young women who didn't know when to stop poking into things that were none of their business. Still, I hated that he was not sharing. I found myself pouting, my lower lip sticking out until it was covered in dust that quickly turned to mud. I wiped off the gritty sand and retracted the lip, but a few hours later, as the silence in our mad dash north persisted, I found that lip was sticking out again as I glowered at my husband.

Oliver glanced back at me and flashed a grin that almost took my breath away. He didn't look well, of course. He looked tired, the patchy yellow stubble on his chin increasing every day, dark circles under his eyes, and still he was pale as a ghost. He hadn't enough blood left in him to give him any color, I fancied, though he should have browned under the blazing sun. Boys like him turned the color of their bandanas in the sun, red like scarlet. But my Oliver wasn't red, nor tan, he was somewhere between gray and cream, and despite his poorly appearance, he was still handsome beneath all his weariness. So damn handsome. My heart beat faster when he smiled at me.

"What's eating you, Flaka? You leave your lip out like that and it's liable to get stuck."

"I'll tell you what's eating me!" I exclaimed, trying to keep from looking like a lovestruck cow in a field. "You lying to me is what's eating me. You keep telling tall tales and beating around the bush. You treat me like I'm a dumb kid."

His expression sobered at that and he studied me, his calm blue eyes sliding up and down my face, the set of my jaw, the posture of my shoulders, drawn back and stiff. "Alright, Flaka. There's things I'm not telling you yet, but I will. I don't even know yet if I can trust you. We've barely met."

"We're married."

"And we've barely met. Both things can be true at once. You'll have to forgive me and give me time. But I promise, when we're safe, I'll tell you everything you want to know about me, and a great deal you probably don't. We've got our whole lives ahead of us, don't we?"

"Maybe, maybe not. We keep having close scrapes like this morning and our lives ain't fixin' to be very long."

"*Touché*, Flaka, *touché*." When he said that a distant look came into his eyes, then he turned his mare away from me and kicked his heels against her flanks and she was off in a flash. That horse could run, that much I'll say, she was like a streak of lightning across the desert, swift like the wind on the prairie. Butterball toddled after her.

When at last it was nearing dark again, with no sign of Marcus since that morning, Oliver led us to a steep rocky bluff, and at the top we made our camp. There wasn't much for the horses to eat up there, so we posted them on the western side of the rock, where a little shoddy grass grew, alongside a tired spring that seemed to dry as fast as it could bubble up a few drops of *agua*. Once the horses were settled there, I climbed back atop the ridge where Oliver was. He was removing his shirt and twisting to peer at the bandage around his torso. I was mighty pleased to see no blood had seeped through this time, though he still looked a bit like death, all green around the gills.

"You did a nice job sewing the wound, Flaka," said Oliver appreciatively. "Just as good as any doctor back East."

I swelled up with pride at that. "You can't live out here long and not learn how to sew up the injured. Most of my work before been done on horses and dogs that get scraped up, though."

"A year; you can at least live out here a year and not know how to sew up the injured. But perhaps you can teach me, when you get a chance."

The sun was fading fast in the distance, turning quickly from a bright, apple red to little more than a speck of orange. The light would linger a little longer than the sun, but not by much. Away to the east, as far as we could see from high atop our outcropping, there was nothing, no sign of our pursuers, and I dared to hope they had turned back, not venturing into Mexico to keep hunting us. From the night before I remembered only the faintest bits of the words Oliver had read, but it was coming back to me as I watched the sun setting.

"*These mortal lullabies of pain, sung by a long-forgotten mind . . .*" The words echoed in my mind, and I think I muttered them aloud, then blushed. I turned from the disappearing gleam in the west back to Oliver. "Before it gets real dark, you think you might be able to read me a little more from that book o' yours?" I asked, trying to feign nonchalance.

The grin that spread across my husband's face damn near split it in two. It went all the way to his perfect blue eyes and made them twinkle. "I can do better than that, Flaka. We can make a trade. You teach me how to stitch and I can teach you to read those words for yourself."

"Nah, I already tried at least a hundred times. I ain't got the brains for reading. That's what Pa told me."

"Of course you do, it just might take one hundred and one times, is all," he replied, his voice full of kindness, but not like he was talking to a child, not condescending-like. Then he took the little book out of his back pocket and waved me close.

I sidled up against him, leaning over those mysterious squiggly lines in the dimness of twilight and watching intently as he ran his fingers along them and sounded each and every word out, slow and patient. Just slow and patient enough for me to start to follow and sound those words out alongside him, for me to begin to remember what noises went with which squiggly symbol. After he sounded them out, he read them aloud in his perfect, husky voice, so low and mellow and soothing, and I thought I would die listening to the beauty of those words as he spoke them. It felt as if the whole damn world couldn't contain such soaring emotions as those words birthed in my soul.

> "I hold it true, whate'er befall;
> I feel it when I sorrow most;
> 'Tis better to have loved and lost
> Than never to have loved at all."

V

El proximo día DAWNED WITHOUT GUNSHOTS OR PHANTOM voices bargaining over my life. I woke up curled close against Oliver, my head resting on the crook of his elbow, as if his arm were a pillow. For a moment I lay perfectly still, trying to remember what had happened the night before. I wasn't sure if we had in fact gone ahead and consummated our marriage vows or not. I quickly realized we had not, and was glad of it.

I was crusted with dirt into my very pores, and any day my courses were due to start. I didn't feel like I could make love, especially not to a man I was so attracted to. I wasn't sure how exactly it was done—though I had a few ideas and had messed around a little in the past with a few farmer boys —but I was pretty darn sure the act was done while you were looking and smelling real fine, and I was anything but that. I rolled over slowly, finding my face only a few inches from Oliver's. He looked boyish in his sleep, touchingly young, almost angelic. His face was smoothed of all the creases of pain and exhaustion that had constantly troubled him in our short time together.

Reluctantly I pushed myself into a sitting position,

knowing it would wake him. Sure enough, he stirred and opened his eyes. For a second he appeared bewildered, glancing around in alarm. Then he focused on me and sighed.

"You alright?" I asked.

"Yes, just for a minute I forgot the whole adventure. Hadn't the slightest idea where I was."

"In hell, just like you was when you went to sleep."

"If hell has such lovely women in it, then I wonder that all men aren't clamoring at the gates to get in."

"Perhaps most men ain't so shallow as to trade their souls for a gal."

"For a woman like you, Flaka Garcia Hasani Kedar, I think I would trade my soul to the devil a million times over."

My cheeks burned, but I think my eyes probably gleamed with delight at the compliment. I started to stand, my stomach rumbling painfully. I had a mind to see what we had left from our stores of food, or perhaps even to look around for a desert hare or a tortoise, or really anything with meat on its bones—even a lizard or a little mouse—but when I turned east I forgot about food in an instant. In the distance, not moving fast, but moving steadily, was the rising dust of riders, and my heart sank into my starving gut.

"Goddamn these bastards!" I exclaimed.

Oliver put his hand over his chest, still grinning like a man in love. "And here I thought I'd married the daughter of a preacher."

"Come on, Oliver. I ain't taking the Lord's name in vain for the fun of it. They're out there. Marcus and his men."

That banished all the amorous thoughts that had clearly been flickering about in my husband's head. He sat bolt upright, turned east and quickly saw the truth of my warning. "He's determined, I'll give him that. I told you he would follow us into Mexico."

"We'll run these poor horses into the grave if they keep

coming after us like this. We need to lose him," I said as we grabbed what belongings we had not lost at our last campsite and scrambled down the bluff to our horses waiting below.

"We'll lose him," Oliver promised. "Just keep close, as close as you can with that little cow you call a horse."

"He'll be sleek and slimmer than your horse by the time we get to Tombstone."

"I'll believe that when I see it," retorted Oliver with a flash of a grin, though there was still that drawn, pained look in the way he squinted his eyes.

That day on the run was worse than all the others. The heat kept searing our bodies as we rode, like we were traveling through an oven, the sun drying us into shriveled prunes, burning away every ounce of moisture in our bodies. Desiccated, that was the word Oliver used, and I didn't rightly know at the time what it meant, but now that I do, I can't think of a word that would better describe what happened to us. Each time I shaded my eyes to look up at the sun I felt my heart sinking. It was as if time had stopped. There weren't no shade to be found, the rocks we had camped by were the last we had seen for hours, and though we lost sight of our pursuers after a while, we knew they were still behind us, relentlessly continuing their chase. In my blurred, exhausted mind, I started to fancy that they weren't even human, to chase us so doggedly. They were demons, demons who didn't need rest, or food, or water, and we would never escape them.

As the day finally began to draw toward its close, I pushed the exhausted Butterball to catch up to Oliver's mare. We had only stopped to drink twice that day in muddy puddles we had found by some miracle. As I drew up to Oliver, who was trotting languidly ahead of me, I shook my head, trying to wipe the grime from my face and my hair, trying to look anything like attractive. Something about my appearance that morning had stoked some sort of desire in him, and I wanted him to feel it again. I longed for him to feel it again, for his eyes to soften with admiration and adoration the way they had at dawn. If he looked at me like that again, I thought perhaps I might forget our troubles. Hell, if he looked at me again the way he had that morning—what seemed so long ago—I think I wouldn't have cared if I died.

But, when he glanced over, it wasn't with that look of desire I hoped for. Instead his brow was creased into a frown and he looked exhausted, impossibly exhausted. He looked like a man about to topple from his horse's back.

"You alright, Flaka?" he asked through chapped, scabbed lips.

"I'm fine. I just . . . I just wonder what the plan is for tonight."

"We'll push as far as we can after the sun sets. Take advantage of the cool and the dark, I think. Then we'll rest, somewhere. I've an inkling we might find a town in another ten miles or so, a little place where we could pay to rest and feed our horses some proper oats."

"Pay with what money?"

Oliver patted his saddlebag. "Don't you worry about that, Flaka. I told you I aim to buy a piece of land near Tombstone. You think I would drag you out here if I didn't have the means to secure that property?"

It took me a moment to figure out what he had said. He spoke real nice, and real easy when he did, but the way he phrased things sometimes didn't make sense to me, and I was even worse at understanding him now because it was so hot and I was so tired. But, I ain't trying to say I would've understood him if I was well rested and cool. I was a woman without the faintest notion of an education. I almost always had to think about his words a long while before they made sense in my mind.

"So . . . you got money?"

He nodded. "I certainly do. More than enough to set us up

for a good many years. That's a question you probably should've asked me before you volunteered to marry me, don't you think?"

"I suppose. How far before Juarez?"

"At this pace? We'll be there in two days."

"And we can visit my sister, Martha? She'd put us up and keep us safe for a few days, I 'spect."

"If she wants to put her kid sister up for a few days I wouldn't argue against it. You know her address?"

"Nah, but someone'll know where to find her if we ask in a neighborhood called Salvacar, I think. That's where she wrote she lived at. Somewhere on the south side of *la ciudad*, I think."

"Is it as far south as Samalayuca?"

"I don't think so, but I ain't much good at readin' maps. You mean the dune fields?"

He nodded.

"I don't think it's so far south. Pa read me the letters from Martha—she didn't mention nothin' about the dunes never. Sounds like she's right in the city proper."

"Good, then we'll head directly toward Juarez." He paused after he said this and seemed to be considering something. "You've heard of the dune fields, Flaka?"

"There's Apache there, I've heard. And scores of killers and bandits. And it ain't safe."

His lips pursed tight and he appeared lost in thought for a long time as we kept riding. Finally he said, "That's what I've heard too. About the Apache, and other rustlers and bandits who take advantage of people that pass through there. But . . . it might be the safest place for us to ride. I don't know that Marcus will follow us across those dunes. Anyway, we can decide once we reach your sister's place and hopefully find a little respite there, in Salvacar."

We stayed that night in a village, if you could call it that. It weren't barely ten *familias* with their hovels built around a dirty well. We fed our horses the best food Oliver's money could buy, which was just moldy oats and old corn. We filled our own bellies too, with beans and maize tortillas that tasted like heaven after so long without a proper warm meal, and then we bought a few supplies we needed from the people there, mostly just more moldy oats for the horses on the next leg of the journey. We slept outside by the town's well. I was becoming accustomed to sleeping on the hard ground under the stars, and, despite the fear and the constant danger, it was starting to grow on me, this life on the road: a wild, free life. The stars were so bright overhead I felt I could get lost in their white, twinkling depths.

Oliver fell asleep the instant his body touched the ground, and I mourned that as I lay, listening to the lonely cries of coyotes in the distance. I wanted him to read with me again. I wanted him to let me sleep with my head on his arm like he had the night before. It had felt more like home than any other place I'd been in my whole life. As if I'd always been alone until the night I slept in my Oliver's arms.

We weren't disturbed by gunshots or the terrible rising dust of our pursuers in the distance the next morning, but we got up before the first glint of dawn. We saddled our horses, who were both looking as refreshed and ready for a ride as they had since the day we started this mad flight.

Oliver brushed against me as I turned to mount Butterball, and I startled at his touch. There was heat emanating from him, as if he had become an oven. I caught his arm before he could move away, feeling strangely shy, not a feeling I think I'd ever had before in my whole life.

"You alright? You feel mighty fevered."

"Fine, Flaka, I'm fine," he returned and flashed me that easy grin, so much more weary than I had seen it before. He was still pale, but there was a flush around his neck and cheeks that didn't look healthy at all. He mounted, but his movements were slower and more laborious than they had been before, frighteningly slow.

An icy, invisible hand seemed to take hold of my throat, along with the dreadful thought that I was going to be left alone. Oliver was going to die in the desert and leave me lost in the wilds. That thought seized me, consuming every other thing in my mind. I don't think I was fearful that I wouldn't be able to survive on my own—I knew I could. I had been proving that every day of my entire life. From the moment my infant feet touched the coarse sand of Texas, I had been training for the day my parents wouldn't be there to watch over me. If Marcus didn't catch up to me and kill me, then I would be fine. There was something else in my fear: horror at the idea of Oliver not being there. Dread that this man I knew so little about but had somehow come to mean more to me than anything else in the world would be gone. The thought of never getting to rest my head on his arm again, and never feeling his body pressed against mine again, of him never reading those beautiful words to me in that low, husky voice of his—for some reason the thought of losing what had come so newly to me took my breath away, and filled me with shivering terror. It was a worse, more gripping fear than I had felt the day we were being shot at by Marcus' dad-blamed *hombres.* I couldn't lose what I had just found. I couldn't not have this thing that I had never had before but that I now needed to keep me alive; this person that had become more important to my life than air and water.

He rode at a slump that day, not cracking jokes like usual, or teaching me new words every time he opened his mouth, just leaning in his saddle, and clenching the pommel hard, like it was going to run away from him. Every time I saw him sway I moved up beside him, ready to catch his tall frame if he toppled.

I found our campsite that night. It was a cave, rocks beneath the sand that opened up into a wide area where we could hide, not big enough for the horses, but at least for the two of us. I helped Oliver off his horse and found he had to lean on me just to stay upright, and he was burning like a candle, his weight threatening to crush me to the ground beneath him. He was mumbling something as I helped him inside the cool little cave that I was so proud to have discovered.

"What's that?" I asked, unsure what he was saying.

"Oh, nothing, nothing," he murmured and there was a momentary clearing in his dull, glazed eyes. "We'll meet your sister tomorrow, I should think, definitely tomorrow we'll reach Juarez. Is she like you?"

"Who, Martha?" I scoffed as I helped him lay down on the hard, sand-strewn ground. "We couldn't be less alike, Oliver. She's perfectly serious, all the time, and angry, always angry."

"Fine, fine, and when will you tell me how she's different from you?"

I laughed a little, recognizing the teasing look in his eyes. Removing his shirt, I inspected the wound. It was bright red, it smelled something awful, and around the horsehair stitches tiny bubbles of pus dotted the surface of the laceration. I dabbed them as best I could, pressing hard on the wound to get more of that oozing, yellow goop out, until he groaned in pain and I dared not push any harder, not wanting to hurt my Oliver anymore. I hadn't minded sewing him up a few nights before, but now when I made him cry out and wince in pain, I could feel agony lancing through me, as if I was the one being hurt. I hated it. I hated the way he was suffering. I could see he was fighting back tears of agony every time I squeezed the wound.

As he lay there before me, I saw the little book in the pocket of his coat. Wanting to hear the beautiful words that gave me such comfort and drowned out the sadness I felt, I yanked the little volume out and leaned over it, tracing each letter, muttering the sounds they should make aloud to myself as best I could remember them. Trying to make sense of it. Trying to make those squiggles come to life the way Oliver did.

I don't know how long I pondered those cryptic shapes, but long after it was too dark to see them. They still danced in my vision when, at last, my eyes closed and I drifted off. I think just before I fell asleep I had managed to sound out one word, perhaps. But it wasn't the way it looked—it wasn't "leh-oo-v-eh," it was "luv." Love. *Amor.* That was the trouble with reading and writing, you tried to sound it out, but when you finally got it, the sounds attached to each letter didn't add up anymore. It was like a silly game; once you knew all the words you could decipher them. The sounds you were told didn't match the word once it came out. Love. That's all it was. It could have been simple, a symbol like a heart, but instead it was laid out in a mysterious code, or a riddle to solve. It was all just a dang trick. No one was actually reading, I fancied, they were just making up things to go along with the squiggles they looked at, trying to seem all educated and cultured.

I slept fitfully, dreaming of giant letters chasing me in the desert, shouting at me, and gunfire, and clouds of dust engulfing me, and then I would wake up to watch Oliver breathe, to listen to his rasping and intermittent, fitful snoring. I was sure that by morning he would be dead. But when the sun dawned outside our cave he was still alive, mostly. He was more bleary-eyed than he had been the night before, and seemed less aware of where we were, why we were there, and what our aim was. I told him three times what had happened and that we were going to Juarez before a flicker of understanding crossed his face. We ate hardtack, I saddled the horses, and then I helped him outside and onto his mare and we set off again, north and west, always north and west.

All that day I kept my head swiveling to watch the road behind us, hoping and praying with all my soul that Marcus had given up. We had outpaced him, or he had pushed too far from Fort Davis, further than he could justify, dead son or no. I knew it was a foolish thing to imagine. Ian Marcus had lost a child, and Ian Marcus was not a man who would forget that. I had never met Grant Marcus before the day I kilt him, but I remember Marcus talking about him once when he visited Pa. I remember the pride in that big, red-haired man's eyes, the way he almost glowed when he talked of his boy. And I had gone and kilt him. *Killed*, that was how Oliver would say it. I had gone and killed him. I had almost forgotten that I was a murderer, distracted by Oliver's illness, the terrible, deadly souring of his wound. But it came back to me fresh that day, with no one to talk to. It came back along with the memory of how much that man I had gone and killed had been loved by someone.

I was lost in these *pensamientos oscuros* when I heard the thump of something hitting the sand behind me, and Oliver's horse nickered in alarm. I turned and found Oliver lying on the ground, staring up into the sky, not moving, his eyes open but vacant. For a second I saw not him there but the handsome redhead, Grant Marcus, dead on the floor when Ma and I had turned him over. I nearly fell off Butterball trying to dismount in a mad rush, and then I was on my knees, shaking Oliver and cursing at him for frightening me so.

After a moment, I saw him draw breath, and then I too was able to draw one. I hadn't realized I was holding my breath until he took in that long draft of air. He blinked and stared at me.

"We there yet?" he asked, attempting to grin.

"No, Oliver, we ain't there. And we ain't goin' to get there if you keep falling out like this. You're going to need to stay sittin' on your horse."

He shook his head. "Apologies, Miss Flaka, er, I suppose, Mrs. Kedar. If those are the rules, I'm not sure I can follow them."

"You've got to, Oliver. I ain't leavin' you out here for the buzzards to eat."

He sighed, staring up at the empty blue sky above with longing, as if he wanted to stay lying there forever. There were buzzards circling too. They had been watching us, following us. Those damn birds can smell death setting in hours before it does. I put my hands on Oliver's shoulders and began to hoist him up. He was practically a dead weight, and clammy with sweat, slipping and sliding through my fingers. He let me lift him and gradually summoned what little strength he had left to assist me. Once he was back in his mare's saddle he began to slump almost immediately.

There was rope in one of Oliver's saddlebags, and with that I tied my husband onto his horse. He didn't say a word while I twisted the ropes around his legs and looped them under the mare's abdomen. I put another coil of rope twice around his middle and fixed it to the horn of his old cavalry saddle. Finally satisfied that he wouldn't fall, I mounted Butterball as the shadows stretched across the desert, making us look impossibly tall, our figures like black giants stretching on for what seemed like a mile into the east. I still kept peering over my shoulder constantly, but there had been no sign of Marcus for two days. It should have made me feel better, but it made me more nervous, my chest wrenching and churning like a living creature was inside, a gopher trapped at the back of a den being menaced by a rattlesnake.

Finally, as the shadows ate up the world around us, I saw the faint lights of a village in the distance, floating and somehow surreal. I blinked hard and rubbed my eyes, staring again, so tired I didn't believe what I saw, though I knew it should be there. But sure enough, the lights stayed no matter how hard I rubbed my fists into my lids. I glanced back at Oliver, meaning to say something, but his head was resting on his chest, and I could tell he was asleep by the awkward way his body tilted in the saddle. His mare was adjusting her walk to keep him upright. I patted her neck and took her reins. She had been following me faithfully all that day, but I couldn't risk losing her now, so close to Ciudad Juarez, where I desperately hoped I would find *mi hermana*, Martha. That had become my one goal since Oliver sickened. I didn't know what we would do after that—I just knew I needed my big sister's help, if she would give it to me.

Oliver had gotten me this far. He had protected me like he promised Ma and Pa, and he hadn't hurt me the way Grant had suggested that he might. He'd been a good husband this past five days or week or whatever it had been, I was losing track of the time. For a girl who'd gone and married a random man who walked onto her porch and started shooting at people chasing him, I thought I hadn't done too badly. Though it remained to be seen if I'd be a widow before I was ever deflowered. I hoped to God I wouldn't. Even ill as he was, my Oliver was handsome. His lean body and pretty face, his blue eyes and tawny hair—the look of him made me hungry in a way no one else ever had before. Hungry to taste that mysterious thing called sex. Hungry to really learn at last how babies were made. These weren't *pensamientos puros*, I knew that, but it was only natural, and he were my husband, after all. I'd been expecting my courses for days, but they hadn't come. Perhaps the stress of our ride had put them off. The longer they stayed away, the more I wanted to consummate the marriage. But it was no good. I didn't rightly know how to do it yet, other than what I'd seen all the farm animals get up to, and Oliver was in no state to teach me the ins and outs of that mysterious act.

Consumed with these vile and impure thoughts, and many more besides of just exactly what I wanted Oliver to do to me, I rode on. I led the mare behind me, through the outskirts of Juarez and eventually, after asking folks along the way, into the neighborhood called Salvacar. I'd been told my sister Martha had gone to live there, with her husband Javier

—Javier Ramirez, I believe. I think it was Javier, or perhaps it was Jorge, I couldn't rightly remember.

The houses were quiet and dark in those narrow little streets, full of dust and shadow devils that you thought were people until you got right up close to them and they turned into shadows proper and then melted into nothingness. But there was some noise and life in that godforsaken desert town, and it was coming from the one place where lights still blazed: the saloon. The sounds of an out-of-tune piano wafted into the street through a slatted door. Someone was clonking out a jaunty tune on the keys, accompanied by scattered verses, hollered rather than sang, and gales of laughter that punctuated what passed for music in this town.

Oliver was sagging onto his mare's neck, and sometimes making sounds, groans or words or mumbles, I couldn't tell. There weren't nothin' for it but to go into that saloon. A girl could get herself in trouble for doing something like that, but I hardly looked like a girl after nearly a week in the wilds of Texas and Mexico, dressed in trousers and a long, dark leather jacket that went down past my knees, crusted with dirt and sweat, my black hair matted under my wide-brimmed hat. I dismounted outside the bar, ignoring the men that stumbled out and bumped against me, intentionally, it seemed, as if they were looking for a fight. Two of them stopped when they saw Oliver and peered at him in the dark. I imagine they couldn't tell if he were alive or dead, and the notion that I had brought a dead man to the saloon made me a mite more interestin' than any old drifter might be.

"*Comprende englis?*" asked one of the men, clearly not a Mexican, and trying to gauge me.

"I reckon I do," I replied, wiping my hair out of my face.

He ran his eyes up and down me, trying to come to terms with my hips and breasts in the garments of a man, and my voice, which was decidedly female. "Whoowee, you a girl?"

"I'm a woman," was my answer, and I lowered my brows,

scrunching my eyes, giving him a look that no man could mistake for inviting.

"And what's this body you're bringing into Salvacar?"

"Ain't no body. That there's my husband, and he's hurt." I took as wide a stance as I could, annoyed with all the questions.

"What'd you do? Shoot him? Where'd you come from? What do you want here in Juarez? You on the run?" asked the second man, a little less inebriated than the first, if I was any judge. He was studying me boldly and with blatant hostility, his lip pulling back from rotting teeth, his face speckled with clumps of patchy dark beard that was flecked with bits of food and debris. He spat on the ground at my feet as I moved to try getting Oliver off the horse. "We don't need any troublemakers in this 'ere town. We don't need any more fugitives neither."

"I ain't no fugitive, and neither is he. And as for all the rest of your dad-blamed questions, it's none of your goddamned business. *Comprendes*?"

He reached out toward me as I was stretching up to touch Oliver's arm. I yanked my little Colt out of my belt, turned, and lunged forward, all the movements blending into one motion. I shoved the barrel of that gun directly into his gut and cocked it. The man stumbled backward a step with an exclamation of alarm, raising his hands.

"Goddamn, girl, take it easy with that piece. You even know how to use that thing?"

"Would you like to find out?" I asked, my voice low and even, though my heart was hammering a thousand times a second and I could feel a tremor in my hand—I just hoped he couldn't see it. I breathed out slowly, trying to still the shakes before the man felt the movements against his bulging belly. The memory of Grant Marcus toppling after I fired flashed in my vision and dread rose up in my stomach and into my throat. I didn't want to kill again.

"Come on, Ellis," said the first man that had approached me. "This girl's fuckin' *loco*, let's get out of here."

The second man sneered at me, spat again, then allowed his friend to draw him away, putting his arms down. I kept my pistol trained on them until they vanished into the night. Shuddering a little, I put the Colt back in its holster, returning my attention to my husband. He had the faintest grin on his face, and his eyes were just open the tiniest crack. I could see the gleam of his blues in the light cast from the saloon door, which stood open a bit, as if welcoming us inside.

"Nice job, Flaka," Oliver whispered, his voice so faint I struggled to hear it. Then he coughed a little and tried to reach toward me, but his hand was still tied to the saddle pommel. For a moment he yanked feebly against the rope, confused by his inability to use his arms. The brief strain of pulling on the ropes seemed to wipe him out completely and he slumped further forward onto his horse's neck.

I cut the ropes that bound him to the mare and then found myself suddenly crumpling under his weight as he slowly slid onto me. I braced my feet and eased him to the ground as slow as I could, letting him lay still beside the mare's feet. The horse, to her credit, didn't seem bothered none with the entire thing. She had begun chewing on the hitching post. There were a few other horses waiting out there, and Butterball had his eyes on a youthful filly. He was dancing about, making eyes and nickering at the lady on the other side of the post and nipping at her face. He was a gelding, but he'd never really believed that.

"The saddlebag, the one on the left," murmured Oliver, gazing up at the swinging stirrups above him.

"What about it?"

"Money," he whispered. "Don't leave it out here." He waved his hand toward the saddlebag in question. "That's our future in there, kid."

"Some future we're going to have if you drop dead

tonight," I snorted as I rose from beside him and began untying the saddlebag.

Once the bag was swung over my shoulder, I took his arm and half hoisted, half dragged him to a standing position. A moment later we were stumbling together like a single dirty, exhausted, four-legged creature toward the bustling, noisy saloon.

As our feet thudded, in my case, and dragged and scraped in Oliver's case, across the wooden porch toward the door, my husband spoke again. I paused to listen, his beautiful, raspy voice sending a shiver through my whole body, tickling my insides with a wondrous glow of warmth. "I told your pa I'd protect you, Flaka, but here you are . . . protecting me instead."

"It's alright. You did your part, so far, anyhow. Now it's my turn," I replied, keeping my voice just as soft as his, then I pushed the door open and we stepped into a place full of such light, chaos, and debauchery that I could hardly believe my eyes.

VI

ALL AROUND MEN LOUNGED AT TABLES AND STOOLS, NURSING tankards of ale that smelled so strong the whole saloon stank of musty corn and rotting apples. They were at cards, and singing and carousing with women in frilly dresses whose ample bosoms burst from their tight corsets. Everyone was laughing and shouting so loudly it made me wince. I thought I had never seen so much color and drunken joy in my whole life. A few people glanced at me, saw Oliver looking fit to die, and began whispering among themselves. Within only a matter of seconds the entire saloon hushed, all eyes on us.

"They're staring at us," I whispered to Oliver as he sagged against me, his head lolling onto his chest.

Oliver pulled himself up, standing as tall as he could. He was swaying on his feet and kept a vise grip on my shoulder to keep from falling. He answered me with a flash of his old liveliness and humor. "Probably astounded at what a handsome couple we make."

He nodded wearily toward an empty table near the door and we shuffled to it. He sank onto the shabby stool as the merriment in the saloon returned to what it had been before we arrived. For a second Oliver remained upright, blinking and looking around, almost dazed, then *mi esposo* let his face rest on his forearms. In a few seconds he seemed completely unaware of the noisy, bustling saloon around him.

The townsfolk and drifters in that tavern kept darting glances in our direction as they swigged their whiskey. After a while a serving girl approached us, her hips swaying. She moved at a brisk, businesslike pace, as if we were an afterthought and she had a thousand better things to do than deal with the likes of us. I straightened up on her approach, but Oliver remained dead to the world around him, listless and probably asleep where he lay across the table.

"Listen here, little fella, *escúchame, hablas inglés?*"

I nodded. By this time I had grown awful weary of the assumption everyone made when they saw the color of my skin that I wouldn't know how to speak English.

"Well, listen here, you best get your friend outta here if he's drunk."

"You got any rooms?" I asked and she took a step back, studying my dirt-crusted face.

"You're a girl?"

I frowned, ignored her question, and asked again, "You got any rooms?"

"We got no rooms tonight, mister, er, miss, er . . . ma'am?"

"Then perhaps you can point me in the direction of the residence of Martha Ramirez?"

Now the lady's face became even more bewildered, and she glanced around over her shoulder and then leaned in, her voice getting very low. "What do you want with Martha?" she hissed.

"You know where I can find her?"

The lady shook her head and then she scurried away, quicker than she had come. People all around were eyeing us again, stares of animosity—another fancy *palabra* Oliver had learned me. I was beginning to feel as tired as Oliver looked, and more than anything I wanted to lay my head down on my arms and drift off like he had. I didn't like how everyone was looking at us. It were positively unfriendly, and a sight near hostile. I didn't like that we were the center of attention, and any of these bastards could identify us to Marcus should he roll through this saloon sometime after us. But there wasn't much I could do. The waitress had obviously known my sister, though she'd been unwilling to provide information. If all else failed I could press the waitress, but I fancied I'd have to ask some other folk. I was just so damn tired. I wanted Oliver to wake up and take charge of everything again in his easy, suave manner.

Then a massive man approached us, walking with a swagger, and I stiffened, instinctively reaching down and loosening my little Colt in its holster, still hidden beneath the long coat I was wearing. The man came to a stop towering over us and the stench of his sweating rolls of fatty flesh nearly made me gag. I lifted my bandana a little and eyed him, keeping my hand on the outside of my jacket where he could see it, though it was resting on the pistol butt.

"We don't take kindly to strangers comin' in here asking after folk. We don't allow drunks and vagabonds in here, less'n they pay. And even if'n you did pay, you can't have a man in here like this, passed out as drunk as a boiled owl. You two troublemakers are goin' to need to shove off."

"I'm looking for Martha Ramirez," I said, sitting real tall and squaring my shoulders. "And until someone can point me toward her home, I ain't leavin'."

"Listen, ma'am, you come bustin' in here with your bottle-nosed husband or sweetheart, prolly carryin' weapons, looking for one of our girls, we ain't about to tell you nothin'. You're looking for trouble. But whatever Martha did for your husband is strictly business. If you can't keep him indoors that's none of Martha's fault."

My mind struggled to make sense of what he was saying. I'm not sure if it was the exhaustion on my part or the way he was expressing himself. I frowned up at him, my forehead creasing, a dull headache building in the back of my skull, both throbbing and piercing at the same time. After a minute I said, "I don't know what you're saying, mister. I'm looking for Martha Ramirez, Martha Garcia Hasani Ramirez. I need someone to tell me where she lives, and then my husband and I will be out of this fine establishment just as fast as we can shuffle off."

The man grabbed my jacket and yanked me up like a cornhusk doll, dangling me in the air before him. In that split second when my feet left the ground, two things happened. The first was that I snatched my pistol from its holster. The second was a blast so loud the whole saloon froze.

I saw a spray of blood burst from the man's upper arm and a look of pain mingled with anger crossed his face. I yanked my gun up, but before I could discharge it, I was soaring through the air. I crashed hard into a table and heard my pistol clattering to the ground a few feet away. It felt as if a mule had done kicked me directly in the spine. I saw the pistol on the floor and scrambled for it, but a booted foot pinned the weapon to the ground. Not waiting to catch the breath that had been knocked out of me, I tossed myself onto the bastard that was stepping on my pistol. It wasn't the first man, just some other interfering asshole.

In a moment I was on the ground, rolling and punching a much bigger person than myself. I think I only managed to take the man to the ground because my attack had surprised him. He struck his head hard on a table on the way down, stunning him, so I managed to pin him down, straddling his chest and punching his face as hard as I could. All around me the entire place had erupted into chaos, men and women shouting and squealing. People had started moving forward, empty liquor bottles lifted threateningly in their hands.

"That's enough," came a familiar, husky voice, raised as high as it could without breaking. There was an edge of danger to that voice that made a shiver of fear run through even me. "The next person that lays a hand on my wife will get a hole straight through their cranium."

It was clear that not a lot of people in the room were familiar with the word *cranium*. In fact, I myself hadn't known it a few days ago, but Oliver had already taught me that one by the time he issued his threat. There was fear and bewilderment on every face in that saloon. I lowered my fists and stood to my feet.

The man who had tossed me was holding his still bleeding arm, and glaring down at Oliver, who remained seated at the table. My husband had managed to sit up, using some inner strength I hadn't knowed he had. He was pale and sweating, but his hand, the hand holding his pistol, did not tremble.

"You've only got five bullets in that gun," sneered the big man. "There's a lot more than five of us here."

"I have two pistols," replied Oliver.

"Well . . ." The big man was taken aback but only for a second. "Well, there's a lot more than eleven people in this here saloon."

"Your counting skills do you great credit. So which eleven of you would like to volunteer to go home in a box tonight?" replied Oliver, the faintest hint of a smile spreading across his exhausted, pale face.

"Half the men in this tavern have guns as well. They'll drop you afore you take two of us."

"You must be a gambling man, mister," retorted Oliver.

I had seen Oliver's easy grace with a gun before, when he was shooting at the bandits outside my parents' house, and again when he showed my pa his ability to protect me. He had that same air about him again, as if he didn't care about a damn thing because he was so sure of his abilities with that weapon.

For a long moment I thought for sure the big man would throw a punch at Oliver, and he would blow the brains out of eleven men as fast as a single heartbeat. But another voice stopped everything, a cry of surprise from the stairs.

"Flaka Garcia Hasani, is that you?"

I looked up and stumbled a few steps backward, as if I were a small child caught with her hand in a cookie jar.

"It's Flaka Garcia Hasani Kedar now," I blurted out, searching for the source of the voice. At last my eyes alighted on her, the only person moving in the saloon, descending down the stairs from the upper floor. I hadn't seen Martha in ten years, maybe more—I knew I was a proper kid when she left with her husband. She was not as dark-skinned as I was, taking more after the Hasani side of the family with a light tan and brown hair that had the faintest streaks of gold mixed in, and a few streaks of white now. She was dressed in a gaudy yellow dress, with extra frills and lace sewed to every hem, a black ribbon around her neck with a central pearl button mounted in silver at her throat. Her breasts bulged out of her corset so much I had to check to make sure her nipples weren't peeking over the dress.

"Kedar?" she asked. The whole saloon melted away before her step and in a minute she had reached my side, ignoring the man I had been fighting, who was still slowly rising. Martha stood before me, drawing herself up. She was tall, handsome, fair, everything I was not. Her gaze slid over the crowd, who almost wilted away from her. "She's my sister, *mi hermanita*. As you were. I'll take care of her."

The room slowly turned back to their drinks, muttering together. There was a reluctance to their movements as if they had wanted to fight a good deal longer. Martha was still staring at me with those wide gray eyes of hers. She always had been a real looker, but now she was more strained in appearance, more fragile, older, and much more careworn than I remembered.

"What the devil are you doing here?" she asked.

I slid around her and darted across the room to Oliver's

side. He was sweating again, and ghostly pale. As the folk in the saloon had turned away, he had begun to sag, his pistol dropping to the table before him.

"I might ask you the same thing," I replied as Oliver lolled into my arms. "In a saloon in the middle of the night? Where's your husband?"

"My husband is drunk lying out on a street corner somewhere, covered in piss and excrement, no doubt," retorted Martha sharply.

I bit my lip, a flash of guilt hitting my chest. I had little memory of the man that took Martha away. He had been a fine dresser, I recalled, and he had smelled of a strong cologne. But the realization that my sister worked in a saloon while her husband was a drunkard in the streets was enough to set my mind reeling. Martha was the smartest of all of us. She had taken to reading like a fish to water, Ma had said, and 'rithmetic too. She had wanted to go east, to get a real, fancy education, but Pa didn't have money for that. He'd indulged her a great deal, but, when all was said and done, she had to marry and become a wife, like women were s'posed to out here. Like we all did.

"Are you a dancer?" I asked.

"We can talk about what I am and what I am not later," snapped Martha. "Let's get you and this man you seem mighty attached to back to my home."

"He's my husband."

"Oliver Kedar, ma'am," whispered Oliver, reaching up to tip his hat brim, his voice barely perceptible. He was fading fast. The fight had been completely pounded out of him. There was nothing left now but exhaustion and pain, pain that I could see plainly was contorting his handsome face.

"Oliver Kedar," Martha repeated, and her eyes narrowed, making her look pinched and cruel, like a mean old school-marm. She swung around to look at me again, shaking her head, then, without speaking, we put Oliver's arms over our shoulders and hoisted him up between us into a slumping but standing position.

A few minutes later we had him on his horse, and he was staying upright—for the most part, anyway. Martha and I kept close beside him at a walk, each one of us pressing against one of his legs on either side of the horse to support him, with me leading Butterball behind. We made our way through those dusty, silent streets, leaving the chaos and piano clanking of the saloon far behind. Martha led us to two disheveled little shacks maybe a mile up the road. Shacks may have been too high a compliment to describe those structures.

The one-room house where Martha lived was cobbled together, boards seemingly tacked together at random with some falling off the structure's frame, leaving gaping holes in the walls. Gaps in the flat roof above let the stars shine in and the cool night air as well. I couldn't imagine how cold it must be in the winter. We ducked inside one shack, the more stable of the two, and Martha looked for something in the darkness. While she rustled about and I kept Oliver upright, I could hear the sound of soft snores ending in faint little whistles, the kind of snores children make. The little ones were sleeping perfectly still against one dark wall. At last Martha lit the lantern she had been searching for, raised it to check on the small, towheaded forms, and then led us outside and into the other shack, even smaller and shabbier. I was reminded in an instant of the story Pa always read at Christmas, of Mary and Joseph and the stable and the manger.

"You can sleep out here. It's a sort of stable, though we only got goats. They prefer it outside this time of year anyway. I'd let you sleep inside the house but there isn't really enough room," Martha explained, showing us a pile of straw to lay on.

I set to removing the horses' saddles as soon as we got Oliver settled. He was asleep before he ever hit the straw.

Martha joined me, uncinching Oliver's mare while I brushed my poor, once-fat little pony. Butterball appeared to have lost near half his body weight on our mad flight through northern Mexico.

"Still riding that lazy little bastard after all these years?" Martha commented.

"He's served me well, and been a truer friend and companion than anyone else I've ever had in the world. You and the others all left when I was barely pint-sized. Never came back to visit, neither."

"You couldn't have expected us to stay for you," Martha replied. "You were ten years my junior, twelve years younger than Rachel, and even Ephraim had eight years on you. We all grew up. You were still a kid. We couldn't just live there forever with Ma and Pa to keep you company. We each had to make our own way in the world. Anyway, we all write when we can."

I didn't reply. Martha didn't know I couldn't read. She'd known I had struggled, sure, and she knew I couldn't read when she left, but she likely wouldn't have imagined that at twenty-one I still couldn't make anything out of letters on paper. She wouldn't have understood, and I was ashamed to tell her. Reading and writing had come as easily to her as breathing, I think, and I remember they had been as important to her as breathing as well. She used to read to me at night, great, wonderful *historias* that took my breath away. Stories I still remembered all these years later, tales of adventure and danger, knights and ladies, high courts and fancy goings-on in far away, magical worlds. Those stories still came back to me sometimes at night when I was trying to sleep.

"Two or three times a year Ma and Pa get letters from you," I said at last as I stacked the saddle, blanket, and bridle in the corner of the shabby little barn. I turned back to her, standing with my hands on my hips. "You ain't never come back to visit since you got married, not even once. You think two letters a year is enough? And never in any of those letters did you mention you had entered the trade of whoring at a local saloon."

Martha, who had turned to face me, slapped me so hard across the face I saw stars burst in my vision. When I turned back to her, holding one hand over my burning cheek, she was alight with rage.

"Don't talk like you know what I'm doing or why I'm doing it. You who went and married a gunslinger without a single prospect in life but to die at the end of a rope."

"Don't talk about my husband like that. You don't know nothin' about him."

"And what do you know about him?"

"He came from back East, and he went to college."

"Yes, and now he lives out here and shoots up banks and stages and saloons and claims to be the fastest gun in all of Texas. Oliver Kedar! You married Oliver Kedar."

"I ain't never heard of him before . . ." I trailed off, not wanting to tell my judgmental older sister about the circumstances of my recent marriage.

"Well, in my line of work men talk, and names get mentioned. I've heard of Oliver Kedar and he's nothing but trouble."

"You fuck some two-bit cowboys pushing cattle through this godforsaken desert and you think you know more about my husband than I do?"

"How long have you been married to him?"

"A week, less than that . . . five or maybe six days."

"And how long have you known him?"

I bit my lip again. Oliver moaned and I turned from my sister to check on him. He was clammy and cold to the touch. He mumbled weakly—words jumbled together in a delirious, nonsensical pattern.

"You have a doctor in this town?" I asked, fear clenching

at my gut. I didn't know what was making me more afraid, the thought of my husband's injury and illness, or the thought that Grant Marcus had been right, and my sister was right too. I had married a gunslinger, with no prospects ahead of him but to die with his neck in a noose. But just then I couldn't think about everything I didn't know about the man I'd bound myself to. We needed food, we needed water, and Oliver needed a doctor, or he would never make it to what Martha believed his inevitable end would be.

"We do, yes. He's probably sleeping right now. And drunk, if I know Belcher."

"Is he near? Could you . . . run and fetch him?"

Martha stood back for a moment, assessing me with those sharp gray eyes of hers. I thought she was going to refuse my request. Her glance flitted back and forth for a few seconds longer between me and my husband, and I think she saw the care that strained my face, and made me look doubtless very old in the shifting shadows of the lantern light.

"Should let him die, would be a kindness to you, Flaka," she said at last.

"It would not be a kindness to me. Listen, I don't rightly know what kind of monster your husband is, Martha, but Oliver ain't that. I . . . I love him." I had not said those words aloud yet in the few days since I had met Oliver, not to him, and certainly not to anyone else as we journeyed across the desert. But I felt a tightness in my chest that I thought was my heart stopping every time I imagined him dying. My Oliver. I wouldn't let it happen, couldn't let it happen, not while I still drew breath. I barely knew him, but somehow in less than a week he had become more important to me and more beloved than any other human in the whole goddamned world.

Martha relented. "I suppose I would still be at the tavern all night anyway, so it's not as if you're keeping me up past my bedtime. I'll fetch him for you, but I'm not sure he'll be of any help. He's an old doc from the war. His best days are behind him. Probably dead drunk at this hour, like I told you."

"It don't matter, as long as he comes and does somethin'."

Martha disappeared into the night, carrying the lantern with her and leaving me crouched on the straw beside my husband. The horses were gratefully munching oats Martha had given them, and the sound of their slow chewing was the only other noise aside from Oliver's breathing. I rested my hand on his cheek and then nestled myself close beside him as he lay curled on his side on the floor. He shivered and mumbled something I couldn't understand. I curved my smelly, sweaty, dirty body around his back, enclosing him protectively with my shorter frame. The aching in my chest was worsening as I felt him breathing, felt the coolness of his body, and feared that any second he would slip away from me forever, before I had the chance to tell him what I had just told Martha.

I laced my arms around him, squeezed him tight against me, and placed my lips beside his ear. He did not stir or shift, giving no sign he was even aware of my presence, let alone of my embrace. I whispered in his ear that I loved him, over and over and over again, though he didn't seem to hear me. As I whispered it and pressed him still closer to me, the thought of Mary and Joseph and their baby in the straw of a stable, surrounded by animals, burst again into my mind. But I would never bear my Joseph's baby, and right then I wanted that. I didn't want him to leave me alone, with nothing but memories. I wanted to make love to my husband before he died. I wanted to be one with him, fully and completely his, and him fully and completely mine.

He shuddered again and let out a low moan of pain as I squeezed him tighter to my chest, and a tear, as hot as fire, slid down my face, burning through the sand and dust and grime that crusted my cheeks to fall in the straw beneath my head. Then another fell, then another, and my shoulders trembled hard as I forced my sobs to be silent.

In my mind I could hear him reading again, those beautiful words that meant something, those words that pulled at my heart. Then I heard the sound of footsteps coming up the lane, and the creaking of the gate of the little compound where *mi hermana* lived. Instinctively I untangled myself from my husband, smeared the wet mud across my cheeks with my hand, and sat up, hefting my revolver. I drew back the cock and waited, hardly daring to breathe. If Ian Marcus had found us now and my husband couldn't defend me, well, goddamn it, I was going to defend him. I owed him that much—to die in his defense if I had to. That was love, I thought, real, true love, to care about someone so much that you'd die for them.

VII

"Flaka, I've brought the doctor." My older sister's voice sent a shiver of relief through me. I uncocked the pistol, though somewhere in the back of my head a flicker of suspicion bloomed. Perhaps she had been captured and was now being forced to soothe me so I would fall into Marcus' trap. These were the thoughts of a hunted person, and I tried to brush them away. It was only natural, but I did not want this constant suspicion and fear to be my natural state; it never had been before. Tension upon tension, the strings of a guitar twisted too tight, drawn to the point of breaking.

"I hear you," I said, my voice raspy from crying.

There was a pungent, sweet smell that washed over the dingy little stable when Dr. Belcher entered. Martha hadn't been wrong, he was practically marinated in alcohol. But he was a doctor. He would help my Oliver, so I could fault him *por nada*. I rose to my feet and stood back, allowing the lantern light to cast its pale gleam over my husband's fitfully sleeping form.

Belcher let out a loud burp, and I supposed that was where he had gotten his name from. He knelt down beside Oliver and rolled him over. The doctor was trembling and glassy-eyed. He fumbled with the buttons of Oliver's *camisa*, until I reached down and helped him undo them. Finally we drew his shirt off, and Belcher produced a pair of scissors from a black bag at his side, quickly doing away with the bandages wrapped around my husband's rib cage. A moment later the wound was exposed, and I startled to see how it bulged out around my stitches, and the purulent stench of rot that it gave off.

The doctor pressed at the wound with one hand, while holding a handkerchief to his nose with the other. He got a few more tiny spots of pus to ooze out from between the stitches, and the pushing against the wound prompted a feeble groan from Oliver. My husband moved a little to get away but stilled after another second, no strength left to fight. I stifled a sob at seeing my easy, carefree, brave, strong husband in such a helpless, weak condition. It weren't right.

"It's infected, my dear girl," explained Belcher and let out another outrageously loud burp. "After he got the wound, how long did you wait to close it?"

"It were more than a day before I had time to close it, maybe two days?" Our flight through the desert had become a blur to me. It might have been three days, but for the life of me I could not remember.

"Better to leave it open at that point. But, I think no real harm was done, though I suppose only time will tell." He fished a thin little knife from his bag and slid it into the wound gently, slicing through the stitches. Oliver groaned again and flinched away. When the cut was wide open again, a gush of thick, white purulence bubbled up, releasing an overwhelming, foul stench into the air.

The doctor pressed his handkerchief harder into his nose.

"You'd best keep it clean and open and draining. Don't put a dressing on it. You can hold warm compresses on it at least a couple times a day. A poultice of slippery elm, pokeroot, blue flag root, and lobelia seeds mixed with a bit of lye if you can find any."

He must've seen the expression of bewilderment on my face. I couldn't even remember the list he'd just given me, let alone hope to find such things in Juarez.

"Oh wait, my apologies, young lady, I may have a mix of the herbs in here." The doctor rummaged in his bag for some time before producing a small fabric sack that he passed to me. "The infection seems already to have gone right through him, though. He's got the look of blood poisoning, I'm afraid. But he appears to be a strong lad, so I think there's a good chance that, with the proper care, he'll recover."

"Thank you, Doctor," I replied as I crushed the bag of dried herbs in my hand, catching the faint sweet, syrupy scent of the slippery elm. An anvil of guilt had settled upon my chest. I had closed that cut. I had made Oliver as sick as he was. I had sealed that poison into his body and into his blood. If he died, then I was the one that done killed him. I could feel tears burning behind my eyelids, but I blinked hard to keep them from spilling out. Not now. I couldn't cry now. There was work to do.

"I reckon he lost more than a few pints of blood as well, but he'll produce more, given time. Don't fret, dear girl, he'll be good as new in a few days, I think. I can't promise anything, of course, you understand that. Sometimes even the strongest and healthiest fall prey to their wounds. Now . . ." He trailed off, looking about with those gleaming, bloodshot eyes and I remembered myself and grabbed the saddlebag Oliver had told me contained our money. It was the first time I had looked in the bag and as I opened it in the light of the lantern I couldn't help myself and drew in a breath sharply.

Martha peered over my shoulder, and her eyes narrowed, her gaze darting back at Oliver's unconscious form. She pressed her lips tight together into a grim line but didn't say anything. There was more money in that bag, real money, both dollars and coins, than I had ever seen in my whole life. I think if I took all the money I had laid eyes on in all my years, added it up, and multiplied it by a dozen, it still wouldn't come anywhere close to the amount in that bag. I pulled out a bill and passed it to Belcher. He held it high in the light, grunted in appreciation, bowed to both of us, and stumbled out the door of the stable and into the night.

"And do you know where your husband came by that amount of money?" hissed Martha as soon as the sound of Belcher's dragging footsteps had faded into the darkness.

"Do you know where your husband is?" I retorted.

She struck me across the cheek again, so hard it stung and I saw stars. She was very good at slapping people.

"Shut up," she snarled. "Or I'll throw you and your husband right back out where I found you and let the good people of Salvacar take care of you. Or better yet the sheriff himself. I don't need you bringing trouble into my home, Flaka. I've enough problems as it is."

"I didn't come here to bring you no trouble. I would've pushed right on through and never sought you out at all if Oliver weren't hurt so bad. Next time, even if one of us is scraping at the doors of death, I ain't coming back here to see you, Martha. That I can promise. Now if you'll leave off and go do whatever you need to do tonight, whoring or servin' drinks or dancin' or whatever it is you do up at that saloon, I'm going to sleep."

I didn't wait to see her reaction. I already knew she would turn a livid purple and clench her fists, and a juicy vein in her neck would stand up so tall it would look like she'd grown a second throat. I had done seen it all before, *hace muchos años*. Martha was mad, and she had a right to be. Her kid sister had come bustin' into her town and found out the hell she lived in, the hell she had been forced to live in. As I lay in the straw beside my husband that night I tried to imagine how hard her life must've been the last few years, and tried to summon up some compassion, but there wasn't much to spare. Not after the way she had talked about Oliver, who had become so much more to me already than she had ever been. I rankled at the words she had spoken about my Oliver—Oliver who cared about me, which was more than could be said about her.

Of my three siblings, Ephraim had always been the closest I'd had to a true friend. He'd always brought me candies when he went into town, and he'd taught me to play the harmonica. I still loved to make that spit fiddle wail out beautiful tunes on lonesome nights, *canciones* as sad as the cries of coyotes in the distance. I felt in my pocket for the little metal piece and considered playing it just then. I hadn't dared on the run, but now we were . . . safe, I suppose, after a fashion, anyway. We were with family. However much she hated me, Martha wouldn't betray me to Marcus. That's not what a big sister does, regardless of how stuck-up and snotty that sister might be.

I could still hear the quiet sounds of Martha's children snoring, so I let go of the harmonica. Wouldn't do to wake up the children, and it would Martha more angry. Then, a few minutes later, I also relinquished my grip on wakefulness, falling into the most peaceful sleep I'd had since we fled from my home. I was safe, safe at last.

The morning dawned with all the intensity of a lit oven, with baking, breathtaking heat. I roused to the piercing cry of a rooster that seemed to be standing right by my ear. When I opened my eyes, at first I didn't see the bird, but then I caught sight of the ruffle of his gleaming red and green feathers through the hole in the roof over my head. Dawn had turned the world peach, like the color of my husband's skin, or at least, the color his skin had been before he got shot in the side and turned all ghostlike. Remembering my husband, I startled and twisted around, looking for him, making sure his chest was still rising and falling, and, once assured that it was, I breathed a sigh of relief and stood up, stretching and yawning.

Oliver was fast asleep, his face peaceful, though it were still drawn and worn by pain and illness. He looked better, I thought, though perhaps it was just my wishful imagination. I rose to go boil water. I needed to make that poultice for Oliver. Outside the barn I found two pinch-faced little children, scrawny and covered in dirt, with wild tangles of brown hair. One was petting my horse Butterball and singing the little gelding a song. It reminded me for a brief sharp moment of my brother and I doting on the old pony when we were kids and teaching him tricks, like how to lay down when you touched the back of his knee just so, making it easier for little ones to climb aboard him. The singer was a boy, I thought, though at that age it can be hard to tell. The other was a young girl, maybe seven or eight years old, milking a potbellied goat while the animal's kids tried to push the child away. The girl sneered up at me with her pinched little face.

"*Quién eres?*" she asked, rudely, I thought.

"I'm your aunt, I do believe," I replied. "Flaka."

"Oh." She stared off as she continued to squeeze the teets of the goat. Then she shifted her gaze back to me. "You must be why Ma is in such a pissing mood."

"More like your ma is in a pissing mood because she has a hard life caring for you," I snapped back.

The girl shrugged, finished her milking and stood up, bucket in hand. The warm milk smelled like heaven, and I heard my stomach rumbling loudly. The girl watched me for a second as I stared at the wooden pail in her hands.

"Come on, then, we may as well cook up some oatmeal with this, while it's warm," she said.

I followed her inside. Now that I could see it in the light of day, I appreciated that the house was a tad more put-together than the stable outside. Straw mattresses were piled up against one wall, and a cooking fire set on a large flat stone spewed black, toxic fumes into the close air of the tiny residence. There were two other children inside, bickering about something, one trying to brush the other's tangled, lice-filled mass of hair. They stopped squalling immediately on seeing a strange intruder in their home, and they gaped at me. Also rather rude, I thought.

"*Quién es?*" asked one of the little ones to the older girl who was setting up a pot on the hot stone by the fire.

"*Tía* Flaka."

"*Tía?*"

"The little ones don't speak English?" I asked.

"They speak it. We speak English and Spanish here all the time. Don't you speak Spanish?"

"*Poquito,*" I returned lamely.

The oldest girl shook her head. "You should speak more. We ain't ever even been to school and we know it."

"Well, I ain't hardly been to school neither, and I don't live in Mexico. *Pueden leer?*"

They all shook their heads as one, giving me an idea. It were a foolish notion, but I wanted the awe of these *sobrinos* I had never met before. I went back outside and returned with the little book Oliver had been carrying. There was a bloodstain along one corner of the cover, and I wiped at it pointlessly, as it was long dry. The children gathered around in awe and I began to pretend I was reading words off the page. I was trying to relay what little phrases I remembered from Oliver reading, but I think the result was the poorest imitation of poetry that has ever been heard this side of the Mississippi. Once they were properly astounded at my abilities, I ate with them, learning a little bit about each ragged, bony child, and finding they were all infested with lice, to various degrees. Once my stomach was satisfied with the oatmeal and I had boiled some water and made a poultice with an old rag the oldest had been kind enough to give me, I returned to Oliver's side.

He woke up enough to drink a good amount of water and then drifted off almost immediately as I applied the medicine to his side. His lips were dry as bone, so I didn't wonder that he hadn't peed at all that day or overnight. Settling down beside him, I held the little volume up, letting the bright sun illuminate the words. Softly I began to sound them out, quiet enough that if *mis sobrinos* were outside they couldn't hear my poor stuttering, but loud enough for Oliver to hear if he was awake. To my surprise, the words started coming together, slowly, painfully, but they were not just squiggles on *la pagina*, I was beginning to find the musical phrases encoded there. After painfully sounding out each line, I went back and said the same line faster, and faster, until the sounds became not just words but entire sentences that began to make sense. It was like learning how to fly, breathtaking and exciting, finding those secret messages amongst those black lines on the page.

That is how I spent the entire day, and I'm ashamed to say I wasn't a great reader by the end of it. But I was putting words together like I never had before. I was stuttering through them and making them begin to sound nice. I could not imagine what had given me this new power over the written word, except that it be my love for Oliver and his patience with me, sounding out words beside the fire. Oliver woke up only three times during the whole day, to drink water, and finally to pee in the chamberpot I had brought from the house, and then he went back to sleep.

The next day Oliver was much the same, waking up to drink water and broth that I brought for him, murmur a few things, and then go back to sleep, but his skin didn't feel so hot as it had before. He was improving, slowly, but surely— he was getting better like the doctor had made me dare to hope. I kept applying warm compresses and the poultices, rationing the herbs as best I could. Despite the foulness of it, it made me happy to see Oliver beginning to use the chamber pot more, and his urine beginning to lighten in color. I saw little of Martha those two days. She worked hard at night and slept a good part of the day. I tended to stay away from her when she was awake and spending time with her offspring. During the mornings I played with the children and tried to eradicate the louse infestations from their hair, but in the afternoons and evenings I practiced my reading skills beside my husband as he slept.

> "W-w-ha'at w-w-ord-seh ah-reh t-heh-es-eh
> —*Godangit*—thees h-av-eh fah-ll . . .n fr-o-
> meh meh . . . mee?
> C-ahn cal-meh d-d-ehs-pah-ir . . . duspa-eer . . .
> an-duh will-duh un-r-hest
> Beh-beh-bee ten-an-tsuh o-fuh ah singuh-sin-
> guh-luh br-ee-ast,
> Oruh . . . sore-rohw suc-huh . . . such . . . a c-c-
> chan-gehi-ling—*Christ Almighty*—chan-
> gehaling be?"

I startled badly as another voice, dry and low but sweet and familiar, began to speak. Not the slow, painstaking words that were dragging from my throat, but rhythmic, songlike, and lovely.

> "Or cloth she only seem to take
> The touch of change in calm or storm;
> But knows no more of transient form
> In her deep self, than some dead lake
>
> "That holds the shadow of a lark
> Hung in the shadow of a heaven?
> Or has the shock, so harshly given,
> Confused me like the unhappy bark

"That strikes by night a craggy shelf,
And staggers blindly ere she sink?
And stunn'd me from my power to think
And all my knowledge of myself;

"And made me that delirious man
Whose fancy fuses old and new,
And flashes into false and true,
And mingles all without a plan?"

Oliver had not opened his eyes as he spoke, but he did at last as he finished that last line, and stared at me with those warm blue orbs, more alive than they had been since before our night in the cave.

"You got all that memorized?" I asked, trying to hide the burst of delight inside me at the sight of him awake and alert in the world of the living.

"I have almost the entire book memorized. Been reading it and only it for a few weeks. I fancy I'll trade it when we find a bookseller or a peddler somewhere, and learn another book by heart. That's how I've been doing it for the past year, since I came out here. A man has to feed his soul, you know."

My eyes widened. "The whole damn thing? And more books besides this'n you've memorized?" I could hardly believe I'd married such a fine, clever, educated man as this feller. And me hardly able to put two letters together.

"I've lost track of the number of books I've memorized. Doesn't come in useful very often, but every once in a while, around a fire on a late night out on the range, men like to listen to beautiful words." Oliver closed his eyes again and seemed to drift off for a second, his breathing slowing.

"Are you alright? The doctor had to come two nights back, open the wound up again. He said you were in a pretty bad way. Said maybe you had a touch of the blood poisoning. You've just been sleeping and sleeping since then."

"Oh? Not to worry. It would take more than one bullet to kill me," replied Oliver, opening his eyes again and grimacing in pain. "The wound hurts like the devil today, and I think it's stinking."

"I'll get some water and wash it up again. I'm supposed to be putting warm compresses on it a couple times a day to keep it drainin'. And a poultice, but I've used all them blue slippery poke flag herbs up on it already. You'll need some food too." I started to rise, but Oliver reached out and grabbed my hand, pulling me back down beside him.

"No rush, Flaka," he whispered, and then he lifted himself up a little and ran his fingers through my hair, behind my ear, and down along my jaw. A shiver of joy and desire ran through me.

"What'cha doin' in there?" came a taunting, high-pitched voice from a space in the wall where a board had long ago fallen out. The strident little voice broke the brief, magical spell of Oliver's touch.

I lunged toward the crack in the boards, frightening my two little nephews away. They skittered off, shrieking with glee, but the moment was over. When I turned back to Oliver, he had slumped a little onto the floor, and now the pain was very clear. He looked around, letting his gaze rove over our dirty refuge.

"It was very kind of your sister to put us and our horses up. We'll have to give her some money for her trouble. It looks as if she could use it."

"You think this is kind? I've known doghouses that were finer than this."

"Come on, Flaka. She could have left us to be beaten to death in the tavern, but she brought us here, where it's safe, and there's a roof, and walls."

"Walls and a roof full of holes." I softened then, thinking

of the night we'd first arrived. "I was starting to think a few nights back about Mary and Joseph and the stable, and the manger, all that. Stories Pa used to tell me from the Bible."

"Well, so my little Flaka is a romantic after all, then?"

"You think Mary and Joseph being together in a stable full of dung and filth and the bloody straw from her having a baby right there is romantic?"

"Not when you put it like that." He grinned broadly. "Is this your way of trying to break the news to me that you're also carrying some sort of immaculate conception?"

"What the hell?" I snapped, reeling suddenly. Perhaps it had been a joke, but something in the suggestion, coming from the man I loved, hit me the wrong way.

"Well, you did up and marry me right quick as soon as you saw the opportunity. Perhaps there's something you wanted to hide from your preacher father and sainted mother."

"The hell are you talking about? I married you because you was a fine-looking, dandy knight that rode up onto my porch, just like in them stories. Fool that I was. I ain't knocked up! I ain't never even been with a man, you ass!"

He was sputtering some apology, his face filled with dismay at how I'd taken his remark. But I was appalled, truly appalled that he would dare suggest such a thing. Sure, I had messed around a little with that hired hand Pa had out at the farm two years back, but I hadn't let him inside my most private parts. Same goes for Sampson, four years ago, that boy from Pecos. He'd been able to suck on my tits and manhandle my nethers a little, but he'd not put his carrot inside me. I was just about as pure as the Virgin Mary herself, and I bristled at the hint that I had been fornicating with anyone outside of the holy bounds of matrimony. I was the daughter of a preacher, after all.

I drew my shoulders back and lifted my nose in the air, forgetting completely that I was the one that had started talking about Mary and Joseph in the first place. I had wanted the conversation to turn towards love, and to tell him the words I had spoken a hundred times over his insensate form the nights before. But not now—the moment had passed. I would not be professing my love to him now, maybe not ever if he was going to be cracking jokes like that, accusing me of being a whore.

I jumped to my feet, glared down at him, then turned on my heel and stomped out to get some water for his wounds. When I returned I slammed the pail down, sloshing some of the water on the floor, and tossed a rag at him before storming off. He could wash his own bloody wound.

Outside I sat on the fence post, playing my harmonica, while Martha's children gathered around in awe. After a while I slammed the instrument against my thigh to clear the spit and asked, "Where the blazes are your ma and pa, anyhow?"

"Pa's workin'," replied the oldest girl matter-of-factly. "I think, anyway. Ma's always gone this time of day. She'll come back around suppertime and then she'll be gone again all night. I think all night. She's gone most nights, 'ceptin' the Lord's Day."

My whole life I had lived with my folks, my virtuous folks, followers of the Good Book, who kept to normal times and obeyed the laws of God and the land. They had modeled for me a good and godly life, a good and godly marriage, but here these children barely saw their parents. Their father was a constantly drunk, useless dirtbag, if Martha was to be believed. Their mother was a whore, just so as they could eat and live their feral little lives with the goats and chickens of their tiny plot of dirt in Salvacar. Perhaps, I reflected, just maybe, I had judged Martha too harshly.

We were interrupted just then by Dr. Belcher. He looked a great deal more shevelled and kempt than he had a few nights before, and didn't smell so strongly of the tangy dew of alcohol. He ambled up to the gait, called greetings in Spanish to each of the children, and then doffed his hat to me, bowing.

"How fares my patient? I trust he's doing better?"

"She musta paid you good for you to come calling again to check on 'im," observed the oldest girl. I pulled a face at her, sticking out my tongue as if I were a kid myself. Then I snapped my face back to normal, remembering myself before this adult physician, and nodded toward the stable.

"He's much better today, thanks to you. I'd be most obliged if'n you checked on him again, though."

"But of course, but of course!" agreed Belcher hastily, sliding over the fence with more grace than I expected from a man of his age and girth.

Inside the stable he tut-tutted over Oliver for a long time, messing with his wound, dabbing at it, and checking his skin and pulse and counting his breaths repeatedly, making a great show of it all, staring at Oliver's chest, then back at his silver pocket watch. All the while Oliver was mouthing "I'm sorry" at me, and looking for all the world like a scolded puppy, and I felt my heart beginning to soften toward him again. Just a little. My temper had gotten the best of me. His suspicions could be forgiven—that was the world we lived in, after all.

The good doctor kept shaking his head and fussing, and mopping at his brow. After seeming to ponder what he should do for a while, he finally dressed the wound with some spicy-smelling poultice that made Oliver's face contort with agony. It must have stung something awful.

"What's this?" asked the doctor, picking up the little book of poems from off the floor where I had left it in my rage. "Tennyson? Fine taste you have, boy. He'll be one of the great voices of our century, mark me there."

"I haven't found words that spoke so clearly to my soul in all my years of reading," said Oliver, brightening at the prospect of speaking to someone else who knew anything about his little book.

"Perhaps I could trade you for this work?" asked the doctor. "I've got a few volumes of the more obscure of Keats' works at home . . ."

"No!" I cut in and immediately quieted my voice as they both looked at me in surprise. "I . . . I want to read it a bit more, I mean. Then perhaps we can send it back, once we reach our plot west of here, in the Arizona Territory."

"Going to Arizona, then? A fine place, I've heard. Though just as hot as it is here. Sometimes I wake up and think I'm not in Mexico at all, but in the ninth circle of Dante's *Inferno*."

"'*Where we came forth, and once more saw the stars,*'" said Oliver cryptically. "But listen, friend, speaking of Arizona, how soon can I be up and off? The horses have rested, and so have I. I fancy I'm well enough for us to push on. Don't want to miss out on the piece of land I've staked my heart and future on."

"I'd prefer and strongly advise you to rest and recover for another week."

Oliver scowled at that, a deep, dark look that cut his broad forehead into lines.

"But I can see that would be expecting a great deal too much," remarked the doctor wryly, reading my husband's expression. "Well, then, give it two more days, at the very least. You hear me there, young lady? Your husband should remain abed and not exert himself for two more full days, at the very least, but preferably a week."

"I hear you," I said as the doctor bowed to us both and accepted another bill from Oliver's saddlebag before departing.

VIII

Just one more day confined to the musty straw that served as our bed was nearly enough for Oliver to lose his mind. The first day he was a little short-tempered, but still exhausted and sleeping through most of the hours. His appetite had returned in full by the morning of what should have been his second full day of rest as prescribed by Belcher. When I woke up he was sidling along the walls, using them for support as he made for the shabby, leaning door of the stable.

I lifted myself up on my elbows. "Where are you going?"

"Just to get some food and relieve myself, if I'm allowed to do so," he said. It was his tone that gave away his annoyance with having his movements restricted, his low voice rising just a little at the end of his statement.

I slumped back, unsure how to negotiate with this man I barely knew. Then I frowned. "Listen, the doctor told you to stay in bed another week, but because you're a stubborn ass he said two days at the very least. Just two days. You've only been in bed one day, so far, since he said that. Just one more day. Can't you do that? It ain't a lot to ask."

"I'm a stubborn ass now? And here I thought the day the doctor came you were about to declare your undying affection for me. I'm fine, feeling much better, honestly. I think we should push on. The longer we stay here the more likely danger is going to find its way to your sister's home. If Marcus comes asking about us in this town, people are going to remember what happened at the saloon. They'll know where we went and they'll come here. Is that what you want?"

"Undying affection? You wish," I retorted, having sorted out the meaning of his words. I blushed, however, and wondered how he had known what I had been feeling while I watched him sleep. "I don't want Marcus to come here, you can bet your life on that. I don't want that at all. But it's been nearly a week since we saw hide or hair of the man. I reckon he gave up."

"That's not the kind of man you're running from, Flaka. He won't give up until you're dead. Or he's dead."

"Then what's the point of running? Why don't we just give up? And how do you know so damn well what kind of man he is, anyhow?"

Oliver opened his mouth as if he was going to utter some scathing response, then he snapped it shut again and his shoulders sagged. Slowly he turned and made his way back toward the pile of straw, moving gingerly, as if his efforts to leave the stable had used up the last bits of energy he had left. Despite his bold words, it was clear that he was still hurt enough and sick enough that we should not push on. Indeed, the more I watched his movement and those rivulets of sweat and the lines of strain that rippled across his face and into his cheeks and neck, the more I felt it would be more than a week before we could press on toward Arizona. We would have to gamble on Marcus giving up, or at least slackening his pace a bit, as it appeared he had done. Perhaps Oliver did not know the man so well as he thought.

I stood up as Oliver took a position of repose upon the straw, staring up at the ceiling, his hands resting on his stomach, his fingers trembling. I gave him the chamber pot that was sitting by the door and set off to scrounge up some food for my wayward husband. Inside the house I found Jorge, or Javier, or whatever his name was, sprawled out on a feedsack by the door. The man stank of piss. The suit he wore had once been fine gray, tailored wool, likely costing an unbelievable sum of money, but now it was riddled with holes, some clearly chewed by rats and moths, and covered in dirt and stains that I couldn't identify and didn't really want to. He looked up at me and leered, his mouth sliding open, revealing rotting, blackened teeth.

"Tengo la hermana fea, en verdad. Ven, siéntate en mi regazo, muñequita. Te haré feliz."

Raising my foot as if to step over his form, I pressed my boot into his flank, crushing his side into the ground. He moaned and then grabbed at me, as if to pull me down on top of him. I have said that I didn't speak Spanish well, but I understood a great deal more than I spoke.

"Come mierda, cabrón," I said and kicked his grabbing, filthy hands away, making my way to the fireplace, where a few dried-out tortillas and some beans sat, cooked hours ago. One of the children must have left them for me, or perhaps my sister had. But I had barely seen Martha the last few days. She spent most of her time out, working at the saloon and perhaps staying late with the highest-paying customers.

It still rankled me to think of my sister as a whore—my educated, clever, snobby big sister. But when I looked at the scumbag lying on the floor of their humble residence, I thought bitterly that to be a whore was probably better than to be fucked by that pathetic, disgusting man. Drinking had washed away his humanity, and I hated him for the life he'd forced upon Martha. She prickled me like a cactus when we did talk, but still she deserved so much more than this.

Returning to Oliver with the food and a pail of water, I was surprised to find my husband still awake. Though he was dirty, and unwell, he still looked a thousand times better than Martha's miserable excuse for a man. I thanked God under my breath for the handsomeness of the man I had married as I knelt down and offered him a tortilla stuffed with beans.

He was still restless after he ate, but I convinced him to work on teaching me to read again, and this kept him occupied for a long time, for I was a very poor student. I was making progress, however, for the first time since . . . perhaps ever. I had learned all the letters by the time I was twelve, but no one had had the patience to teach a nearly full-grown woman after that. If I hadn't learned to read by twelve, Ma once said, I wasn't going to learn, and there was no point wasting daylight trying. Too many other things to do around the farm. Being able to read wasn't going to keep me alive in Texas. She was a practical woman, my ma, and her views were no doubt colored by her own inability to read. But Oliver was not practical like that, and he didn't mind spending hours and hours tryin' to teach my dumbass how to string letters into words.

We stayed up late that night poring over the words of that little book by the light of a lantern. Finally my husband began to teeter on the edge of sleep, his lids drifting closed and his head nodding onto his chest from time to time. At some point in our reading he had propped himself against a bag of oats for the horses. I had laid my back against his chest, finding, much to my delight, that I fit perfectly there. I held the book open before me while he peered blearily over my shoulder.

After completing a particularly challenging sentence, I glanced up, looking for confirmation of my efforts, but found that he was sleeping, his breathing slow and even against my back. My stomach was grumblin' mighty loud by then. Close and comfortable together, occupied with learning me to read, we had plum forgotten about lunch, and dinner too, it seemed. I slid out from Oliver's arms, pleased that he didn't wake up from my movements. Then I stood and set the little book on the ground, open to the page we had paused on.

It was nearly dark, and I was surprised to find Martha inside. Usually she would be at work at this hour. She was seated cross-legged on the ground, holding her youngest son's hand while he slept. She had a distant look in her eyes as she stared at the boy. She seemed lost, old, and terribly careworn. She didn't stir as I moved across the house, pausing to dig among the pathetic assortment of food by the fire. It was just a little bit of rice and beans, soaked but uncooked yet. The children must've gone and eaten everything that was cooked, and I didn't blame them none. They were scrawny little ragamuffins, more than a bit undernourished. They needed the food more than me and Oliver.

I sighed and began setting up the fire again, preparing to boil the rice. After a few moments of my clattering about, I heard Martha stirring. She stood up and moved over to crouch beside me on the floor at the stone slab that served as a stovetop.

"I didn't mean to be loud," I said, though she hadn't said I was annoying her.

"It's fine. These little ones wouldn't wake up if there was a Comanche ambush or a cavalry charge. They're like stones when they sleep."

"I reckon that's because of the hard days they have." I bit my lip hard as soon as I said that, realizing how it might sound, as if I blamed my sister for the struggles her children went through.

"If I could work every minute of every day to make their lives easier, I would. I want Harriet to go to school, Flaka. She's so clever I can scarcely believe it."

"Gets it from you," I said, flashing a smile at her that I think made her brighten a little—at least the lines in her face softened. "Will she go?"

Martha let out a sigh, scraping her fingers through her

long, fair hair. "Not unless the doors of heaven open up on us and bless us with more money than I could imagine. I barely make enough to feed them. And Javier takes the rest for his booze."

"I'd like to kill that man," I muttered darkly.

"You and me both," said Martha, and then she laughed, a harsh, bitter sound in the quiet little hovel. "Oh, Flaka. I don't mean to be unkind or judgmental of you and your husband. I only want you to have a better life than I've had. I don't want you to be forced to work in a saloon, making love every night to filthy, uneducated cowboys just to keep your children alive while your husband rots in some prison somewhere, or lies out on the road, loaded to bursting with foul liquor."

"That's not the kind of man Oliver is." My voice was firm as I said it. I sounded sure, surer than I felt.

"How do you know?"

"I just know it, Martha. That's all. You can tell with some people. You can jest tell."

"I thought the same of Javier when he first wooed me, Flaka. But it was all a lie. So many lies. Lies upon lies. And now we're here, living like this. Living like animals."

"After we buy this land Oliver wants, I'm going to send back as much of that money as we can spare to you. Harriet's gonna go to school, Martha, I promise."

"I don't want your husband's blood money."

"It ain't blood money."

"Then where did he get that much loot? Tell me that, Flaka? If he didn't kill someone or rob someone or both, then I can't imagine how a common boy like that came by such a sum."

"He's not a common boy, Martha! That's what you jest don't understand. He comes from Boston, from back East. It's probably . . . family money." I realized as I spoke how silly and foolish that was. Just why had the bandits been chasing Oliver when we first met, and did it have to do with the money he carried? And why, after a week of marriage, had Oliver still told me so little about himself? My sister was right, and I felt the heaviness of my mistake in my bosom and the pit of my stomach, as if I had swallowed a desert tortoise. Pictures of the future flashed through my mind, a future filled with babies I couldn't support, and, more horrifying than that, a vision of watching Oliver hang for crimes he hadn't told me about yet.

A gunshot cracked the night air and we both dropped to the ground. My hands were trembling madly. In a second I was back at my parents' home, gunshots whistling around, and Grant Marcus coming toward me. I forced my mind to the present, to the tiny, shabby hovel where my sister lived, and the unknown threat that was shooting outside.

"The fuck was that?" I whispered, wincing at the loudness of my voice.

Martha had already scurried across the floor to soothe the children. The little ones had woken up and started crying immediately after that first gunshot. There were more gunshots now, every minute another earsplitting noise. Outside a howling desert wind was picking up, whipping at the sides of the house, making it groan. The wind gave the world a strange, hollow sound beyond the doors of that tiny shack.

"Pistol's under the firestone," hissed Martha.

My fingers scrabbled in the dirt for seconds that felt like ages, searching around the warm edges of the stone, where a few coals still glowed. At last I found the soft spot, a tiny cave beneath the rock, and I yanked the weapon out of its hiding place. It was truly the oldest damn revolver I had ever seen, probably an antique long before the war in the sixties. Another gunshot split the air and the children whimpered louder. My heart thundered in my chest, thumping so hard I thought Martha could probably see my breasts leaping with every beat from across the room.

"Bullets?" I whispered urgently.

"Same hole!" called Martha.

I dug around in the hole again, coming up with a small, heavy tin that clanked when I moved it. Inside there were about two dozen bullets, not more. Another gunshot rang out and I startled and dropped a bullet I was trying to load in the weapon. There hadn't been any crack of timber, nor thud of bullet into wood that I had heard. So where were these bastards aiming? And who the devil was shooting so close to Martha's house? In my gut, I felt sure that it had to be Ian Marcus. He had found us after all. And if he had found us and was shooting at us, he had probably been watching and knew where in that little compound my husband and I were hiding. Then my heart leaped right up into my throat, cutting off my ability to breathe for a few seconds.

"Oliver!" I called hoarsely into the darkness as soon as I caught my breath.

"I'm alright."

A wave of relief washed over me at his low voice, just loud enough to be heard, almost cracking as he raised it—a strained but beautiful sound in the night. There was another shot, and I shivered, listening for him again, afraid that any second a bullet would find its mark in my husband's chest or head.

He called out, "They're turning this shed into a pincushion. Perhaps it's time to stop availing ourselves of your sister's hospitality?"

"Stop doing what?!"

"Leave, Flaka. It's time for us to leave!"

"We can't leave now! That bastard'll hurt Martha and the children!"

"No, he won't, Flaka. He'll let them alone to chase us. But we have to leave. It's the only way to save them. Understand?"

Then I heard the noise of the horses moving in the darkness and the shuffling of saddles and jingling of harnesses. Oliver was saddling up the mare and Butterball, and we were about to be pushing on. At least he had those two extra days of rest that the doctor had insisted on, I reflected, feeling grim. Hopefully it had been enough. Two more shots split the night air and the wind rose still more, whistling as it tore through the night.

"Flaka Garcia Hasani, come out now and we'll stop shooting," came the harsh voice I had heard a few nights before. It was a voice that sent a shiver down my spine and every hair on my body stood up on end. The deep, gruff voice of Ian Marcus. He was here, somewhere outside the shabby fence around my sister's tiny home. "The longer you delay the more likely these good people here are going to get hurt."

I heard Butterball let out a squeaky whine, the little noise he made when his cinch was tightened. Oliver was almost ready. I clenched the gun in my hand and skittered across the ground to Martha's side. It felt useless to have the revolver. I couldn't see nothin' outside the house. What in tarnation was I supposed to shoot at?

"She's not coming out, Marcus," called Oliver.

Marcus chuckled and then replied coolly, "Then you're going to die, Oliver. You're a rat caught in a trap. How are you going to get out of this? Send her out and I'll let you live."

"If we leave they'll follow us," I whispered to Martha. "You'll be safe here."

"Who is chasing you, Flaka? What in God's name have you gotten yourself into? That man's asking for you, not for Oliver."

"Because Oliver didn't kill his son. I did," I replied and felt a strange pride rise up inside me at the declaration. It oughtn't have given me pride, to say I had killed a man, that I was the wanted one of the couple, that I was the fugitive, when all of Martha's fears for our future were for my husband's misdeeds. But I did feel that proudness inside me. I felt it real strong. Because she thought I was a kid and I weren't anymore, and Martha ought to know that. She ought to know that I was growed up, that I could make my own mistakes, that I had gone and killed a man, and I was the danger, not Oliver. I wasn't some child brought on a dangerous trail against my will. This was the path I had chosen when I pulled that trigger in a moment of terrible fear. We were wanted, but not because of anything Oliver had done. My sister had misjudged where the real danger was. I straightened up, pulling back my shoulders. "I promise, he'll chase after us and he won't hurt you if we push on."

"How do you know that?"

"Oliver says so."

"I don't trust your husband."

"You don't have to, Martha, you just have to trust me," I replied and then I turned and raced for the door. I pushed it open slowly, and it creaked on rusty hinges, making me cower a little behind it. As the door opened, I paused, my eyes sweeping around in the black. The sliver of a moon gave just enough light to illuminate the fencing, the yard, the house, the chickens roosting in a corner of the rickety fencing, barely disturbed by all the ruckus. I heard Martha say something behind me, and I thought I felt her hand brush my shoulder, but then I was away into the night, darting across the yard, from one small hiding spot to another, a pile of rocks, a wheelbarrow, a heap of moldy straw. It was a stupid wild dance with death, gunshots ricocheting off the shoddy barriers I put between myself and Ian Marcus as I kept moving toward the stable.

The stable door stood open, but still a few yards away. I leaped across a few feet of open space, from behind a rotting barrel, and bullets pounded the earth behind my feet, dust flying up as they struck the sand and rocks. I threw myself down, pressing hard into a foul pile of manure and straw, almost swallowed up by that filth. Silence fell, save the wind howling eastward. I waited, letting my breathing slow, watching the quiet world around me. Nothing stirred. Nothing changed. The cry of the wind grew a little higher, drowning out any noises I might have caught. Far away, I thought I could make out the lonely howls of coyotes, carried for miles on that wind.

Taking one last deep, gulping breath, I lunged forward and gunshots rang out again. I threw myself through the air, toward the open door of the stable, striking the ground and rolling and tumbling, my ribs screaming out in pain from where I hit the floor. As I passed through the door, I saw the flash of fire, as if a torch were being hurled into the air, and then I was inside the dank, musty depths of the shabby structure, and Oliver was helping me up and running his fingers all over my body, searching for holes or blood. A warm tingling started in my loins at his touch, but I shook my head, trying to clear that lustful surge away. It was foolishness. We were about to die and here I was thinking about Oliver's penis, of all the dad-blamed things. Though, I suppose for a girl about to die who'd never had proper sex before, it may have been only natural.

Against my better judgment, I pushed Oliver's groping hands away. "I'm alright. I'm okay. They didn't shoot me," I whispered. "I'm alright. You?"

"Never better," he replied, then his head swung to the side as we heard the crackling not of pistol shot but of fire. Flames were already licking up the side of the little stable, hungrily devouring the dried, decaying old boards, replacing them with rippling orange.

"Martha's stable!" I cried and grabbed up an empty feedsack, running forward to begin putting out the flames. Oliver's hand, like a vise around my wrist, stopped me in my tracks.

"We can't save this building, Flaka. We can only save

ourselves, and save your family by leaving. If we escape, I can send enough money back to Martha to build a house ten times the size of the one she has and a livery fit for a queen."

My mouth dropped open. I didn't know what a "livery" was. All I knew was that I was leaving my sister with her barn on fire and her children under the gun from some monster in the darkness. But Oliver was clinging to my wrist, squeezing it so tight I thought my hand would break right off, staring at me with those earnest, desperate blue eyes. I nodded, sagging, feeling bleak and wrung out, and I let the feedsack fall to the dirt. The horses were becoming uneasy, crammed in that small space with the smell of smoke all around. The gunshots had finally let up outside. They were burning us out and they'd blast us with every bullet they had left when we rode out of that burning stable.

I squared my shoulders and moved toward Butterball, stroking his nose to soothe him. Then I swung up into the saddle, crouching low over his neck, making myself as small a target as I could. A smart man would aim for the horse, though, I told myself, and no amount of scrunching low would change the size and girth of Butterball.

"We'll split up and go in opposite directions," said Oliver, already mounted on his mare. "They won't know which of us is on which horse and they'll have to divide their fire. I'll find you, even if we get separated for a while. You understand?"

I nodded, feeling breathless and shaky. "But, Oliver, what about your wound?"

"I'm fine, Flaka, I promise I'm fine," he said, grinning that easy, reckless smile of his, the one that melted my very soul every time I saw it. "And I'll find you. Listen, make for the south side of the city, and toward the dunes, toward Samalayuca, but don't go into the dunes without me. I'll find you. I promise."

He edged the mare close against Butterball, and reaching over he took hold of my face with both hands, tilted my head up, and pressed his lips hard against mine. A wave of joy swept over me and I pushed my lips against his hard in return, loving the taste of him, the intoxicating smell of his sweat and his dirt. Then he released my face and turned his horse directly into the licking flames, kicking his heels into her flanks.

When he burst away into the night I thought an entire army must be after us, as the sound of guns discharging echoed out, shot after shot after shot. Every bang sent a bolt of terror through my heart, as I imagined any one of them finding their mark. The first kiss Oliver and I ever had might very well be our last. Then I heard hooves beating away fast into the night at a gallop and breathed a sigh of relief. The horse at least had made it alive through the volley of gunfire. I prayed under my breath that the rider had as well. There were more noises now, though, coming from the town. The folk of Salvacar were waking up and coming to see what was happening, and all that attention would hopefully drive Marcus away. For a second I wished we had waited just a moment longer. I heard men yelling and then the hiss of quickly intaken breath, close inside the shed with me. Still on Butterball, I whirled around, aiming the little pistol into the darkness of the stable.

"Don't shoot. It's me," gasped Martha. "My God, Flaka. My barn!"

"It's alright. We'll help you build it again. Oliver said he'll send you enough money to make a library fit for a queen, or something. Once we reach—"

"No!" she hissed, raising a hand with the palm outstretched, coughing a little as the smoke grew worse. The heat was cooking us alive and Martha's face glistened with sweat as she gaped at the flames consuming her stable. "Don't tell me, Flaka. If you don't tell me where you're going, then I can't tell anyone else. Here, give me the gun. You can't take that from me."

I reached down, finding my own loaded pistol already packed on Butterball's saddle, and then handed the ancient revolver across to my sister. She stood back, eyes flashing with fear and anger.

"Thank you . . ." I whispered. "And, Martha . . . I'm sorry. I promise I'll make it up to you. We'll make it up to you. I promise."

"*¡Cállate!*" she snapped in reply, her forehead wrinkling and lip twisting up a little with disgust. Then her expression softened and she said, "Just, for the love of God, shut up. Don't bother making promises to me that you can't keep. Just . . . just don't die, Flaka."

I nodded, clenching my *boca* tightly closed. Then I turned Butterball and burst into the night, to be greeted by a hail of pistol shots—though not quite the same amount that had met Oliver. A moment later I was galloping away, knocking over the curious people gathering to see the fire and the fight, and then I was free of the crowd and off into the dark streets of Salvacar.

IX

That night alone in the streets of Ciudad Juraez was the worst of our flight, so far. Gradually the noise of the fire and crowd died away behind me. I knew I was being followed, but I made a mad, twisting path through the streets, winding in and out of buildings and hovels, hopeful to lose them. Every time a shadow moved I startled and pointed my revolver at it. It was very late before I finally felt sure I'd lost them and I slowed to a steady pace. I wanted to be out of the city on the southwestern side by the time the sun rose. I wanted, more than anything, to find Oliver, to make sure he was alright. I could still taste his lips against my mouth, and feel the warmth in my whole body from that kiss, as if I had become a living flame, hotter than the fires that had burned that barn around us. Indeed, part of me thought the fire might have started from us, not from some torch hurled by Marcus' men. *Un beso de fuego.* How I longed for my Oliver all through that terrible, lonesome night.

The great torment of that night was not knowing if my husband were alive or dead. It was the most bleak damn night I could remember in my whole life. We had that all-too-brief moment of awesome glory when we finally kissed—that moment when I felt like I had done touched heaven itself—and that made the loneliness after all the more terrible. I tried to cling to the hope of another kiss, just like the first. What I wouldn't do for another kiss like that, for a thousand such kisses. But I was being eaten up by the horrible thought that there wouldn't be no more kisses at all, ever, exceptin' maybe mine on cold, dead lips if I ever found my husband's corpse.

He had fled before me, and all of Marcus' guns had been trained on him. Every gun had fired at once. It stood to reason they would have hit him. It stood to reason at least one person among Marcus' crew would have found their mark. And they had followed him into the night, with only a few left to pursue me when I rode out. Oliver had once again put himself in harm's way for me, and I felt fiercely that I weren't worthy of such devotion, not nohow, no way. I had put my sister and her children in danger. I had cost them their stable and everything they had stored in it. I was a selfish monster—a brat, as my oldest sister Rachel used to call me when I was little. Putting my sister in harm's way, Martha, who had been so begrudgingly kind to me and my husband when we came to her doorstep with only the promise of danger and ruin as payment.

I didn't deserve the love of such a good, smart, kind, self-less man as my Oliver clearly was. I didn't deserve that anyone should sacrifice theirselves for me, let alone him. He hurled himself into the path of a dozen bullets, just to protect a murderer who was running away from what would have been justice. I had killed and I should pay the price, like Cain did for slewin' Abel, as the story Pa told me went. Though, perhaps I was already paying that price, wandering the world as a marked woman, with no safe place to rest my head, no safe place to rest at all. *Una vagabunda.*

All that night I pushed through my loneliness and onward, and before the sun rose I was riding in the desert, away from the sleeping city, toward . . . toward nothing—

toward a greater loneliness, I s'pose. Tombstone. Oliver had said we were going to Tombstone. I didn't know the way, except that it was west and north, and I fancied I could probably ask along the way if I didn't find Oliver soon.

The desert south of Juarez was just a vast expanse of sand stretching on forever. There were scattered cactuses standing tall in that wild desolation, but there weren't nothing else, nothing but baking, unlivable heat, and fine white sand. I knew vaguely where the dunes of Samalayuca should be, still further south and then west, but I weren't sure it was a good idea to travel those dunes, even with my Oliver, certainly not alone. There might be other good folks, pioneers, traveling along that road, mayhap, but there would certainly be killers and robbers. And one woman riding by herself across the desert did stick out like a sore thumb. I shook the canteen fixed to my saddle and was pleased to find it full. We had been keeping them both full as much as we could, unsure if we would have to leave in a rush. But in the saddlebags themselves there weren't much that would pass for food. I would need to hunt if I wanted to eat. But there weren't no animals to speak of out there, 'ceptin' little hopping mice, the occasional circling vulture, and rattlesnakes.

I ran into my first rattlesnake a few hours into the ride, as the sun was nearing its highest point. Butterball kicked a rock the snake was trying to find shade under and must've startled the fellow badly. I yanked Butterball up as he shied anxiously away, practically running sideways. The snake coiled and uncoiled, making himself into a swirling spiral of motion, his tail shaking so fast it became a blur. Then he was still, save the rattling of his tail, his upper body half raised off the ground. He stared up at me, poised to strike, his black, forked tongue flitting in and out of his mouth.

I raised my pistol and pointed it at him as he darted his head at us in a warning. But we were outside the range of his fangs. I cocked the gun, and then I swear I heard my ma's voice.

"They're more scared of you than you are of them."

I uncocked the gun and studied the animal, with its beautiful pattern of shifting gray browns in diamonds along its back terminating in a black tail. It was slowly sliding backwards now, away from us. Beating an uneasy retreat from the horse and the woman that had disturbed its rest. I s'pose I might've eaten it, but I didn't have much of a taste for rattler. I stared into those gleaming black eyes with their narrow slit pupils until I couldn't see the detail of them no more as he slithered off. Then I sheathed my gun and turned Butterball away.

We had a few more near encounters with snakes, none quite so near as that first one. I saw a hare too, but he was fast as the wind and I couldn't get a bullet off near quick enough, and didn't want to waste one. I rationed my water, only sipping at it now and again. But I was powerful hungry when the sun began to set over the desert. As the blazing light of the sun—which had been burning me to a crisp all day—began to fade, a strong wind started kicking up, and I thanked God for it. I wasn't sure if God was out there in the desert, where no church nor monument nor cross stood, but if He were, then He sure was looking out for me. That wind, though it stung my sunburned cheeks and hands, would blow my tracks into nothingness and Ian Marcus wouldn't be finding me nohow. But, I also feared that *mi esposo*, if he were still alive, wouldn't find me neither.

I made a little camp under an outcropping of rock that jutted out like a hand reaching up from the desert, some giant troll long ago swallowed up by the sand. 'Twere one of the few large stones as far as I could see, which made me a bit leery of it. That single rock would be the first place anyone out there would try to camp, or would look if they were searching for a person in those flat fields of endless sand. Still,

I had to stop somewhere. I put hobbles on Butterball, gave him a ration of the oats from the saddlebag, just a scant amount, though, a couple mouthfuls, and then he began to wander, searching for food among the tumbleweeds and cacti. I hoped he found some—poor pony deserved some good eats. I also gave him half of what the canteen had left in it. I'd never make it out of the desert if my horse died of dehydration, after all. There had to be a spring or a well somewhere out here. I would have to find one the next day, or both of us would be in a bad way real quick.

While I was setting up my blanket roll, I felt an unmistakable wetness a'tween my legs, and sure enough, my damn courses had finally come. I packed my drawers with rags and settled down under the cover of the rock, my pelvis aching and cramping with the pains of my monthly as the wind howled above me. The sand felt warm and comforting where I curled up with my blanket. In the saddlebags, I had scrounged up some hardtack to nibble on, left over from the things my ma had packed for Oliver and me. I also found a little piece of paper, the document that legalified my marriage to Oliver. I puzzled over the words slowly in the waning light, but then the last gleam of sunlight faded away completely and even if I could read, I couldn't see the paper no more to try, so I stowed it in my coat pocket.

My fingers brushed against cool metal in my pocket, and I felt a rush of longing to play my harmonica. I chided myself a little. It was a dad-blamed foolish thing for a fugitive to be making a human sound out there. But I was lonely, and afraid, with only the yips of the coyotes and the howling of the wind to keep me company. I hadn't heard a human speak since Martha told me not to die, and I was beginnin' to feel that loneliness heavy around my neck, like a weight dragging me down into the sand, into a depth of despair I hadn't yet known. I set my dry lips to the mouth organ and began to play a song *en la noche*, nothing special, a soft, crooning cowpoke tune that carried like a mournful dirge upon the wind. I played for only a little while, until at last, sunburned, exhausted and completely dried out, I tucked my harmonica into the pocket of my coat and drifted off to sleep.

I woke up to the sound of spurs jingling and low, male voices speaking around me in a mixture of Spanish and English and some other language I didn't recognize. Even before I opened my eyes, I reached for the old Colt that had been at my side. Panic surged in me as I found the holster empty. Then I did open my eyes, gaping down at the empty gunbelt for a second. Dry swallowing, I raised my head to look around. There were eight men gathered by a small tumbleweed fire, and the smell of sizzling meat and heating biscuits reminded me how empty my stomach was. I glanced around quickly, searching for anything I could use as a weapon. The men seemed to be paying no attention to me at all. They were looking at the fire and the food.

Real slow and easy, I began hoisting myself up off the ground, onto my hands and knees. The hard, sharp heel of a boot struck me hard in the back, knocking me down. I tried to roll over and grab the foot of my assailant, but whoever it was had planted his boot hard in my back and kept me pressed into the sand.

"Your prize's up, Tom," said a gruff voice, and if leering had a sound it would have described that man's tone.

I tried again to get up, struggling under the weight of that boot, terror clawing at my throat. It wasn't Ian Marcus, but someone had found me out here, and I was alone, with no way to protect myself.

"About damn time. These little Mexican gals sure can sleep," said another voice, higher-pitched, almost whining. "I was starting to think I'd have my way with her and she still wouldn't wake up."

"Most women wouldn't, with your little carrot in them," joked the man standing over me.

Again a terrible sense of fear lanced through me. These men meant to rape me, to do what Ma had warned me men do to women they find alone and unprotected. I tried to roll over again and this time the man pinning me down let me. I scrambled to my feet and took a few running steps, but my guard neatly tripped me, and then all the men were laughing. I crawled a few steps, coming up against two tall boots. The owner of the boots knelt down as I stared up at him. He was a white man, brown-eyed and dark-haired, with a coarse, bristling beard. He took my face in his hands, craning my neck toward him. I pushed myself backwards, scratching at his cheek with one hand.

Someone kicked me so hard in the side I think it musta done cracked a rib. Terrible pain tore through my chest, and tiny stars danced before my eyes as I curled up.

"She's a fighter, Tom," proclaimed the bearded guard standing over me.

"She can fight all she wants," said the whiny voice of the one called Tom. "Ain't going to do her much good, short little thing like that against nine grown men."

"You . . ." I gasped—speaking sent bolts of agony through my chest. "You don't want to fuck me."

Tom chuckled at that as I uncurled enough to look him boldly in the eye. "And just why not?" he asked.

"I'm on my damn monthly, you bastard. So unless you want blood all over your damn dick, you don't want to fuck me," I continued, still gritting my teeth from the waves of pain in my side.

"Is that so? Mayhap we'll just take your pants down and see if you're telling the truth."

I lunged upward again but received another kick, this time to my face, and I fell to the ground with a whimpering cry. I lay still for a moment. My nose was bleeding and the world was spinning all around me. Someone pressed their knee into my back and I felt them fumbling with my pants and the buckles of my belt. I pushed backward, shoving the man off me, and reached inside the pants myself, bringing my hand out stained with blood. The men drew back a little then, their faces scrunched with disgust.

The weasely little man called Tom spat on me and jerked his head to a few of his thugs who set to tying my hands behind my back. I relaxed a little. To be honest, I hadn't been entirely sure my courses would frighten them away, but I was sure glad they had. Never had I been so thankful for the curse of womanhood. That gave me *seis*, maybe *siete días* to escape before these bastards had their way with me.

"You speak mighty good English for a Mexican," Tom observed.

"Speak mighty good English? It's my first language, you dumbass," I snapped back and received yet another blow to the face. "And I ain't Mexican," I continued, shrugging my shoulder up to the corner of my mouth, trying to wipe away the trickle of blood from my lip and nose.

"Is that so? Then mayhap you got a family that would be willin' to pay a few dollars for the return of their gal, mostly unscathed." He laughed a little at the last two words and I shuddered.

"That's right, I do. I got me a man who would pay you hundreds for me, but only if I'm unscathed, like you said."

"Well, I can't promise the last bit, especially once your bleeding dries up. My men are hungry for the comforts of a woman's body. Where can we send notice to this fine fella you supposedly got?"

My mind raced for a few seconds, then I said, "Tombstone. You can send notice to Tombstone, up in Arizona Territory. To Mr. Oliver Kedar."

By then I was sitting up, my hands roughly tied behind my back, and I saw every one of those bastards change color real fast. Tom's eyes narrowed and he flushed. Most of the other men paled a little under the dirt and grime that coated their faces.

"Oliver Kedar?" asked Tom, and there was the faintest tremor in his voice. Then he licked his lips and laughed. "Sure, of course this dirty little whore in the middle of Samalayuca, dressed like a man, is Oliver Kedar's gal, of course. You just heard that name from someone and are tryin' to use it to scare us."

A shiver of dread passed from my neck to the pit of my stomach. I didn't rightly know why these men were scared of Oliver, but it was plain that his name had struck dumb terror in them. That was another point for me, then. Or was it a point against me? What kind of man had I married that these evil men in the desert feared him?

"I am Oliver Kedar's wife, duly and legally married. You don't believe me, you can go ahead and check the paper in my pocket. And if Oliver Kedar finds you with me, or if you hurt me, he won't leave a man of you alive."

Tom shook his head, a nervous grin twisting across his narrow face as he tried to bluster in front of his men. "We'll just see about that." He dug around in my pocket and yanked out the scrap of paper that made Oliver and me husband and wife. It took him a long time to make sense of the words—I fancied his reading skills were little better than mine—but after a moment his eyes darted at me and the fear there was plain as day.

He grumbled and shoved the paper back in my pocket. "That prob'ly ain't even legal."

"It's legal and you know it."

The men were all murmuring among each other by then, in various *idiomas*. A few of the men were Apache, some appeared Mexican, and a couple were plain old white men, toothless and dried out by their lives as bandits in the harsh dunes of Samalayuca. This news that somehow they had picked up the wife of Oliver Kedar didn't sit well with any of them. I squared my shoulders. It really didn't sit well with me that these evil killers and criminals in the desert were so afeared of my husband, but I had to act like I knew why they were afraid of a man I felt only the deepest affection for.

The bandits all turned away from me, their voices raised and clamoring as they bickered with Tom. Some of the suggestions I heard didn't exactly set my heart at ease. Several of the men proposed leaving me tied out there under that rock. The others said they ought to slit my throat and leave me for the coyotes. I sat there, smarting from the kick to my chest and face, just listening to it all. But I was dull and slow. They mumbled too much and mixed in too many words from their Apache and Spanish for me to make sense of it all. They feared my husband, but I could not make out why. There were snatches of stories, hints of things Oliver had done. After a few minutes I forced myself to stop trying to listen, just focusing on my breathing. It was funny to me that even with him not there, still my husband was protecting me, just like he'd promised. Then a memory from Oliver's book leaped to my mind, and I quietly murmured the words through my split, bleeding lip as best I could remember.

> "But I remain'd, whose hopes were dim,
> Whose life, whose thoughts were little worth,
> To wander on a darken'd earth,
> Where all things round me breathed of him."

Tom turned back when he heard me mumbling. "Fuck," he said loudly. "She sure is that bastard's woman. He's the only gunslinger I know of that spouts poetry." He went quiet after that for a long time before finally saying, "But still, Kedar might pay a proper ransom for his little gal. I think we ought to take her on."

There was a great deal of grumbling that followed this, but at last the men agreed. They saddled Butterball and hoisted me up onto the pony's back. They weren't so rough as they had been before, I noticed. Throughout that long, hot day, riding in the dunes of Samalayuca, I mulled over snatches of verses I remembered from Oliver's reading lessons. I think those poems kept me from going mad. Most of that day I wanted to cry. But I couldn't. The bandits gave me no water nor food, and I was nearly fainting when we came to rest that night. I couldn't even say the word *water* by then, my lips and mouth were as dry as the sand around us.

They camped at the base of a great dune, tossing me roughly to the ground on one side. As an afterthought, one of the men did put a canteen to my mouth and let me get a couple sips of *agua*, though not nearly enough. I hadn't pissed the whole day; I knew it was because there weren't no moisture inside me to piss out. Dully I lay on the hot sand, not feeling hungry anymore, feeling dead, and tired, and hopeless. There was blood staining my pants as I hadn't had the chance to change out my rags. I felt like a corpse. They would push on, through the desert, and kill me without even trying by starving me or letting me perish from thirst. I had been saved a little by my attachment to Oliver, but Oliver wasn't coming. I was alone, and I was going to die.

X

Someone grabbed hold of my shoulders, hauling me up off the ground. My eyes snapped open to find the world was fast turning from gray to that baking hot desert brightness. One of Tom's men was yanking at me and I let him drag me to my feet. Then they shoved me toward Butterball. The men were scrambling to mount and kicking their heels into their horses, sending them as fast as they could across the sand. Someone picked me up and tossed me over Butterball's saddle like a sack of oats. They tied me to my pony's saddle and then we were off, loping after the others.

I was still barely awake, but I turned my head and quickly saw what had started this mad race. There was a plume of rising sand behind us, pursuers, coming on quick. Tom waved his hands toward a higher dune and we wheeled and rode up it, as fast as our exhausted, heat-stricken horses could go. A gunshot rang out and I saw one bandit tumble and drag, lifelessly thumping behind his animal, still attached by the reins and the stirrups.

As soon as we reached the top of the dune the bandits dismounted, sending their horses down the hill behind them. They threw themselves onto the sand, guns ready, firing down at our pursuers, who backed off a little, just out of pistol shot range, though a rifle would still have covered the distance between us. Someone snatched me from Butterball, cutting the ropes that secured me to him and hurling me to the ground. Unable to catch myself with my hands bound behind my back, I landed face-first in the gritty sand and raised my head, trying to spit the dirt from my mouth.

A bandit went down near me with a terrible scream. Seven. There were only seven now. I winced as they died around me, caught between my desire to be free of them, my fear of who these new strangers might be, and the loathing I felt about men killing men. The specter of Grant Marcus appeared in my mind again. The flicker of hope I had felt at the thought of being freed by these attackers was in vain. I would just be in the hands of some new and perhaps more terrible captors. There was nothing to be gained from this battle for me, exceptin' mayhaps they'd kill me and I wouldn't have to be beaten and raped as it was looking like my lot was going to be from here on out.

I squinted down the dune, biting my lip. There were about fifteen of these attackers in all, hiding behind a few scattered rocks, cactuses, and tiny sprigs of bushes on the sand below our hill. A few of them had wheeled their horses about and were moving at a slower clip around the dune, meaning to flank us from the side or attack us from behind. Cutting off any escape route.

My captors were digging into the sand, trying to make some kind of wall between them and these attackers. The horses were squealing and moving away from the battle, further down the dune behind us. I shifted onto my back, wincing as my weight laid on my awkwardly twisted arms. I decided my best hope would be to try to get to Butterball, who, alert to the attack and edging away from the gunshots, had stayed closer than the other horses and kept flitting his ears toward me.

I took a couple painful rolls, feeling fire in my rib cage where I had been kicked the day before, and then I froze as a shower of sand sprayed my face from a bullet that had struck too close for comfort. A strong hand gripped my ankle and someone yanked me backwards, behind a pile of sand. I struggled, but there weren't much I could do, tied as I was. More gunshots rang out as I turned to see who had dragged me back from my desperate escape attempt. The man called Tom was smirking at me. He looked almost hungry.

"You ain't going nowhere, no way, missy. We're keepin' you here for insurance."

There were more gunshots and more bullets struck the sand around us. I wedged myself deeper below the little hillock Tom and his men had made at the top of the dune and waited, breathless. There were too many guns out there for it to be Oliver. It was either Marcus or some other bandits. But I didn't want Tom to know that. The longer he thought it might be Oliver, the longer he would keep me alive as a bargaining chip.

There was another loud crack of a rifle and one of the bandits fell back, screaming bloody murder and writhing in the sand, blood pouring from his neck. He kept screaming until Tom himself turned and blew the man's brains out to make him stop. I drew back in horror from the spattered blood and brain bits mixed into the sand. Tom chuckled as he looked at me, then popped his head up and shot over the barricade.

"I did that to my partner. Been ridin' with Fred for more than a year," said Tom, his voice laden with threat. "Don't think I won't kill you too, girl."

"I ain't tryin' to leave," I returned sharply.

"Ahoy there!" called a smooth, confident, deep voice from behind a rock below us.

"I hear ya," Tom hollered in return.

"Well, then, listen. We don't want you. We want the girl. Send her out and we'll let you live."

"I ain't sendin' this girl out, no how, no way, less'n you pony up some loot for her. Is that Oliver Kedar down there?"

All the noise of gunfire had stopped, and around me the bandits were reloading their guns and dabbing at the sweat on their faces with bandanas and sleeves. A few started taking drinks in the brief respite, guzzling water and letting the drops of it fall to the ground around them. I licked my dry lips with my cracked and furrowed tongue, yearning for just a drop of liquid.

A brief laugh sounded from below us. I knew for sure then it was the voice of Ian Marcus, a man who no one dared say no to back home. The voice of a man used to always gettin' his way. He had found me here, in the dunes of Samalayuca.

"I am not Oliver Kedar, and I am certainly not going to pay you for that murdering young whore. The way I see it, you send her out, or I'll come up there and murder every man of you, and take her. Your payment for giving me the girl will be to keep on living."

My stomach churned, twisting in hard, roiling knots. I hated that Marcus wanted me alive. He had his own plans on how to kill me, and I didn't think it would be quick like a bullet to the brain. I was starting to feel like a crawdad that had fallen out of the pot and into the firepit. The way I saw it, there weren't no hope for me no how. No Oliver to come to my rescue, no chance of escape, no matter what played out in the next few minutes, I was *una mujer muerta.*

I started thinking of all the times I had talked back to Ma and Pa, and guilt rose up inside me. It felt like a salty ball of phlegm deep in my throat. Then I thought of Oliver, and that kiss, and what else I had wanted to do with him in that fleeting moment. I would never know the pleasures of married life. My face sagged a little and I closed my eyes as the gunshots started again, more of them this time, a lot more, popping and blasting all around. I saw myself back in my parents' bedroom and Grant Marcus advancing on me, and every time I heard a gunshot ring out, I saw his eyes die and his body crumple and I shuddered at the horror of it, the horror of what I had done, killing a man in cold blood. All this fighting, over me, a killer. I heard more screams and thuds, and when I finally opened my eyes again, six of Tom's bandits were dead, and only three remained alive—Tom, the bearded man that had kicked me the day before, and a slim Apache with a face set like stone.

"I've had just about enough of this, all over some fucking worthless little cunt," said Tom after counting his dwindling supply of ammunition in a brief lull between the gunshots. He lunged forward, grabbing my neck and yanking me upright. Then he rose to his feet, pushing me ahead of him, his pistol held against the side of my head. "You'll let us ride out if we give you this bitch?" he hollered as the gunshots stopped.

"That's what I said," returned the cool, even voice of Ian Marcus. "Give me that girl and you won't be feeding the coyotes tonight."

"Alright, then, come up here and get her." When Tom said this he pushed his gun harder against my head. The metal was hot and burned the side of my face.

Across the expanse of sand, a form appeared, impressively tall and broad-shouldered, with a paunch overhanging his gun belt. Ian Marcus strode toward us purposefully. He was dressed in black, with his pistols holstered, carrying his rifle, his hat pulled low over his piercing blue eyes. He walked so slowly, it seemed like an age passed before he was standing a few yards away, regarding me with the most contemptuous stare I think I had ever seen. I felt like a piece of meat he was sizing up to buy.

The two men behind us were shuffling a bit, and I hoped for a second that they would kill Ian Marcus, though that wouldn't exactly help me. I'd still be the prisoner of these bastards, destined to be raped and mistreated until Oliver came—if Oliver ever came. If Oliver was still alive.

For a few seconds no one spoke, and I thought Marcus would just gun me down right there. But what happened next was so fast I almost didn't believe it. Marcus yanked one pistol from its holster and fired off two shots at the last of Tom's men left alive, then, almost in the same movement, he swung his rifle, striking Tom's head, who fired a shot that buzzed past my scalp as I dropped to the ground. There was a warm rush of oozing blood through my hair and down the side of my face as I scrambled in the sand, trying to slither away. I rolled behind that pathetic little barricade of sand Tom's men had made and swiveled about, taking in the fight between Ian Marcus and the much smaller Tom.

Both were disarmed. Tom must've dropped his pistol when Marcus hit him, and Marcus had tossed both his weapons aside, like he wanted a fistfight. He had a broad grin on his face, a grin that went all the way to his eyes, making them crinkle with merriment. It reminded me of Grant Marcus' face, right before I shot him. Back and forth the two men punched at each other. Tom circled the other man, making quick jabs at Marcus' hulking torso, jumping in and then leaping back to avoid a fist. Marcus was just swinging and smiling, hardly bothering to block or dodge Tom's frantic attacks. The power of Marcus' punches, when they landed, sent the weaselly bandit flying.

Below us, I could see Marcus' men, running toward the fight, toward me. I began rolling, trying to get to Butterball. The bandits' horses had scattered, but when the gunshots had stopped they had begun instinctively returning to where their masters had been. I didn't make it far before Marcus' goons yanked me to my feet, holding me still as we watched the battle between Tom and Marcus continue.

"You said you'd let us go," hissed Tom through bleeding lips.

"I'm not a lawman, and I don't much see the point in keeping my word to thieves and murderers," replied Marcus, still grinning as he swayed back to avoid another desperate attack from the smaller man.

By then I could see what Tom was trying to do. They had moved far from their dropped guns, and he was maneuvering the fight back, toward his revolver on the ground; slowly but surely, dancing in and out, circling, herding Marcus like a dog herds sheep.

Finally, having got Marcus within a few yards of the gun, Tom made his move, lunging for the pistol. He almost reached it. His hand was mere inches from the metal barrel when Marcus' boot struck his gut, sending him flying away from the weapon. Then Marcus dropped onto him, planting himself on Tom's chest, and went to work, pounding the little bandit's face over and over and over again. The sound of fist against bone and flesh made me wince, then came the sound of bones cracking and splintering, and Tom's whimpers of pain, and finally the squelching of a clenched hand against unyielding, pulpy, bloody flesh and then Tom whimpered no more. He didn't move, he didn't breathe, his face an unrecognizable mass of blood, his skull dented into a shapeless form by Marcus' mighty blows.

Marcus rose, cracking his scarlet knuckles, still smiling as he turned toward me. I cowered back against the man holding me. Marcus had ten men still alive with him, almost all hands from his ranch that I'd seen in Fort Davis or Acantilados from time to time. I recognized both the men that had been with Grant the day I killed him. There was another man there that I didn't recognize, dressed in a gray suit. He appeared almost stunned by all that had happened and was mopping at his brow with a handkerchief. Marcus stepped up, towering over me. When I looked down he grabbed my chin, yanking my neck up, craning my head so my eyes met his. I thought he was going to bludgeon me to death the way he had Tom.

"So, you're Flaka," he said, his booming voice softening a little.

I glared, and when I spoke my voice was harsh and rasping from lack of water. "You've done met me before."

"Yes, well, you didn't make much of an impression on me, apparently," he replied. "Had I known you would one day kill my son, I would have shot you the first time I saw you hiding behind your mother's skirts."

I clenched my teeth together, trying to look defiant, to look brave and strong, but inside I was scared, I was afraid to die. "Well, you didn't, and here we are, so what you gonna do now? Take me back for a trial? What I did I did in self-defense."

He let go of my chin and backhanded me so hard I stumbled into the man behind me, the world turning black for a second. Slowly my vision and senses returned, though the world still swam a little.

"Yeah, I'm taking you back for a trial," replied Marcus. "Ain't that right, Marshal Evans?" Here he turned back to the man in the gray suit, who nodded mutely, staring at me with something that was near pity. Then Marcus leaned close to my ear and whispered, "But, somewhere along the way my men are going to get a might squirrely, I think it'll happen about the first time we find a tree out here, and then you're getting hanged. The boys loved Grant, you understand, you can hardly blame them. And this little US Marshal here won't be able to stop them. These boys aren't going to put the knot on the side of your neck, either, they're going to gum it up, because they're stupid. And your neck isn't going to break— no, you're going to kick and squirm as you dangle from that tree for a good ten, maybe fifteen minutes until you strangle out, nice and slow, while we watch. We'll probably burn your body afterward. Then I'll go home and apologize to dear old Jozef and his wife that neither I nor the good marshal could control my men, and that'll be the end of this."

The men were all grinning cruelly at me, save the marshal. The fear and dread churning in my stomach was getting worse, like there was a roaring fire burning a hole through my gut. "And that'll bring your son back? Killing the girl that shot him in self-defense?" I asked, keeping my head up, my voice bold, still feigning bravery that I didn't feel at all. I didn't want to die, but more than that I didn't want to die by strangling slow from a tree while Ian Marcus enjoyed the show.

"That's enough talk from the murderer, I think," said Marcus, nodding toward one of his men, who removed his bandana and jammed it into my mouth, tying it tight behind my neck. I felt like a horse with a bit that was too tight. I tried to spit it out, but it was useless. The bandana tasted foul, of dirt, sweat, horse manure, cowboy saliva, and chewed tobacco.

They shoved me over to Butterball, who they had caught, and hurled me up over his saddle, onto my stomach. Someone wrapped a rope around my neck, joking as he did so about how it was just practice for hangin', to get me "used to the feelin' of it." He ran the rope through the loops of the saddle, over the top and around the horn, then under Butterball, and finally around my feet on the other side. If I didn't balance just right or if I moved my feet or legs even an inch, the rope yanked my neck up, strangling me until I could adjust back to the only position that let me breathe.

I was trussed like an antelope that had been shot on the plains, coming home to be cleaned and gutted for dinner. And I were still bleeding from my monthly, my pants soaked through with blood, unable to change my rags. I was fucking helpless. The pain in my ribs was excruciating, and my airway kept getting cut off every five or ten minutes, making me panic and struggle vainly. Each time it happened I was sure I was stuck and wouldn't be able to loosen the tightness, wouldn't be able to breathe again. At least I would die long before we ever reached *un arbol* out there in the dunes. There weren't no trees in those endless fields of sand anyhow. Two times that day I passed out from the tightness of the rope. One of the times I came to with Ian Marcus loosening the cord a little and adjusting me roughly in the saddle. I looked at him with eyes that I was sure were bloodshot and crazed from pain and suffocation.

"Don't want you to strangle too soon, bitch, I like seeing you suffer," he said, chuckling and patting my cheek as he spoke.

I wanted to tell him he was a monster, he was evil and hateful. I wanted to tell him I was glad I'd killed his son. But all I could do was growl behind the filthy bandana and fight back the tears of helpless rage that threatened to spill down my grimy face.

Every once in a while I caught sight of the marshal, looking all green around the gills and mournful. He kept looking away when my eyes met his, like he didn't want to be a part of this at all, like he was ashamed of being there. But I couldn't hope for much help from that quarter; he was just one man, and Marcus still had nine.

It was nearing dusk when Ian Marcus at last found what he was looking for: an outcropping of tall, sandstone rocks, and an old, dead *arbol*, dried out, without bark or leaf, looking as ominous as anything I'd ever seen. They cut the ropes securing me to Butterball and I fell with a thud onto my butt, then I let myself topple to my side, feeling like I had no strength to keep myself upright anymore. I lay there, staring dully at the world around me as it dimmed into twilight. At least by then, from lack of food and lack of water, and my ability to breathe being cut off half the day, I was barely present in the world. Death probably wouldn't hurt too bad. In fact, it might be a real relief, all things considered.

I was vaguely aware of Marcus' men tossing a rope up over the highest tree branch, and then someone grabbed my arm. The marshal was making some nominal protests, playing his part, but Marcus' men menaced him with guns until he stood back, arms raised, looking down. I wriggled a little, but only half-heartedly. I didn't have no strength to fight anymore.

My legs were untied and I was dragged, kicking feebly, and then dropped face down before the tree where I was meant to die. Someone put that noose around my neck and it found its way into the raw marks from my long day trussed to the saddle. Marcus' men yanked on the other end, hoisting me up from the ground to my knees as I gasped and fought the thick cord. Then they hoisted again and I gasped and struggled still more. Another unyielding, unstoppable yank came on the rope and I was all the way onto my feet. I thought briefly that they must've untied my legs the better to watch me kick. The next pull and I'd be off the ground.

I swept my gaze over the world, taking my last look through bloodshot eyes at the windswept sand and the orange glow of the setting sun, turning the desert and the sandstone around us a shade of brilliant red. I wished I'd said a real goodbye to Ma and Pa and told them how much I loved them. I wished I had fucked Oliver. I wished I'd had just a little more time, just another day, just another goddamn *minuto*. I heard Martha's voice clear in my head: "Just don't die, Flaka." She would be so disappointed in me.

Then, just as my feet began to lift off the ground, I heard gunshots, the squeal of horses in pain, and the thud of bodies falling on stone and sand. Men were flying in every direction and the rope eased, letting me drop to my knees, able to breathe again, gasping for air that had never tasted so damn good before. The rope was slack, and in that second of relief I lunged upward and stumbled forward, making toward the horses, toward Butterball, dragging my leash behind me. Many of the other horses were already dying and dead. Whoever was shooting was aiming for the animals. Butterball was still alive, but he was running away from the slaughter of his companions. More gunshots rang out and I dropped to the ground behind the still-warm body of what had been a very fine horse. Hidden there, I looked around, feeling wretched and half-dead. Another two shots sounded, and now every single one of Marcus' horses was dead and I could see three of his men lying unmoving on the ground as well.

"Now who's the rat in a trap, Marcus?" came Oliver's voice, raised as high as that low baritone could go, carrying across the sand, echoing off the rocks around me.

Slowly the nauseating terror began to wash away, replaced by hope like the rising of the sun on the first day of spring. I found the strength at last to maneuver my head free of the noose, dislodging the bandana up onto my nose, and the second my mouth was free I whistled as high and clear as I could. Butterball, the last horse out there left alive, pulled up sharp and turned back toward me, uncertain, his ears twitching back and forth. I whistled again and he began to sidle toward me nervously, eyeing the dead horses with a look of blind panic, the whites of his eyes showing and his flanks streaming with sweat.

A shot blasted out from behind me, Marcus' men aiming at Butterball. I began to slither toward my pony as best I could, then I started rolling. Another loud bang split the air, and was answered by my husband's bullets. I rolled until I was underneath Butterball. There I raised my head and tapped it against the back of his front knee. The pony knelt. I hadn't asked him to do that in years, not since I was a kid, but boy was I thrilled that he still remembered the trick. I slid my legs over Butterball's back, grateful that Marcus' men hadn't taken the time to unsaddle him. Once I was on his back, slumping over his neck, I urged the pony away, toward where Oliver's voice had come from, toward safety. Butterball obliged the squeezing of my legs, breaking into a quick trot. Two more gunshots rang out, sending sand flying around us.

"The next one of you that lifts so much as a hair out from behind those rocks I will blow their brains out. You know I can do it," called Oliver. His voice was coming from a smaller stone outcropping some forty feet away from the sandstone and dead tree where I had almost met my maker.

Butterball picked up his pace. In a few seconds we were behind the rock, where Oliver waited. He reached up to help me down, yanking the bandana the rest of the way off my face and then cutting the ropes binding my arms behind my back. My hands free, I wrapped them around my husband's neck.

I was sobbing, honestly sobbing, at how close I'd come to death. Oliver was hugging me back, and then he undid a canteen from around his shoulder and pressed it to me. He must have seen the dryness of my lips. But even as he helped me and hugged me, my husband's blue eyes and the barrel of his gun remained fastened to the spot where Ian Marcus' men crouched.

"Did they hurt you?" asked Oliver.

"No, not really," I said between gulps of life-giving *agua*. "Not seriously. My neck's a bit raw, and I think I've got a busted rib. I've been kicked a few times, slapped too. And a bullet grazed my scalp, but that ain't nothin', I don't think . . . but . . . oh God, Oliver . . . I done been through hell since last I saw you."

Oliver's eyes widened and his face turned a dark shade of red. I could see a big vein bulging out along his forehead. He studied me up and down, seeing the bruises, the cuts, the place where dried blood caked my hair, the raw mark around my neck from the rope. I must've looked like a demon straight outta hell. But Oliver looked better than when I had last seen him, more recovered from his wound, less pale.

"I will kill every single one of them," he threatened, the words spoken real low and distinct. His voice had become almost a growl.

"No. No, don't do it. They don't have any horses. We may have already killed them by stranding them out here. We best jest move on," I said quickly. "Let's just run, Oliver. No more killing."

He ground his teeth together and then fired again, and I heard a scream of pain in the distance. He was an incredible shot, and he shot to kill, not to injure. His accuracy, at such a distance, in the fast-fading twilight, with minimal targets to aim at, was unbelievable. I remembered then the fear that the bandits had of him, and the ominous *palabras* of my sister Martha about what she'd heard of Oliver Kedar. And in that moment, looking at his stoney face, dark and cool with rage, I felt, for the first time, a real thrill of fear about what my husband was.

"Please, Oliver. We can't kill them all."

"I can," he insisted. "I can kill them all. Even Marcus. Especially Marcus."

"Please, I don't want you to kill them. I just want to get away, Oliver, that's all I want is to get away from here, with you. To be alive with you, and safe. End this damn nightmare once and for all. That's all I want. I don't want no more killing. Please."

He paused, turning his narrowed eyes away from the gunmen huddled behind the rocks. After a moment of studying me, the tight lines in his face softened. "You're sure, Flake? You want to end this nightmare, there's no more certain way than to turn all those men out there into corpses."

"I'm sure. I just want both of us to get away from here alive, Oliver. Away from here and to our farm in Arizona. If you go out there and try to kill them and you get shot, where does that leave me? I'll be alone again and they'll catch me and string me up. If you go out there and don't die and manage to kill them all, then a lot more people will be looking for us." My raspy, dry voice choked as I spoke.

After a long moment, Oliver nodded, and I turned and mounted Butterball, my entire body shivering uncontrollably. Oliver checked that both his guns were loaded. Then, on his signal, we rode out, him firing into the rocks as we galloped past and out of gunshot range as fast as we could, and away, westward, into the wild, desolate dunes of Samalayuca.

XI

The first thing we did was find cover where I could change into another pair of Ephraim's pants, this time stuffed with rags, and I just left my old pair, crusted with dried blood, out there on the dunes for the coyotes. Then we pushed on, running like hares before a fox. I was afraid all that night, in a way I had never known fear before. I constantly looked over my shoulder and must've checked a thousand times to make sure Oliver was still there, riding beside me. My heart kept pounding as if it was going to come out of my chest even when we were miles from our unhorsed pursuers. If I'm being honest, I didn't calm down properly for the entire rest of our flight across the desert and into the Arizona Territory.

The only things I found that soothed my terror during the week after my capture was the sound of the harmonica and of Oliver reciting poetry, some from the book he carried and some from his own memory. I think Oliver understood how terribly shaken I was. In the evenings when we camped, we took turns keeping watch. Oliver would kiss me goodnight, with the same adoring passion as the kiss before our flight from Ciudad Juarez. Those *besos* were like salvation from the darkness that had fallen on me. In his arms I felt loved, though we had never made love to each other yet. His touch was warm and adoring, not like the brutal, rough grip of the men who had tried to hang me in the desert.

My reading was getting better, smooth enough that I could even enjoy the words a little bit, and linger over the beauty of them. The verses sometimes took my breath away with how lovely they flowed. It was like a song or a piece of art, but made with squiggly lines, not the thrumming of a guitar or paint on a canvas. I don't think, until that desperate trip across the desert, I had ever thought of books like that—of how beautiful they could be. I was learning so many new words—words I'd never heard anyone say before in my whole life. I fancy I was also starting to sound like a right educated woman when I spoke, real genteel-like.

At night, as I was drifting off to sleep I would go through some of them words I'd learnt over and over in my mind, while I gazed up at *las estrellas*. Those stars. I didn't feel like I'd ever looked at them before the way I did lying out there in the desert. They'd never seemed so beautiful and real before. They must've been a thousand miles away, maybe even a million, but they were so bright that even that far away you could still see them, staring down at you the same way they had stared down at that spot in the desert for hundreds and thousands of years, long before I was ever born, long before my oldest ancestor was ever born. Before the white men came to the desert when it still belonged to the Indians, the Comanche and the Apache and other tribes besides. Before any of this. I reckon those same stars will be staring down long after I've passed on, too, long after we're all gone, white men, the Comanche, the Apache, the Mexicans, all of us. Them stars will still be up there, untouchable, always watching, watching it all, silent judges of how we human folk live out our stupid, brutal, absurdly short little lives.

Before bed each night I would play the harmonica, and

Oliver loved to listen to it. He would sit quiet by the fire—if we had one—and listen with his eyes closed, still as a rock. I don't think anyone had ever listened to me play the way he did. He really listened, almost as if he was becoming one with that old harmonica's tunes. It made me feel strange, like I was one of them people who wrote those pretty words in the book. I was some kind of artist. But the book will go on like the stars, long after I'm dead, and them tunes I played in the desert jest vanished into the wind the instant the notes left my mouth organ.

One night we camped in a rocky gully, by a little chuckling crick. We were getting into Arizona and there were red rocks and trees dotting the landscape, no longer just the baking, empty desert. The stars shone especially bright above the rim of the little gulch where we camped. After we ate, I played "Auld Lang Syne," letting those wailing notes carry for miles. The gully gave the harmonica such a beautiful echoing sound, it made my heart ache.

Oliver just watched me, real quiet and calm, never taking his eyes away as I ran my lips over the cool metal. I had played that one for him a few times, and I knew he liked it. As I got to the end I had a flash of something, I guess you'd call it inspiration. Another song came to mind, one I hadn't played in a long, long time. Slowly I started the tune, a low, mournful lullaby. A flicker of recognition glittered in Oliver's eyes. Then he started to sing, the purtiest damn thing I think I'd ever heard in my life, him crooning in that low, husky voice. It damn near took my breath away. I wished I coulda stopped playing and jest listened to his voice, but it sounded better with the two of us together.

> "Beautiful Dreamer, wake unto me,
> Starlight and dewdrops are waiting for thee;
> Sounds of the rude world heard in the day,

Lull'd by the moonlight have all passed away!

"Beautiful dreamer, queen of my song,
List while I woo thee with soft melody;
Gone are the cares of life's busy throng
Beautiful dreamer, awake unto me!
Beautiful dreamer, awake unto me!

"Beautiful dreamer, out on the sea,
Mermaids are chanting the wild Lorelei;
Over the stream let vapors are borne,
Waiting to fade at the bright coming morn.

"Beautiful dreamer, beam on my heart,
E'en as the morn on the stream let and sea;
Then will all clouds of sorrow depart,
Beautiful dreamer, awake unto me!
Beautiful dreamer, awake unto me!"

I slapped the harp against my thigh, getting the spit out, while wearing a big, stupid grin on *mi cara*. Oliver had closed his eyes, leaning back against the red stones around us, his lips curving up at the corners.

"You sing all them purty things and know all the words to a thousand fancy poems," I said after a while. "But I jest can't reckon that with the way I've seen you kill men, I guess."

Oliver's blue eyes snapped open again, glowing strangely, brighter, it seemed to me, than the very stars above us. "What are you asking me, Flaka?"

My jaw worked for a few minutes while I tried to sort out just what exactly it was that I wanted to know. Finally I had it, and I rolled the words out slow. "I kilt—killed one man, in my whole life, Grant Marcus. I killed him in my own home.

And not a day goes by that I don't see his face in front of mine, loomin' like some kind of awful ghost that I jest can't escape, no matter how hard I try to forget. But I watched you kill on the farm, and when you came to rescue me from Ian Marcus, and you . . . you don't seem like it bothers you none. In fact, when you did it you looked like you plum enjoyed it."

"I didn't enjoy it," replied Oliver, slow and even, his gaze drifting from me to the little flickering fire. "Maybe I used to, the freedom of it, the power of it. But I don't enjoy it anymore." He paused for a long time before finally asking me, "What do you feel when you read the poems with me?"

I thought on that for a minute, then said, "I don't rightly know that I have the words to explain it. But I feel something deep stirring inside me, right here, in my gut and in my chest. Something . . . strong. It's like a connection to the words, to the way the writer felt when he wrote them. I feel . . . human, I guess. Like I'm the same as the writer, somehow, though I ain't. I couldn't never put words together the way he does. But the feelings he describes so well are . . . real feelings I've had too. So, I guess I feel like I'm connected to the poet that writ them words. Like, even though we ain't never met and we never will, we're both people that have felt those same deep things inside us. So, even with all our differences, we're the same, in a way, we have the same . . . soul, maybe. If that makes sense."

"It does," replied Oliver, and now he was looking up at the stars, so bright in that black velvet sky above us. "I told you that I love the space and the freedom of the West, a place where a man can be a man, where a human has the room to really feel his humanity. But sometimes the space is too big, and men lose their connection with other men. They can kill and it won't keep them up at night, because they feel no kinship with the ones they killed, or kilt, as you like to say." He glanced at me and smiled fondly when he said that, in a way that made my heart melt.

"It's easy to lose that connection," he continued. "That brotherly love of other people out here, that knowledge that we're all the same species, fighting the same battles, all on the same quest, and once you lose that, it can be hard to find it again. When I read books and poems—poems where I can hear the voice of someone speaking to me, speaking in beautiful ways that I never could about what it means to be a person—that just helps me remember what I am, and who I am, and that we all have that same deep soul within us, and I don't lose that.

"I try only to kill when it's necessary, to protect myself, to protect you, and in between those killings that I can't yet seem to avoid, I keep reading these words and memorizing these poems, and as long as I do that, I think I won't lose the meaning of what it is to be a person. I'll still shoot a man to defend myself, but I don't want to. I hate that I have to. It's a sad thing, because that same spirit and soul that gives the words to men like Tennyson and Byron and Dante, that allows a woman to play songs the way you do on your harmonica, that very same spirit lived in all those men I've killed. But, if they raise their gun against me, I'm not going to just let them shoot me down."

"So . . . you've made your peace with killing because of some poems?"

Oliver shook his head. "Have you ever seen a dog fight?"

I blushed a little but nodded. They used to have them in Fort Davis, before the mayor decided it was immoral. I went there with that boy called Sampson once, just to see what it was all about.

"Then you remember what it's like, those dogs that are bred and raised to kill, how they fight? Ruthless, brutal, unstoppable. They just keep tearing and shredding the other dog until there's nothing left. And no matter what else is going on around them, they won't stop. Ian Marcus is like that. I've seen him kill his own men when he was in a mood.

I've seen him beat men to death for crossing him. I've watched him lose sight of everything around him when he's intent on a kill, lose all of his senses, just killing, blind to all else in the world besides his prey, and somehow lost afterward for a while, once he's completed the murder. Like he doesn't know what to do when it's over, so intent was he on that one thing. It's like madness in him, I swear. I don't know if it's because he lost his humanity or he was bred and raised to kill, like those fighting dogs. Grant was the same. A killer through and through, like it was in his blood."

As he spoke, the memory of Ian Marcus beating the bandit flickered back into my mind, the sound of the fists against pulverized flesh. The little spitting sprays of blood with every bludgeon. I winced a little and forced myself back to the present.

"So, what I'm saying is, I've made my peace with killing to defend myself and to defend the ones I love. I haven't made peace with killing the way Ian Marcus does, hunting a man or a woman for weeks or months for revenge. Brutalizing them when the opportunity arises, losing all sight of everything, losing all sense, living for murder. There's no justification for that, and there's no peace that can be made with that sort of killing. Nor, despite what Marcus thinks, is there any peace to be found in vengeance."

Then Oliver lay down in his bedroll and fell asleep. I thought on his speech a long time as I lay on my back, staring up at the shimmering, lonely stars above us. I was sure I could hear the beautiful howls of *un lobo*, not a coyote this time, crying somewhere far in the night, lulling me slowly to sleep.

XII

WE SAW NO MORE OF IAN MARCUS AND HIS ILK IN THAT LAST week of riding. Butterball must've lost a full half of his body weight on that entire trip. He hadn't been ridden like that in years, maybe ever. He was never really a cow horse, just a riding pony for a little kid, getting from place to place. He had to be getting close to thirty. Ephraim had learned to ride on him before me. I'd had him since I was three or four years old, I reckon, when I was so little I had to clamber atop a fence to mount him. I hated that I could see the ribs showing in his once-plump flanks. We had tried to stop and feed the animals at every little homestead we could find along the way. Still, it was a lot of exercise for an old pony.

All that to say, I felt a mite bit guilty when at last we entered Tombstone, what with Butterball looking so thin and ragged and wore out, and Oliver's mare too, though she was in better shape to begin with. Folks stared at us as we rode through the streets of that little town. They gaped, and at first I thought it was because of my emaciated pony, or how dirty the two of us were, but after a little while I realized it was because I had a scab mark like a noose around my neck and I was wearing pants. Women don't often wear pants out here in the West, less'n they have to. It does happen, but not commonly, and women rarely look comfortable in trousers. because they ain't tailored for our bodies. But I had become so used to the pants they just felt as natural as skin to me by the time we reached Tombstone. I hadn't thought about a skirt in weeks, riding through the heat and all the hell of the desert. I started pulling faces at the folks gaping at me, sticking my tongue out and crossing my eyes like a child.

Oliver turned around and saw me scrunching my face up and sticking my tongue out at a girl with braids who looked to be catching flies with her mouth hanging open so far. He halted his horse and frowned at me.

"You want to draw more attention to us, dear wife?"

"I reckon I couldn't attract more attention than I already have, no matter how hard I tried."

"Well, I believe you're wrong about that, and I would appreciate it if you kept your tongue behind your teeth."

"Turning into a bossy husband now we're getting close to our lifelong homestead?" I snapped back, annoyed with him for scolding me. I weren't no child.

"Not at all. You know I've never pushed you to do anything in all our two-odd weeks of marriage. I only want to protect you, Flaka, and the more people that remember seeing us on the street the easier time Marcus is going to have tracking us down if he comes here."

"He ain't followin' us no more. You scared him off with your threats by the rocks. Plus we left him without a single horse alive. Hell, he likely died from the heat out there in them dunes."

"You're very confident in my ability to frighten off a man much more powerful than myself. I'm flattered, believe me, but I am not so certain as you that he has given up, nor that he is dead. He may have just altered his strategy."

"If you're so worried about it, then what are we doin' in this town full of gawking farmers?"

"I need to pay for the plot of land and the little house I've had my eye on. For that we need to visit the bank, which also serves as the land office in this town. Do you have a problem with that plan?"

"No, it's fine," I returned scornfully and focused on the road in front of me, resenting Oliver as I never had before, and thinking about all that he was still hiding from me.

I hadn't pressed Oliver anymore about his past in all our days in the desert. It sounds stupid, especially now, but in those weeks of riding in the wilderness I'd grown closer to him, comfortable and happy near him. We joked constantly, but the closer and lighter our relationship became, the less I wanted to know the truth about who he was, and the badness that lurked behind those easy smiles. I didn't want to believe there was anything dark in his past. I didn't want to believe that he was anything but a kind, poetry-reading cowboy from Boston.

The bank was inside the pioneer store, a large shabby-looking wooden building, set prominently on the corner of the two biggest streets in that little town. I felt proud that I could read all them building signs in Tombstone. Feeling that pride rise up in me, and remembering who I had to thank for that new skill, I pushed my questions and that brief rising resentment about Oliver's past deep down inside again.

We hitched our horses outside the store. Butterball instantly went to cribbing on the hitching post, and I bopped his nose gently before we walked inside, carrying our saddle-bags. In the pioneer store I got the same raised eyebrows from the shopgoers that I'd been seein' out on the street, due to my pants again, I assumed. But no one said nothin'. I fancy they didn't have the balls, because I didn't look like anyone they wanted to start a fight with.

We moved to the back of the store, to a little door where a wooden shingle hung with "Pima County Bank" carved across it and below, in tiny added letters "& Land Ofis".

Inside there was another wall that had one door set with iron bars like a prison. Behind that door a clerk sat pouring over his *libros*, scratching on the pages with a quill pen. The man was practically buried in a hazy cloud of dandruff that he continually added to by running his fingers through his thinning gray hair. He seemed oblivious to our entry, though we weren't quiet. After a few minutes of no response to Oliver's loud "harumphs," I turned to the door behind us, opened it wide and swung it closed again as hard as I could into the frame. The whole building trembled.

The clerk looked up, eyeing us over his spectacles. He peered for a long time, as if trying to assure himself that we were real people. Then he slammed shut the enormous tome he was scribbling in, sending a cloud of dust into the air, enough to make both Oliver and me cough and gasp.

"What can I do for you young'uns today?" asked the man in a shrill voice.

"Do you have a list of the plots of land that are for sale? Plots that were sold back to the bank?" asked Oliver, making his voice extra loud in case the man was hard of hearing.

The man frowned over his spectacles for a long time. "I ain't deaf, young man, I'll have you know."

"Certainly. Could have fooled me, though. We were waiting for you to look up for ten minutes."

"The ability to concentrate on one's task and complete it is the mark of a thorough and careful banker. I shouldn't think you would want a banker who was easily interrupted from any task, would you now, young sir?"

"Of course not," Oliver allowed, humoring the man and winking at me. "But I am interested in a particular plot of land, about ten, maybe fifteen miles from this town. Along the San Pedro River."

"Prime land up in that area," remarked the banker, again pushing himself back from his desk and regarding us with disdain. "All those plots have been claimed, I believe."

"The one I'm looking for was sold back to the bank."

The banker frowned. "Doesn't come cheap buying land up there."

"The particular plot I want was still available a year ago when I was last through these parts. I . . . put a security deposit on it."

"With me or my partner?"

"With your partner. I would have remembered you."

"My partner's been dead for four months now. Some troublemakers from somewhere south of here came in, shooting up the place and trying to steal some land contracts and money."

"Did they steal them?"

"No, they didn't. But Melvin was a meticulous keeper of records. If what you say is true, I can find the deed for the plot you're interested in. You'll just have to give me a little time."

Oliver spread his arms wide. "Take all the time you need, sir. I've waited a year already. I'm in no mad rush now."

I settled myself on a stool near the barred window, and within an hour my stomach was grumbling like mad and I was beginning to regret Oliver's generous allotment of all the time the stodgy banker needed. Twice while he was shuffling through the heaps of dusty books, I swear the man nodded off. Oliver just sat real quiet on a stool across from me, leaning back against the wall, not saying a word, a strange look of contentment on his face. I reckon after a year of planning to buy this piece of land he was just plain happy to finally turn that *sueño* into reality. About the third time the man appeared to nod off, I stood from my spot, stretching my sore muscles and then moved across the narrow room and kicked Oliver's leg. He looked up with wide eyes, as if he had forgotten all about me.

"What's gotten into you?" he asked.

"If we're going to spend the next few days waiting for this

old man to finish scrounging around in his books, maybe we ought to look up a room to stay tonight, and see if'n we can't get a bite to eat around this town. I wouldn't half mind a bath, neither."

"As my lady demands, then," replied Oliver, rising. "Hey, old-timer, we're just going to take a look around. What time do you close?"

"I can stay open till six o'clock for you. The store closes more around four o'clock most Wednesdays, so Allen can get his cattle watered. Just tell him on your way out to leave the outer door unlocked for you. Ain't no trouble."

"We'll be back before six," Oliver promised.

Out in the dusty streets, the heat of the day had driven most of the curious townsfolk back into the welcome shade of their homes. There were only a few people still standing around, talking loudly. Tombstone was not a genteel town. It was a rough place. There were women, but not many. I had seen a scant few, mostly barmaids, along with a handful of more respectable-appearing ladies. The respectable ones were older, hard women with lines along their sunburned faces, worn hands, and strained, muscular arms under their thread-bare calico dresses. I looked into those judging, sharp eyes, set in deep hollows above their cheeks, and I wondered if, given a few years as a homesteader, I too would look like that.

This was a land that dried women up long before their time, and sanded men down to a fragment of themselves before they reached what should have been their prime. They were the crispy remnants of once bright-eyed young folks who had come to this territory full of hopes and dreams— folks like us. They had survived their attempts to tame the Arizona Territory, but the land had beaten them, transforming eager youths into wan ghosts, bland and worn like desert tumbleweeds. I don't suppose none of this were all that different from the land and the people around Fort Davis, but it felt different.

Oliver and I walked to the local hotel, which also served as a saloon, and he paid for a bath for the both of us. I swear I hadn't never felt nothing as close to *los cielos* as that bath, washing the grime of three weeks of hard travel from my body. I think I turned three shades lighter from when I went into the hotel until the time I exited. I changed into a white frock, trimmed with lace, a dress that made me look a bit like a doll. I really oughtn't have brought it in my saddlebag, and it was wrinkled and dirty from its time crumpled in there. But I had grabbed it on my wedding day when I was packing because it was the only dress among my possessions that had even a tiny resemblance to the finery of a wedding gown. Now I wanted the people of Tombstone to know I was married to the tall, handsome blond I was walking with, and that I was good enough for him.

When I stepped back into the saloon lobby in my fine white dress with my saddlebag slung over my shoulder, there were no more stares, or rather, there were more stares, but of a different, more lewdly appreciative sort. They looked at me as if I was the freshest piece of meat for a hundred miles. The gazes of men moved from their saloon women toward me, sweeping up and down my body. A few even licked their lips. Expressions that brought back the memory of Tom and what he and his bandits had meant to do to me.

I scanned the crowd for my husband, gradually feeling more and more tightness building in my throat and chest, panic clawing at my insides to get out. There was no sign of Oliver, only the staring eyes of dirty, hateful men, and the spiteful, jealous glances of aging barmaids. I began to walk across the saloon, toward the door. The clear, vivid memory of all that had happened in the dunes of Samalayuca burst into my mind, along with that tearing fear eating my chest, the fear that my husband was missing, again. I kept swinging my head from side to side, searching for him in every shadow and corner of the saloon.

A hand grabbed my arm, roughly, and I yanked away, spinning around and reaching for the saddlebag hanging on my shoulder, where my revolver was stowed. The man behind me took a step back, holding his hands up high as if to calm me. He was a short man, shorter than me, with a ridiculously tall hat upon his head.

"Easy, lady. I don't mean to hurt you, I just don't think I've ever seen a lady so pretty this side of the Mississippi."

"I'm married," I replied, narrowing my eyes.

"Of course you are, I wouldn't presume. A nice, fancy lady like you, of course you're married. But, listen, just listen. I'm Richard Burns and I think you're new here. Tombstone is a dark, ugly place in the world, and you ought to know that if you're settling out here."

"We are settling out here."

"Right, yes, that's why I wanted to speak with you. The men out here live short, ugly lives, though we wish that weren't the case. Anyway, this here saloon and hotel is mine, and . . . well, God forbid, but if anything should happen to your husband at any time, you'd be welcome to work here among my girls. The money's good and the folks here are pleasant. There's hardworking, nice girls here, they'll make you feel at home."

I think my mouth was gaping open wide enough that you could drive a cattle herd through it. I'd never been propositioned such a thing in my whole dad-blamed *vida*. I couldn't believe the boldness of this stranger to suggest to a young woman that her husband was going to be killed just for being a young man in that wild, lawless world and that she should then become a barmaid. I was shocked that any man would be so brazen as to proposition me like that on my first day in Tombstone.

I opened and closed my jaw several times and finally managed to choke out, "Where in the Sam Hill do you think you come off—"

"Flaka."

Hearing the soft, low voice of Oliver sent a wild thrill through me. The thrill of having made it to our destination alive and the thrill of being clean, and dressed up real purty, in my Sunday best. It would be the first time my husband had seen me clean, I think. A ripple of excitement ran through my stomach, the flutters of butterflies. Oliver weren't dead nor missing. I didn't have to become a saloon girl like this man suggested. I almost sneered at the saloon owner. My heart began to patter madly in my chest and a strange catch was forming in my throat. I was afraid—excited and afraid—just terrified that Oliver wouldn't like how I looked now that he finally saw me all cleaned up. I spun around, scanning the room, but there was no sign of him, until he spoke again.

"Flaka, is this man bothering you?"

I blinked hard, taking in the vision that was talking to me, the fine, polished dandy from back East that was approaching. I hadn't seen Oliver because this man looked nothing like the grimy cowboy covered in dirt and sweat that had walked onto my porch three weeks before. He was clean, close shaven, and his tawny hair was freshly cropped. He smelled milky smooth, like soap, and he was wearing a beautifully tailored pair of gray pants, a white shirt, and a gray jacket over it all. His suit was a little wrinkled, but I didn't care about that. He had become a new man, buttoned to the nines with a thin black tie twisted into a bow around his neck. He was perfection, and he was mine. All mine.

I forgot the proposition of Richard Burns; I forgot that Richard Burns even existed. There was no one else in that room but myself and my husband, no one else in the whole damn world except Flaka and her perfect, splendid Oliver.

My husband slipped across the space between us and gently chucked me under the chin. I snapped my jaw shut, still gaping at him with my eyes, though.

The man named Burns drew away when Oliver darted

him a withering glance, and then my husband pressed his lips close to my ear and whispered, "You clean up real well, Flaka."

I grinned broadly, stupidly, I think. "You don't look half bad yourself," I said, and then I blushed, wildly conscious of my loud, unpolished manner of speech. I felt my cheeks burning as I turned and looked around at all the people staring at the two of us. I almost stuck my tongue out at them, but I couldn't do that. Not now. I was a full-growed and married woman, not a child. I had the most handsome man in the entire town, with the most teeth in his head of any of them, indeed, he may have had more teeth in his mouth than all the teeth combined in the whole damn hotel. I didn't care what they thought of me, as long as they admired my . . . Adonis, I think. That was one that Oliver had taught me while we were riding, a verse from a poem he had memorized a long time ago.

I had thought when I heard the poem that the words applied to Oliver. But since then I had forgotten those verses. When I saw him cleaned up like that, the words sprang back to my mind.

> "Thrice fairer than myself (thus she began),
> The field's chief flower, sweet above compare,
> Stain to all nymphs, more lovely than a man,
> More white and red than doves and roses are;
>
> "Nature that made thee, with herself at strife,
> Saith that the world hath ending with thy life.
> Vouchsafe, thou wonder, to alight thy steed,
> And rein his proud head to the saddle-bow;
> If thou wilt deign this favour, for thy meed,
> A thousand honey secrets shalt thou know."

I didn't rightly understand half the words, especially

"nymphs" and "vouchsafe". Lots of *thys* and *saiths* and old-timey ways of talking. But I did know that I wanted to rein Oliver's proud head to my saddle-bow and make him drink the secret honey and mead. As I held his hand, I felt a warmth between my legs that I scarcely understood. I had never knowed real love's touch, and I could tell there was something greater and more beautiful and more mysterious about the experience than my ma had told me. There was something wonderful about it that seeing the pigs breeding just didn't quite explain. I could tell it was good by the way I felt whenever Oliver was near me, excited in ways I hardly understood, short of breath, my heart beating in great, slow, pounding thumps within my chest, gasping for the life that would come from becoming one with him. This thing called intercourse I felt I needed when I was near him, I needed it more than I needed air, more than I needed food and water, more than I needed anything.

Gradually my heart steadied and the churning excitement in my abdomen quelled, though I still felt warm in my breast and my groin. I clung to Oliver's arm proudly and we promenaded—which I believe is the fancy word that fancy folk use for a walk—across the street and into the bank. I expected a crowd, people rushing to close their business with the inefficient clerk before the day's end, but there was no one there. The store was empty too, as the banker had told us it would be. There was nothing but dust floating in a beam of light that pierced through the grimy window, casting its wispy golden glow across the book open on the old man's lap.

The banker glanced up at us after a few minutes, during which I could sense Oliver already getting impatient again. Oliver had told me only a little about our plot of land and the small house there, but I had got the idea that he had hardly thought of anythin' else since the first time he laid eyes on that little green spread by the river. Come hell or high water, he meant to reach there today or tomorrow, though I think there were at least fifteen miles to go.

"Hmm, may I help you young people?" asked the banker, scratching his head and setting up another spray of dandruff. The cloud was so overwhelming I coughed a little but tried to delicately muffle it into my sleeve. I was a fancy, high-falutin', homesteadin' woman now, not some common farm girl.

"The deed, old man. Don't you recognize us?" asked Oliver.

"What deed?"

"The deed that was kept aside by your dead partner, Melvin, for a man named Oliver Kedar, you idiot."

The old man took stock of us again, and after a moment of staring with all the intensity of a studious schoolchild looking at the blackboard, his lids lifted a little and his eyebrows went up. "Oh! Had a bath, then, and a change of clothes, have you? I confess I scarcely recognized you."

"My God, man, do you have the deed or not?"

The banker dug around among his papers and books, tutting and clucking and murmuring to himself about the impatience and shortsightedness of youth. At last he triumphantly withdrew a yellowed envelope from the stacks. Oliver leaped forward, sticking his hand through the grate and snatching the envelope from the old man. My husband's eyes greedily drank up the words on the form, words that would've taken me hours to slowly decode. Then Oliver smiled, that easy smile of confidence and assurance, the same smile I had seen him give from behind his bandana on the porch to my parents' house the day he first walked into my life. The day I married him.

As soon as he finished reading the document Oliver withdrew a massive wad of bills from his pocket and thrust it at the banker. "That is everything, the entire amount, as drawn up by your partner a year ago."

"Well hold on, my dear boy," blustered the banker. "You

can't just go throwing money around like that. We need a witness, and a notary, and all things proper. I have to count every penny you've given me and take into account inflation changes and taxes, etc."

"Take your inflation and your etceteras to the gallows, my good man. What you're proposing will take hours, maybe days, and believe me, I've waited long enough."

"There's a proper way of doing things around here," continued the banker in annoyance. "And if you steal that deed without the proper filing and paperwork, I shall be forced to report you to the sheriff."

"My God, man, come off it. I'm not stealing the deed, I just bloody paid for it!" snapped Oliver. He had nearly sworn. I don't think "my God" is fully a swear, but both that and his exclamation about the gallows was very nearly swearing and these two phrases were wildly out of character for my husband. I had learned so little of him in our short marriage, but I knew he was educated, knew many fine words, and never swore, that much I knew for sure. He barely raised his voice, unless I was in danger.

There was a loud thud behind us, and I spun about to find three men standing in the doorway. They were dirt-covered cowboys, all wearing bandanas over their faces. As they burst into the room the banker let out a gurgling exclamation of terror. Perhaps he knew them. Or perhaps he simply knew what was about to happen. Behind the bars he dove under his table. Before I could react, one of the men grabbed me in his arms and pressed a gun to my head. I struggled, but he pushed the cold metal harder against my ear, bending my neck sideways until I stilled. I was caught again, just like in the dunes. I was fucking helpless, fucking worthless, and it made me mad as hell.

The man wasn't looking at me, though, he was looking at Oliver, who stood with his back to the teller's barred window, his hands raised high. I twisted in the robber's grasp again, but I couldn't get free.

"Fucking stop wriggling, bitch, or I'll kill you," said the man. "That goes for everyone in this bank. If you don't cooperate with my partners, we'll kill the girl and the two of you as well."

The other two bandits pushed past us and made for the teller's window with their guns drawn. The banker was still huddled in terror under his little table, I couldn't even see him anymore. I hoped the little man was going for a gun he had stashed somewhere in case of robbery.

The man holding me smelled like a strange mix of sweat, licorice, and tobacco. The odor was so strong it made me gag. When I twisted in his grasp again, he raised the revolver and struck me hard across the face with it. I yelped from the stinging pain and felt the warm flow of blood down my cheek and along my neck.

"Damn you, woman. Listen! Stop wiggling and stop fighting, or I swear to God I will shoot you," he said, his voice low, gruff, and angry. "I want every scrap of money in this place, Caleb. Everything you've got."

The banker, whose name must've been Caleb, let out a terrified little squeak from somewhere behind the window. My gaze moved to Oliver, who was staring back at me, his face turning strangely pale, and a vein in the side of his forehead jutting out, seeming to throb with repressed rage.

The big man holding me was smooth and assured, like he had done this before, many, many times. His two accomplices, however, seemed frightened, and shaky. Neither of them had spoken yet. They were fiddling with the door to get to where Caleb huddled, but the door with the barred window was locked from the inside.

What happened next was so fast I can still scarcely believe it. I was trying again to wrench myself free of the bank robber's grip, twisting and fighting, and I saw him raise his hand to pistolwhip me again, the cords and sinews in his arms bulging under his sleeve. He was going to hit me real hard, probably enough to knock me out. Just from the corner of my eye I saw Oliver's hand moving toward the pistol holstered at his side, in a belt underneath his jacket. The robbers hadn't thought to check the clean-dressed, close-shaven, dandy-lookin' Oliver for weapons.

Faster than the man holding me could strike, he was dead, shot in the face, a cascade of blood and brains spattering upon my pretty white dress and the side of my face as he toppled back. I lost my balance, tumbling down with his falling body, but not before I saw the other two robbers drop to the ground as well, lifeless and inert, dead before the reports of the gunshots echoed in the air. In a second the room was absolutely quiet. Then I scrambled to my feet, detangling myself awkwardly from the dead man and swiping my hands across the blood and brains on my face and dress, trying vainly to clean up the mess but only smearing it worse.

"Sign the form," Oliver ground out through clenched teeth, thrusting the deed through the barred window at the banker. There was a faintly sad expression on his face as he glanced down at the bodies, but it vanished as quickly as it had appeared and all his attention was back on the banker. "Sign the bloody form, Caleb, and take my money and we're leaving."

"My God!" howled the little old man, standing and peering past Oliver at the lifeless forms on the ground. "Mr. Kedar, you'll have to wait now. There's three dead men on the floor of my bank!"

"You think I don't know that? I put them there, you incompetent old fool. I need you to sign this deed and my wife and I are leaving."

"But we must get the sheriff!"

"Listen to me, old man. Pull yourself together and listen." There was a low urgency to Oliver's voice, almost soothing, as if he'd had this discussion with frantic, terrified towns-people a thousand times before. "I saved your life just now, and every penny in this bank. I need you to sign this, take my money, and tell no one that you met with me today. Hide the copy of the deed. You owe me that. You owe me a great deal more than that, but that's all I'm asking for. Don't tell the sheriff. Don't tell anyone. Tell them you killed these men. You've got a revolver back there, haven't you? Good. Then tell them you killed these men. I don't honestly care what you tell them, as long as it's not the truth. Just sign the form, take my money, and let me go before a whole crowd comes bursting through your doors to see what all that commotion was about."

For a second longer the banker hesitated, then, his lip trembling, he snatched the deed from my husband's hand, scribbled quickly across it with his pen, set Oliver's money on the desk, and then handed the deed back. My husband took off his hat and bowed to the old man before grabbing my wrist. We slipped out the back door of the bank, just as the front door of the pioneer store swung open and the crowd poured in to see the massacre my husband had wrought.

XIII

"YOU DIDN'T CHECK TO MAKE SURE I WAS ALRIGHT," I ACCUSED as we shuffled quickly through the alleyway, back toward the saloon where we'd stalled our horses.

"I didn't have to. I knew who I shot," replied Oliver. The assured, easy air of a gunslinger had come back to him. After a glance back at me, he paused and reached out to touch my swollen cheek gently and the laceration under my hair. I flinched away. "How's your face? That brute hit you pretty hard."

"I'll live," I answered brusquely, pushing his hand aside and walking on.

While Oliver went inside to pay, I washed my dress and my hair as best I could in the horse's watering trough outside the saloon. Everyone in the whole town was at the bank by that point, 'ceptin the saloon owner. The store itself was hidden around a corner, but I could hear the commotion. I watched the street warily as I scrubbed the scarlet from my hair and wrung it out. When Oliver led the horses out he tossed me his mare's saddle blanket.

"To cover the gory parts," he explained.

I unfolded the blanket and wrapped it around my shoulders, drawing it tight across my chest. The smell of soap from my bath was all but gone, replaced by the metallic scent of blood and the coarse odor of horse sweat. Glancing down I was pleased to see that it had worked. The blood and brains were hidden from any prying eyes. I swung up into the saddle, sitting sidesaddle now with my dress, my left foot in the stirrup and right leg hooked over the pommel.

We skedaddled out of that town as fast as we could. Evening was falling and the shadows of the little buildings stretched out long and tall, making the town look bigger than it really was. I had to kick Butterball hard to get him to keep up with Oliver's mare. My husband was rushing on this final push in our journey, at last having achieved what he had worked for and desired for so long. As the dimness of twilight faded into black around us, I called ahead to him, "How did you learn to shoot like that, Oliver?"

"How does anyone learn to shoot like that?" he replied over his shoulder. "Practice, Flaka, years of constant practice."

"But why? What were you before you came to my doorstep three weeks ago?"

Oliver bit his lip, slowing his mare to a walk, and gave me a sidelong glance. He didn't speak for a long time, but finally he let out a low sigh. "I was no one, Flaka. I was the son of a whore in Boston. My father came from out west, and he took a shine to me, even though I was just a whore's son. He bought me a gun when I was twelve, and I learned to shoot it really well, just practicing, constantly practicing. My father paid for my schooling, so I went to university, but when my mother died I came west, to seek my fortune. To see if I could become a great man like my father."

"Do great men sleep with whores?"

"Great men sleep with whomever they please."

"And who is your father?"

"No one—at least, no one to me anymore."

"Did you become a great man by coming west?"

Oliver snorted. "No, I became a gunslinger. I worked with evil people who robbed and stole and shot up people who didn't deserve to die. I made a lot of bad choices, and I hurt a lot of good and honest folk."

"Did you rape a girl in Fort Davis like Grant Marcus said you did?"

He shook his head slowly. "No, Flaka. I didn't do that."

It was not a lot, but I felt satisfied after hearing his brief confession, as if I finally knew my husband. It felt good to have him confide in me, even if there were no specifics. It was still so much more information than I had known three weeks ago when I married him in my parents' farmyard. He was a gunslinger, at last he had admitted that, and a man who had done things he wasn't proud of. That should've made me anxious, afraid of him, but it didn't. If I'm being honest, it made me want him even more. We had been on the run so long, and he had been ill, and then I had been on my cycle and in that state of just dread sickness of soul that I can't hardly explain. There hadn't yet been a time and a place for us to make love, but I yearned to have Oliver Kedar inside me —I yearned to be a wife in the carnal sense of that word. To be one with my handsome, fine-talkin', fast-shooting gunslinger.

Perhaps my reaction was wrong, or foolish, or naive, but it was the reaction I had to learning more about my husband. I couldn't judge it then, I just felt it, riding beside him, deeply aware of his breathing, his scent, his height, his yellow hair and bright blue eyes, his presence, more intoxicating than moonshine. I loved Oliver Kedar, and I was loving him more and more every day that passed. What had happened in the bank, his speed with his pistol, faster than I had ever seen a man shoot, and his accuracy, every shot a kill, had left me awestruck. I had married myself to perhaps the fastest gun in the West. Despite what Martha had said and all her dour warnings, colored by her own sad life, I knew that I had made the right choice, that here was a man who would protect me and love me for all of our lifetime together. Here was my knight in shining armor. Here was a man so fast with his gun that I would never have to fear losing him like the saloon-keeper had suggested.

"Oliver, can you teach me to shoot like that?" I asked suddenly, on a whim, almost playfully.

He shook his head and there was a thoughtful sadness in his face that I could just make out in the moonlight, a deeper sadness than I had seen there before. "You don't want to know how to shoot like that, Flaka, believe me."

All night we rode, and it was still dark when we crossed the rushing waters of the San Pedro River, the water icy cold against our legs. The rocks were slippery beneath our horses' hooves, but Oliver never paused, pushing through fast while Butterball floundered in the raging current. We had crossed a few rivers in our journey but none as fast as this one, and none so full of refreshing water. I was midway across when Butterball did slip. For a second I thought he would regain his balance and be fine, that we would both be fine. Then we kept tipping and I let out a little yelp before the water swirled up around my face and mouth, filling my nose, my throat, and pouring into my lungs. I floundered amidst the thrashing of Butterball's legs and hooves, splashing and coughing and fighting as panic welled up inside me. There weren't no rivers nor lakes to speak of around my family homestead, and I had never acquired the skill of swimming. My body came loose from the saddle but I could not free my left leg from the stirrup no matter how much I thrashed.

Suddenly I felt Butterball find ground and break free from the rushing water, yanking me forward. He dragged me up onto the shore, where I coughed and sputtered, scraping and bumping against slimy rocks covered in green algae. In a second Oliver was by my side, soothing my pony and freeing my twisted, aching leg from the stirrup.

"Couldn't resist one last attempt to get yourself killed?" asked Oliver gently, laughing at me but in a way that made me feel loved and cared for, not patronized.

I was shivering like mad. Oliver slipped me out of my wet leather coat and draped his own dry jacket over me—he hadn't much needed it, except at night over the last few days. I coughed up muddy river water and said, "I weren't tryin' to get rolled on, nor was I tryin' to get taken hostage by that damn bankrobber." I was still trembling all over, perhaps more from *miedo* than the cold.

"Alright, we've pushed hard enough tonight. This is as fine a place as any I've seen to camp at," said Oliver. "Just rest easy for a few minutes. I'll untack the horses and get a fire going."

It took a little while, but soon I was holding my hands up to warm them by a crackling little fire while the horses rested and grazed along the river bank in their hobbles. Butterball was still blowing out, his flanks heaving from the effort and fear of his near watery grave. Oliver sat beside me, letting me rest my back upon his chest, his arm wrapped around my sopping shoulders.

"Will you read for me?" I asked after a while, starting to feel a little warmer.

"You ought to read for me."

"I ain't good enough yet. It still sounds like a little kid reading, sounding everything out real slow and stupid-like."

"No, that's not true," whispered Oliver and pressed his lips against the back of my neck, and more goose bumps sprang up. But these were a different type of goose bumps, not from the cold. In fact, my neck felt fiery hot where he'd kissed it. "You sound beautiful when you read, Flaka. But, first, why don't you take off those wet things? You'll catch pneumonia for sure, cold as you are."

I had it on good authority from my ma that cold wasn't what caused pneumonia, despite what people said, but I let it be. My husband was breathing on my back and it was tickling, and making not only the hairs along my neck stand up, but every hair on my body seemed to be standing on point by then, all of them waiting, tall, erect, poised for whatever was to come. I reached back and began to undo the buttons of the dress on my back. After a moment Oliver gently grasped my hands and set them on my lap and took over the task. I think his fingers were trembling a little as he worked the wet buttons through the loops, though perhaps it was just my imagination that he was as excited as I was to have me naked in his arms.

I felt the loosening around my shoulders and peeled the wet garment off my chest, letting it fall, exposing my stays beneath. I think my breasts had swollen in those last few minutes; they seemed to bulge, begging for freedom from my stays. I looked up at Oliver, who was drinking in my exposed bosoms, tracing his fingers along the curve of my neck and shoulders. He smiled at me, bending to nip teasingly at my lips, then press his mouth against my chest. He smiled even more then, letting his breath tickle my breasts. I reached my hands up and grasped his neck, pulling him deeper into me.

Oliver chuckled and then looked very seriously at me and asked, "You're sure this is what you want, Flaka?"

"More than anything!" I exclaimed, and I fell back onto his jacket, laid out on the rocky river shore, and pulled him down on top of me. We fumbled for a few minutes with our garments, forcing ourselves to stop kissing each other like starving animals, just to keep undoing stays and belts and buttons, and slide shirts and corsets off. It was much easier to remove men's clothing than ladies, I noticed. He pulled his shirt off, letting me kiss his chest, then he rolled me over to undo the lacing on my back and release me from my corset. I twisted and yanked myself free from the whalebone harness and then free from the petticoats. And, just like that, I was naked at last, every part of my body exposed to the flickering light, and Oliver, still in his trousers, paused, his eyes glowing with appreciation, with love, as he cast his gaze up and down my form.

He pressed his body into me, scouring my mouth and neck with his tongue and sucking at my breasts with his lips, lips that burned like fire. His hand found its way into the soft spot between my legs, found that center of pleasure so easily, so perfectly. A moment later I was twisting in joy, casting my head back into the dirt, moaning from the glory of the sensation. I had been told that only whores moan, but if that was the case, then I was a whore—I was Oliver's whore, his plaything to pleasure. I became an instrument in his hands, and he played me like a skilled musician, sending my whole being dancing in circles of delight. After a moment, desperate for more, desperate for all of him, I gently pried his hand from my vagina, looking up into his eyes. Then I undid his belt buckle the rest of the way and slid his trousers down. He kicked them free and I found myself staring at his bulging, erect penis, gleaming, somehow beautifully, in the light from the fire.

I don't know what possessed me, but I wanted every bit of him inside me, I wanted to consume him. I wrapped my lips around his member, and a moment later it was pressing into the back of my throat, filling my mouth, making me pant for breath through my nose. But I didn't want to breathe, I wanted Oliver. I thrust my head back and forth until at last I heard a faint groan from him and knew I had done well. I was giving him the same delight he had just given me; I was pleasing him. Then he pulled my head up and slid down beside me, kissing my mouth so hard I couldn't breathe. An instant later I felt his penis sliding between my legs, and I was full and I gasped from a delight mingled with a pleasant pain so intense I had never experienced anything like it in my entire life. I was staring up at the heavens above me, and he was thrusting himself into me again and again and again, so hard and fast and exhilarating. It was like riding the wildest, bucking stallion.

I stared up at his eyes and then past him into the sky and the flickering stars above as he slowed his thrusts, escorting me on an agonizing journey of rapture until I cried out as it seemed my whole body was consumed by the fires of an ecstasy unlike anything else on earth. My eyes closed and my neck arched back. He was panting and moaning above me, and then it was over, and he was out of me. Never in my life had I felt so madly satisfied, so unfathomably happy, as Oliver bent over me and kissed my lips and my chest and took my hands and pressed them both to his mouth before he toppled over and lay beside me, gazing up at the stars with a faint smile on his face.

We didn't say anything after that, just lay there tangled naked in each other's arms under the canopy of beautiful stars above, more happy, and content, and together than either of us had ever been before in all our lives, I think. We had known one another, and it had been glorious, and we would know one another forever. Here was bliss, here on the banks of San Pedro River was pure, unadulterated, heavenly bliss. We had found the hope of a future better than any we could have imagined when we fled my parents' farm.

When morning dawned, Oliver was already dressed, though I was naked yet beneath the bedroll. He was cooking and the scent of fresh *pescado* filled the air. I sat up, pulling the blanket instinctively to cover my nakedness. He grinned and winked at me.

"No need for that, Flaka, no one here is going to complain if you leave your breasts exposed."

I let the blanket drop, and the sun dappled its light across my chest as Oliver brought me the *pescado* he had cooked. We curled up together, him clothed and me naked as the day I was born, and ate and laughed like children on a picnic. We had done something that I had never done before and there was an awkward, beautiful intimacy to our interactions following that experience the night before. I looked around me, taking in the sunshine, how it shimmered and speckled off the ripples of water in the river; taking in the rising hills around us, the greenness and lushness of the riverbank rising above us and a willow tree dangling its tendrils into the water, letting the current pull it along, north, away from us. I wondered if the water would carry the story of our love-making to distant places and burble that tale to others resting along the riverbank. It was all foolishness, I suppose, but it didn't feel like foolishness. It felt like heaven.

I dressed reluctantly, packing my scant belongings as if it was a burden, never wanting to leave the magical, beautiful place where I had become one with my Oliver. At last we were both mounted, and Oliver turned back to survey the river, and the sloping greenness of the river bank merging with the red stones. He blew out a sigh and that distant, wistful look came into his eyes again, the look I had learned always appeared before he began to recite poetry. He began to speak as I expected, his voice quiet but firm.

"We leave the well-beloved place
Where first we gazed upon the sky;
The roofs, that heard our earliest cry,
Will shelter one of stranger race.
We go, but ere we go from home,
As down the garden-walks I move,
Two spirits of a diverse love
Contend for loving masterdom.
One whispers, 'Here thy boyhood sung
Long since its matin song, and heard
The low love-language of the bird
In native hazels tassel-hung.'
The other answers, 'Yea, but here

Thy feet have stray'd in after hours
With thy lost friend among the bowers,
And this hath made them trebly dear.'
These two have striven half the day,
And each prefers his separate claim,
Poor rivals in a losing game,
That will not yield each other way.
I turn to go: my feet are set
To leave the pleasant fields and farms;
They mix in one another's arms
To one pure image of regret."

"Seems a sad poem to speak over a place of such happiness," I remarked.

Oliver smiled. "That's the point, sad and full of joy all at once. I meant to make love to you first in our new home, Flaka, the place we're going to grow old together, so let me offer my apologies for deflowering you upon a rocky riverbank."

"I wouldn't have had it any other way," I answered, and we rode on, for the last leg of our journey together.

Danger had a way of finding us, even without the pursuit of Ian Marcus, who hadn't shown his face since he captured me in the desert in Mexico. But, once we had crossed that river, once we had known each other intimately, I felt as if we had found peace at last and there would be no more badness. A memory came into my head of a phrase my pa had said once, a quote from someone, a book, or a verse in the Bible maybe, I didn't know. "Let us cross over the river, and rest in the shade of the trees," he had said, and I had always remembered it, but never had I felt it so truly as when we left that riverbank and rode out into rest, into *paz*, into a new and hopeful and bright future, a future that stretched on as endless as the desert behind us. We were free, and we were one, and we were young, and we were beginning our lives anew after passing through terrible tribulation.

It was another two hours of riding before we climbed a berm to find a small, crumbling cottage, surrounded by fallen fencing and a half-built barn. The motley collection of human structures rested atop a green spread of flat land, perched high above the river, but looking down on those glistening waters. It was a tiny slice of paradise—heaven come to earth. It was my home, however disheveled, and in that moment when I first laid eyes on it, I too saw the possibilities more than the reality: the possibility of a beautiful life and a family, a spread of our own with our own cattle, expansions to *la casa* to fit a bustling crew of little ones, the barn that could be full of our stock, the fences repaired, and the lush, verdant garden above the river. The whole world and our whole lives rolled out before my eyes as I drank in that little home nestled on the red stone bluff.

Oliver glanced at me, and I could tell that he could see all that had passed through my mind. Together we spurred our horses across the last stretch of green that lay between us and our home. A loud gunshot rang out, splitting the air, coming directly from our new *casa*. Instantly we spun our horses around, making for a rocky cover a few dozen yards to the north. In a moment we were crouched behind a stone outcropping, holding our horses' reins, staring at the house, both of us breathless.

"Marcus?" I asked, my eyes wide with fear.

Oliver shook his head. "He would have called out by now. Just a squatter, I would think, though I don't see much signs of life around the cabin." He studied the lay of the land for a moment, then ducked as another shot rang out and a bullet struck near his hand. "Definitely a rifle, and definitely coming from inside the house. I can make it around the back, there's a window there," he whispered. "Do you think you can distract him from this side? Just move around a bit, occasionally shoot at him. Don't do anything stupid."

I nodded emphatically, my throat tight from fear. It had been too good to be true after all. We had almost reached our longed-for happily ever after, but danger and death had found us here too. Perhaps we were just an unlucky couple. I scoffed at that thought as I took two shots at our home. It wasn't that we were unlucky. It was that I had killed Grant Marcus, and perhaps I would always be paying the price for that one mistake.

I squeezed the trigger again, watching the bullet crack against a wall. I couldn't hit with any sort of precision at this distance. But that wasn't the goal, I just needed to distract the shooter. I had not thought of Grant Marcus in a while. Perhaps it was like Ma had always said, whenever her children were upset about something—like the loss of a beloved pet. She had always said that time would make the memory dull. That time would heal the wound left behind. She had always been right about that too. And now time had done passed since I killed a man, so that sick feeling weren't so fierce and breathtaking as it had been when I first shot him. Now here I was, fixing to start my life in the Arizona Territory by killing again.

I flattened myself against the slab of stone, listening as more bullets pinged off the rock protecting me. My heart thundered loudly in my chest, loud enough, I thought, for even the squatter to hear the noise of it. I could see he was firing from just in the corner of the west-facing window. There were brief flickers of movement there, though no particularly clear features of our squatter that I could make out. I wedged myself between two of the rocks, bringing the gun slowly up to aim at the window and waiting for another flash of someone or something through the dingy panes, half of them broken out. I was holding my breath, I realized, and the image of Grant Marcus' face as he dropped to the ground, deader than a doornail, kept flitting through my mind. Still, I remembered how easily Oliver had killed, how he had even made it appear admirable, even beautiful, in a way. He brought such grace to the skill of killing. I could do that too. I could separate myself from the knowledge that the man out there was a human, a person, I could make him a thing, just a thing that was tryin' to kill us, a thing squatting in what should have been our peaceful, beautiful home, a home we had paid for. I steadied the gun, taking slow, deep breaths. A galling thought startled me then for the first time. Yes, we had bought the house, but with what money? Where had Oliver come by such a sum? Was this place really ours? Ours enough to kill over?

The movement behind the window happened again and I forced that thought out of my mind and squeezed the trigger. The gun leaped in my hand, startling me with the finality of the jolt of it, like I was holding lightning itself. But there was no cry of pain, no dull thud inside the house. I'd missed, and I felt relieved at that.

I saw Oliver dashing through the grass behind the house and then heard a loud shattering crash, like someone smashing through a window, then the crackle of multiple gunshots, and then silence. My heart was back in my throat again. I stood and began to edge myself forward across the yard, trying to stay behind shrubs and bushes as I moved. I didn't know who had triumphed in that last brief scuffle. I didn't know if Oliver was alive. I dove to the ground as the door of the little cabin opened and then peeked up, holding my pistol before me.

Oliver was standing there, grinning, though his hands were covered in blood. I scanned him up and down, looking for any wound. There were just a few scratches I could see. My stomach twisted, remembering the last time he had been wounded, how little I had cared at first when I locked him in the chicken coop, but how terrifying that wound had become as my love for Oliver blossomed.

"It's alright, Flaka. You can come up. He's dead," said Oliver. Behind the smile there was that faintly sad expression I was beginning to recognize. He always looked like that after he killed a man.

I stood, dusting myself off, and ran forward. To my surprise Oliver caught me as I reached the door and hefted me off the ground, into his bloody hands. Instinctively I put my arms around his neck as he carried me across the porch. I must have looked bewildered because he grinned at me and explained, "A man always carries his bride across the threshold, it's tradition."

Carrying the bride over the threshold of a house where a dead man lay while the husband was covered in blood must be the Arizona twist on that tradition. After a moment my eyes grew accustomed to the dimness and I could make out the finer details of our new home. The dead man, a bearded, ragged, dirty old-timer, lay in a pool of blood near the window, staring sightlessly at the ceiling. There were shafts of light piercing through the shabby roof, through the walls of the building where my bullet holes had punctured it. The place was otherwise dingy, little bigger than Martha's hovel in Salvacar. There was a bed without a mattress, a couple broken chairs, and a table with three legs, along with a few scattered bits of the dead squatter's belongings, a jug on the floor, a torn jacket and ragged bedroll.

Oliver stepped into one beam of light, shining through the largest hole in the roof, and for a moment I was blinded. Then all I could see was my husband's handsome, weary face, smiling at me, a warm, soft smile, full of adoration. Suddenly I forgot the dead man by the window and let Oliver kiss me, his lips opening and closing around mine. Desire for him rose up inside me, washing away everything else, washing away all consciousness of the horror and grubbiness of our surroundings.

He set me down and took off his jacket, using it to cover the dead man's face, and by the time he returned to me, swiftly yanking his shirt off as he walked, I had my pants halfway removed. In a moment he had relieved me of my shirt as well and pushed me up against the wall, still nipping at my face and neck and chest with his insatiable mouth. I had a flicker of a thought that it was wrong to do this in a house where a freshly dead corpse lay, but then Oliver was on his knees and his lips found the edges of my vagina, and his tongue found its way to that spring where pleasure comes from, and I was powerless against the waves of delight that washed over me. A few moments later I was on the floor kissing his chest and neck, and tearing ravenously at his belt, forgetting everything but my desire to have my husband inside me again, here, in our new, perfect, beautiful home—the place we would spend the rest of our lives together.

XIV

A KNOCK AT THE DOOR STARTLED US FROM OUR LOVEMAKING. WE had finished with our throes of ecstasy and were just playing with each other on the floor by then. The instant the knock sounded, Oliver tensed and then scrambled for his gun and his pants.

"Who's there?" he asked as he stuffed his perfect penis and long legs back into his trousers. I was also rushing to get my own garments rearranged into some sort of order, but not so urgently that I couldn't appreciate his beautiful body as he hid it within his clothing, to my great sorrow.

"I should ask you the same thing," retorted a man's voice outside the door. "Ain't no one lived here in all the five years Susanna and I been here, so I'm assuming you're a squatter. Or two squatters, I should say, based on the number of horses you got out'chere."

"Then you would be wrong in your assumption," replied Oliver, and with one last glance at me to make sure I was at least decent, he opened the door.

There were two people standing outside on the uneven, yawing porch, a young man and a young woman, older than the two of us, sure, but not yet thirty if I was any judge. The man had a thick black mustache and narrow eyes. He was shorter than Oliver by a head. The woman stood behind him, dressed in a worn blue dress that hugged her plump form close. She had a freckled face and long, straight brown hair falling past her shoulders.

Oliver studied them for an instant and then holstered his pistol, holding out one hand that was still covered in dried blood. "Name's Oliver, Oliver Robinson." He cast a quick glance at me, but I nodded. My husband was a gunslinger and I was a fugitive. Oliver didn't have to explain why the sudden name change had to be.

The man frowned as he looked us up and down, his brow creasing beneath his black hat, then his face smoothed and he took Oliver's hand.

The woman was studying me closely, and looking down I realized that Oliver had managed to smear blood on my neck and jaw during our lovemaking. I looked a real sight, I was sure, my dress all askew and rumpled, the scab marks on my neck still evident from Marcus' rope, and now fresh blood on my face. I also imagined our new neighbors could probably smell the sex we'd just had.

"I'm Edmund," the man was saying as he shook Oliver's hand. "Edmund Gardner, and this here's Susanna, my wife. We live about a mile up this h'yere creek."

"A pleasure to meet you, neighbor," said Oliver. "This is Flaka, my wife. We bought this place yesterday. I've had my eye on it since about a year ago. I've been saving up to purchase it ever since."

I also shook Edmund's proffered hand, still watching Susanna, who stepped forward and, to my great surprise, gathered me up in a warm embrace. For a second I was lost in those enormous, bountiful breasts, and I felt a warmth fill me —it felt damn near a sense of belonging, the warmth of finally coming home after a long journey. Susanna would be my first *amiga* in the Tombstone region, of that I was sure. I could tell from the sincerity of that embrace. She squeezed me as if to let me go would make me disappear.

"There was a squatter, however," said Oliver, pointing back toward the still figure on the floor, covered by his jacket. "That's why you heard all the shooting. But I can show you the deed if you want proof that Flaka and I own this place."

Edmund shook his head vigorously. "No, no, I can tell you are good Christian folks. I can see it in your eyes. I think if I did anything to make you feel unwelcome, Susanna would never forgive me. She's just been a-longin' and a-hankerin' for a woman to befriend out here. It's lonely out in the wilds for a female, ch'a know."

I grinned broadly; this, then, was the reason Susanna had squeezed me so hard. "I think if you'd hugged me any harder, Oliver'd be a widower right now and you'd be back to waiting for someone to come and befriend you."

Susanna blushed, her freckled cheeks turning scarlet red. "I know, I know, I just . . . couldn't help myself. When did you all arrive?"

"About the time you heard those first shots," Oliver replied.

"Well, we must see what we can do to help you folks get settled in and feel welcome," proclaimed Edmund. "Perhaps disposing of the body would be the first step?"

"Oughn't we to take him into town for the sheriff?" Susanna asked. I was noticing that she blushed almost every time she spoke, and it made me like her all the more.

"Sheriff's got enough on his plate right now without dealin' with dead squatters," Edmund retorted. "Let's jest bury him and let that be an end to it. Anyone squatting out h'yere alone prob'ly don't have no family waiting for him anyhow."

"You're a cynical man," observed Oliver. Together the two of them gathered the dead form in their arms, still limp and floppy, and took him outside. I'm still not sure where they buried him, because the next few weeks I hardly strayed from the yard.

Those first weeks passed in a blur of endless work, what with putting the dilapidated *casa* in order. I hadn't had the least notion afore about how hard it was to be a settler and build something from what amounted to almost nothing. For things we needed Oliver would go into town by himself, borrowing Edmund's wagon. Susanna came over twice a week to help us with projects, Edmund less often because he had his own work to do on their little plot up the crik. Oliver sent money back to Martha, just like he had promised, and I hoped that when the money arrived she felt a fool for thinking him anything less than the world's most perfect husband. I had won this round, and she had been wrong. Oliver was everything a husband ought to be, and my favorite part of every day was when his reeking, sweaty body returned from what would be our bountiful fields one day or from errands in Tombstone and I made love to him. My ma had never told me proper about the best part of being a wife.

Susanna kept insisting that I come and visit her home, and when I finally did, riding Butterball to their little shanty two miles downriver, I was amazed to see how well they had set their place up. Despite all the hours and days—and by then weeks—that I had put into our home, it came nowhere close to the domestic comforts of Susanna's little abode. She had curtains, beautiful curtains printed with flowers, she had windows that were cleaned to the nines and all with glass in every pane, and little flowers and cactuses planted all around the edges of the house, and all that on top of her garden which was also blooming madly with vegetables, peppers, tomatoes, corn, cucumbers, and also bright, colorful flowers I ain't never seen before.

When I came into the house, gaping at all the lovely comforts she had put in place, she yanked me to the side of the main room, over to a small table draped with a beautiful, checkered tablecloth. There, in the corner, she showed me two long spools of fabric leaned up against the wall.

"We shall make curtains for your home too, Flaka. Curtains!" she proclaimed triumphantly, like a general after winning a great battle.

I stared at the crisp fabric, real linen, printed with green ivy and yellow flowers circling around it in a cheerful design. As my fingers touched the starched cloth, for an instant I was home, sewing with my ma in the parlor. Then I saw Grant Marcus' face, and saw Oliver and me fleeing in the desert like mad, desperate to escape death. I think a tear started in my eye. A moment later I was really crying, sobbing even, staring down at the floorboards, my shoulders shaking hard, and I felt Susanna wrap me in her arms.

"What is it, Flaka? Did I say something wrong?" she asked, concern evident in her tone.

"No, no," I said, shaking my head. "It's jest . . . everything, you know, everything. Oliver and I been through a terrible time coming here. I don't know why I'm crying. It's plum foolishness."

Susanna rubbed my shoulders and my back. "There, there. It's alright. I do understand. Edmund and I been through trial after trial out here as well. We done lost three babies since we started living out here, you know. I know it's hard, awful hard."

I choked a little and spoke through my tears. "Three babies? Oh, Susanna, I'm sorry. Why am I crying like a fool when you been through something like that?"

"It's alright, they were never alive, just came out still. I don't let it bother me none, not anymore, leastways. When God wants us to have little ones, He'll give them to us and not take them away like that. Those ones were never mine. I'm sorry I brought it up. I'm not trying to burden you or make your sorrows seem smaller. I just want you to know, we've also struggled and had it hard and I do understand how you're feeling, better than anyone, really. And I'm just so deeply happy to have you here now, a friend and a sister in this wild, bleak place."

"It sure is wild and bleak, but it's beautiful too, ain't it?" I said, smiling a little and sniffling, trying to stifle the tears. I must have looked and sounded like a real fool, but Susanna just glowed at me and listened real good. "It's like we came through purgatory and finally get to have our just reward."

"I think that's exactly what happened," replied Susanna. "But you're here now, and all that's over. It's just hope and goodness lying ahead of you now, Flaka. The worst part is over."

And, like the dad-blamed idiot I was, I believed my first, dearest *amiga* out there in Arizona Territory. I believed that the worst part was over, and only joy and happiness lay ahead now. I believed that the danger had finally passed us by. I shoulda knowed better. Susanna and I both wiped the tears from our eyes and set to work making the curtains for mine and Oliver's perfect home in paradise.

XV

We had lived on our little homestead for a mite bit longer than a month, and the memory of Ian Marcus and that blasted son of his that I had killed was finally fading, fading away into nothing. The days had fallen into a steady rhythm, Oliver working hard to clear some fields most days, me tending the house and garden and preparing food for his return. On my insistence, Oliver had started teaching me to shoot fast and accurate, the way he did, and that was the only reminder of the horror we had known. I weren't nowhere close to Oliver's skill, but I was getting better every time we practiced. Some days I worked alongside him in the fields, but on this particular day he had gone into town for a new axe handle. I was left alone and didn't mind it much. I had even finished a project, repairing the stools inside the house, and for a while I was just sitting and reading that poem again, getting lost in the prettiness of the language and the rhythms of it, like music.

A knock sounded on the door and it startled me. It wasn't Wednesday. Wednesdays Susanna came, and other days beside, but most commonly Wednesdays and Saturdays. Sundays I saw her at the little meeting house six miles up the way where many of the rural folk out here gathered for church. I thought hard as that firm knock sounded again. It was most definitely Thursday. I had definitely seen Susanna yesterday, and there was no reason she would be coming up to visit me again so soon. Plus the knock didn't sound like her. It sounded different, harder, much more solid and confident than Susanna's gentle patters.

Cautiously, feeling the first flutter of fear in my chest that I had felt in weeks, I went and got the shotgun down from where it hung on the wall of the main room. We kept it loaded, as a precaution. Going to the door, I slowly eased it open. A man was standing outside, just one man, facing away from me, surveying the property. I made double sure there was only one man with a quick scan of the yard. I hefted the gun up to my shoulder, eyeing his back.

"I'd advise you not to shoot me," he said softly. "I'm a lawman and you'd bring terrible justice down on this little homestead if you killed me."

My jaw dropped open as a flood of recognition washed over me. The voice, the form, the figure standing there, the dark hair protruding from beneath the hat; I knew that person, though I hadn't seen him in years. Finding him in this place, so far from anywhere else that we had known together, sent me reeling. Of course I had told Oliver he lived out here, but with all our busyness fixing the house and yard, I had plum forgot to try to look him up. I almost didn't believe it was him.

"If you don't turn around and give your little sister a proper hug, then I damn well will shoot you," I said as I set the gun down, leaning it against the door frame. Hearing my voice, he spun about in surprise and I launched myself into his arms before he could recover himself or make sense of what he was seeing. He stumbled backward, then steadied, squeezing me tight.

"Flaka? Is that really you, Flaka? What in God's name are

you doing out here?" He kept repeating that question even as he clenched me against his chest. He held me so tight, as though if he were to ease his grip even for a second, I would vanish into the air around us.

"Of course it's me, dummy," I retorted, and stepped back from him, spreading my arms wide so Ephraim Garcia Hasani could see, beyond all shadow of doubt, that it was his little sister, eight years his junior, but the closest companion of his childhood.

I had been no less than a living shadow to Ephraim when he was a boy, aping his steps, following him and his *amigos* everywhere, getting into scrape after scrape as the boys had tried to evade his incorrigible little sister. But for all his running from me as he grew older, he had loved me. I knew that from the way he read to me when the other boys weren't there, and built me forts of blankets, and played pretend Texas Rangers versus Commanches with me. Ephraim had always loved me, and I loved him, far more than my older sisters. But I still couldn't believe he was here, standing on my porch. Then I saw the dull silver badge on his chest and I think my heart stopped.

"Is Oliver alright? You didn't . . . you didn't come out to tell me that he's . . ."

"Oliver Kedar?"

"Yes, Oliver Kedar. Oliver, my husband."

"Your husband?" Ephraim's forehead creased, as if he was struggling to put together some puzzle in his mind. He even took a little step back when I said Oliver was my husband.

"Yes, my husband, *mi esposo*. Is he alright? What are you doing here? And with that fancy, shiny badge?"

"I . . ." Ephraim was slack-jawed. He looked down at his badge, up at me, then at my house, like he was looking for an answer to some impossible question in the air around us. He snapped his mouth shut then, collecting himself. "As far as I know Oliver Kedar is fine. But Flaka, you can't be married to him."

"Well, I am."

"Well, you can't be."

"What the hell right do you have to come to my home and tell me who I can and cannot marry? You took off as soon as you turned sixteen and I ain't never seen you since."

"I wrote home, didn't I? Oliver Kedar is a bank, stage-coach, and train robber, and more than that, he's a murderer. He's a wanted man, Flaka, in three states now."

"Shut up!" I cried. "That ain't true. Is that why you came out here, then? To arrest my husband?"

Ephraim clamped his mouth shut this time, studying me with those kind brown eyes of his. Ephraim was taller than all the rest of us Garcia Hasanis, broad-shouldered, with lightly tan skin and dark hair that fell down into his eyes. He had gotten all the good looks and most of the brains in the family as well, I thought. But I hadn't never in my life expected to meet him on my doorstep in Tombstone with a shiny metal star on his chest. I wanted to hug him again, but I was angry at the same time. He had no right to come barging onto my front porch and telling me who I couldn't be married to, especially seen as how I had already married that person.

"It is true, Flaka," he insisted finally, his voice very low and careful. "Oliver Kedar is a gunslinger and a bank and stage robber wanted in Texas, Colorado, and Missouri, and he's about to be wanted in the Arizona Territory as well."

"Why?" I said. "He ain't broken no laws here. I been with him the whole time."

"I'm sure he has. I'm sure he's broken a passel of them. But a lawman, a marshal from out by Fort Davis, came looking for him and brought Ian Marcus with him, who said Oliver and a woman he was harboring had killed Grant Marcus, Ian's son."

"Then leave Oliver alone and arrest me, Ephraim. I'm the

one that went and killed Grant Marcus," I said, jutting my jaw out.

"Flaka, I ain't going to arrest you. You're just saying that to protect your man, but he doesn't deserve your protection. He's got a record of crimes ten miles long if it's an inch. He's a bad man, Flaka."

"You don't stop talking like that and I will shoot you!" I cried.

"He killed his own brother, Flaka."

"His brother?"

"Grant Marcus, Oliver's brother."

Now it was my turn to draw back in shock. I confess I couldn't take it anymore. I spun around on my heel and walked back into the perfect home that I had rebuilt with my perfect husband and plopped myself down on a stool, pressing my elbows into the table, staring blankly at nothing, trying to make sense of everything, or just anything. I suddenly understood the way Ian Marcus spoke to Oliver. The father that had fucked the whore in Boston that Oliver had mentioned was a great man in the West—all the pieces were falling into place. If he'd lied about this, it stood to reason he'd probably lied about everything else as well, about where he got that money from, about the girl Grant had accused him of raping and killing. My husband, my perfect, beautiful husband. In that second he became nothing but a monster to me. The son of a man who had chased me across countries, hunting me like an animal for months.

It is a wonder how fast love can turn to hate. In a split second, in the blink of an eye, the most passionate, consuming love can twist and contort into utter disgust, into the most deep and abiding hatred, wiping away every shred of affection in an instant. I didn't just hate Oliver then, I wanted him dead. Perhaps it was the heights of the love that had preceded that new revelation that caused the depths of anger to be so devastating. The higher they climb, the harder they fall, I think the saying goes.

I sat there, all numb and stupid, gaping at the wall, while Ephraim held my hand and listed off the many, many crimes of Oliver Kedar. Things Martha had tried to tell me, but I hadn't been willing to listen then. I remember hearing those things my brother said, but distantly, like the roll of summer thunder, far, far away. In my head I kept seeing scenes from our flight across the desert, over and over again, things Oliver had told me, the books, the poems, all of it just the disguise of an evil man, a screen of tricks and smoke to hide what he truly was. The same murdering blood that ran through Marcus' veins ran through the man that fucked me every night. For every tender moment we had known, Ephraim had some sinister tale to erase that memory. I had been fooled. I had been a fool. I was still a fool. And Oliver Kedar had played me for the fool I was. My head hurt, and a rolling nausea passed over me, like the waves of a lake washing against a pebbled shore.

"Do you hear me, Flaka? You haven't said a word."

"I hear you," I whispered after a long pause. I was dull. I was stupid. I was dense. I was like a rock rather than a woman. My husband had lied to me, and I had known it all this time. I had known since the moment I married him that I knew nothing about him, and rather than changing that, he had continued to pour obscurity upon what little knowledge of him I did have. Here was *una sombra* that would never lift from my heart.

Ephraim's lips twisted downward at the corners, and creases formed in his brow, and his brown eyes seemed almost to deepen as he looked at me. Then suddenly he wrapped me in his arms and hugged me against him, my face lost in his chest.

"Don't arrest him, Ephraim," I said. My voice, half muffled by his shirt, was throaty and raspy. There were unshed tears in my eyes, brimming, about to spill down my cheeks. "Let me tell him. Let me send him packing."

"You would do that?" my brother asked. "You're going to send him away and then what are you going to do?"

"He lied to me. I'm going to send him packing. That's all. Just give me a few days and he'll be gone. I . . . I'm angry as hell at him, believe me, Ephraim. But I don't want him to hang, and I certainly don't want my brother to be the one to hang my husband."

Ephraim nodded after a long moment of thinking on it. "Flaka, you know I'd do anything for you. There's lots of other folks tearing up this county, and Oliver ain't the worst of them. I reckon I can stand to let one man get away."

"How did you find out he was here?"

"Well, he does play it safe around town, I've learned. He's been using a different name in Tombstone, Oliver Robinson. But for legal documents Kedar has to go on those forms. Let me back up a little, though. See, I ain't the real sheriff, just a deputy. The real sheriff got injured a few months ago and I've been acting sheriff ever since. How I found out about Oliver, well, it was something that happened more than a month ago now. Three men broke into the bank and tried to rob it, but somehow they all ended up dead. The bank clerk said he'd killed them. But I knew he couldn't shoot worth a darn, and his gun was clean and unfired. But try as I might I couldn't make heads or tails of what had actually happened. Whoever shot those men had done a hell of a job, too. I pressed that banker, but he wouldn't give me anything, so eventually, with other things to do, I just let it be. They were bad characters, known to the law office. It didn't really matter. Whoever had shot them had saved the bank clerk and a fair sum of money.

"I had put the whole thing clean out of my mind, but then, last week, Ian Marcus showed up with a US Marshal, asking questions, lots of questions, and telling me about his son from back East, a man called Oliver, a man with a real flair for trick shooting. I figured it all out pretty quick from there. I pressed the bank clerk again and he finally showed me that damn copy of that deed. But I didn't tell Ian. I . . . I don't entirely trust the man, Flaka. He's keeping things from me, and he's a hard man, you know. I needed to come out here for myself first. I didn't know you'd be here, though Marcus must've known it was you. He didn't want to tell me your name, in case I refused to help him, I reckon."

"Rather foolhardy, don't you think? Coming out here alone when you knew what Oliver was capable of? After all the things you'd heard."

"I've had to become something like brave to serve the townspeople and homesteaders out here, I guess." replied Ephraim, grinning a little.

"You were always brave," I replied. It was true, Ephraim had always been full of courage, standing up to boys twice his size when anyone smaller was being bullied or harassed. He was born to be a sheriff, to help those who couldn't help themselves.

"It wasn't so brave, I . . . after what happened at the bank, and hearing the bank clerk tell me about him, how desperate he had been for this pretty little plot of land, I knew he couldn't be all bad. There was a lot of good in him, I figured. I wanted to talk to him myself, give him a chance, you know. Hear him out. I thought there might be more to the story."

"Thank you, for that," I said, my voice still real low. I felt if I raised it anymore it would crack and I would go straight to sobbing. "Ian Marcus still doesn't know we're here, then?"

"And he won't find out. He's a vengeful son of a bitch, Flaka. He'll kill you for sure if he finds you."

"I killed his son, Ephraim. You shouldn't be here looking for Oliver, you should be here arresting me and settin' me up for a proper hangin'." Then the tears began to rush out of my eyes, pouring down my face, while I told Ephraim the story of how I had killed Grant Marcus and all that had happened that wild day almost two months before. It seemed like a lifetime ago, but telling the story brought back the memory of Grant's death, at my hand, as fresh and as gutting as when it had happened. That awful moment when I had gone and killed a man in cold blood. I kept weeping, and choking, and sometimes having to stop in telling the tale as I sobbed, smearing snot and tears onto the sleeve of my dress. Then I told my brother how I had married Oliver and how we had fled across the desert, and almost died ourselves what seemed a hundred times, and how when we finally came here, it was like the best thing that had ever happened to me, in all my life. When I had finished the story I fell silent again, sniffling and crying, but quiet, my body still trembling from half-suppressed sobs, sometimes escaping in loud, lurching gasps.

Ephraim glanced at the little book sitting on the table beside us, Tennyson's poem. With Oliver's help, I had finally read the whole thing. Now when I read it for practice it was all bits I'd read before. He picked it up and rifled through the pages, glancing over the words with interest. He set it back after a while and turned to me again. I was just beginning to pull myself together, squaring my shoulders, my tears finally drying. My mind was made up. I had to tell Oliver to leave, and he had to go. I was angry with him, but more than that even, I was afraid for him. I was afraid that he would be hanged if he stayed where he was. I wasn't going with him this time though. He had lied to me, and what kind of man lies to the one he loves?

"Flaka," said Ephraim, his tone gentle but somehow firm as well. He was staring into my eyes again. He reached out and touched the pale scars along my neck from Marcus' ropes. "What you did was as plain a case of self-defense as I've ever heard. But it don't much matter what I say, and it don't even matter that Ian is traveling with a marshal, a sworn officer of the law. He's probably paid the man off. If I give you to them as a prisoner, you will not make it back alive to Fort Davis to stand trial, and even if you did, Ian would have paid the witnesses and paid off the judge as well to convict you and hang you. Bribes work out here in the West, they work real damn well, and Ian Marcus has a lot more money than anyone else I know. He could buy the whole state of Texas if he wanted, I swear. But what you're describing to me is self-defense. You did nothing wrong. I'll send Ian home, tell him Oliver Kedar never came this way. I'm . . . I'm deeply sorry about your husband, Flaka, about all of this."

"It's okay, it's alright," I replied, my voice so soft I thought only I could hear it. *"Better to have loved and lost than never to have loved at all."*

He glanced at me in surprise, then followed my gaze to the book of poetry on the table. "You know how to read?"

"Oliver taught me."

"I've never read this, but I haven't found a work by Tennyson that hasn't moved me deeply. I'd love to read the whole thing. Do you mind if I borrow it?"

"Please do," I whispered, my voice still a little breathy and choked, but strengthening at last as my resolve hardened. "When you come to return it, Ephraim, it's just going to be me living here. No one else."

"I'm sorry, Flaka. Are you sure you're safe here with Oliver? Safe to tell him off and send him away?"

I flashed a grin from my tear-stained face. "If there's one thing I can do, Ephraim, it's tell someone off, you know that. Oliver does love me. The rest of it all might be a lie, but he loves me, that's sure. He'll listen and he'll leave if I tell him I don't want him here no more. He'll be sad, but nothing a little whore in Mexico can't make him forget."

Ephraim's eyebrows shot up as he looked at me and then around at our cozy little home. "I doubt that, Flaka. I suspect it'll take more than a whore to make him forget all this."

XVI

IT WAS LATE WHEN OLIVER RETURNED HOME, WELL AFTER DARK. I was sitting on the same three-legged stool where Ephraim had left me, staring vacantly at the saddlebags on the table that I had packed for my husband. I don't even know how long I had sat there, staring at those bags, my mind nothing but a blank slate. He came bursting into the house, in his usual cheerful, exuberant manner. He was carrying a rectangular wooden box in his grimy hands, waving it about like he was a cavalry flag bearer. I didn't smile when he approached me, just babbling on about his day. The lantern on the table was burning low by then, almost out of oil.

"Old man Clancy died yesterday, and the whole town is talking about it," Oliver was saying. "Everyone's in such a fluster. He was one of the real founders of this silver town, you know. Now with him gone they're trying to figure out what to do with his holdings. Apparently he had the richest stake in the territory, or so people believe. But anyway, you probably don't care much about that. Look what I bought for you!"

He opened the box and displayed a gray dress made of

some sort of silk fabric, shimmering in the low light of the lantern.

"What the hell am I going to do with that?" I asked, letting no expression cross my face. I was afraid that if I did change my expression it would crumble into tears. I had to stay like this, stiff, unreadable.

"Well, we're pretty well settled here now, and soon we should start taking invitations to parties and other events. I thought we might even go to Mr. Clancy's funeral. Everyone for miles around will be there. This is our home, and you're a fine lady, and I want you to feel like one. I still remember how beautiful you looked that day in town when we first arrived. I would be so proud to have you on my arm at the next social event around Tombstone, Flaka."

I swallowed hard and found that my throat was dry, the spit sitting like a ball above my Adam's apple. My brows knitted close together, and my lips drew tight and straight as I looked at my husband. He leaned in, like he was fixing to kiss me, and I felt that faint thrill inside me, that yearning I knew so well. But I quenched my desire and pushed him away. I wanted him, more than anything I wanted my Oliver, but it just couldn't be. He was a liar, a barefaced liar.

He blinked as I shoved him away, his expression one of both shock and hurt. For a second he looked like a little boy who'd been scolded, an expression that sent another bolt of pain through me.

"You lied to me," I said, trying to keep my face a stone.

"What do you mean, Flaka?" He seemed genuinely bewildered. He was a great actor, my husband.

"You, Oliver Kedar *Marcus*, lied to me."

That clamped his mouth tight shut as he studied me in earnest. After a moment, he drew up a stool and sat across from me, his fingers drumming on *la mesa*. When he spoke at last, the light was so dim that I could barely see his face. "Who told you that Ian Marcus is my father?" he asked, his tone gentle, infuriatingly gentle. He was trying to handle me, now that he had been unmasked.

"The sheriff told me."

"The sheriff was here?" There was alarm and fear in his voice now. My Oliver was afraid of something, then. Maybe his courage was all put on too, part of his endless parade of *mentiras*.

I nodded. "Aye, he was here, Oliver. He came to arrest you and to find out about the woman Ian Marcus claims killed his son. He came out here and he told me all about your past. About the shootings in Texas, the stagecoaches and the banks. I even heard you done robbed a train in Colorado."

"Not by myself," offered Oliver, as if that was some kind of consolation. "Listen, listen. You've heard the litany of my crimes—"

"I don't know what a litany is."

"The list, I suppose I should say, you've heard the whole list. But you haven't heard what I have to say about it, about how it happened, and why it happened. Just listen to me, Flaka, please, just listen."

"I haven't heard the how or the why or anything about it because you didn't tell me nothin'," I said accusingly. My voice was breaking. He reached out and took my hands, but I yanked them away. "I packed your bags, Oliver. I want you to get out. In fact, you have to. If you don't leave now, the sheriff will be back in a few days, and when he comes back he's going to arrest you, and you'll hang, Oliver. You'll hang." That was all I could say—if I had spoken anymore I would have busted into a sob. I waited, breathing slow and even, letting the wave of pain in my soul pass.

There was perfect silence betwixt us, save the sound of a fly buzzing about the room. Oliver broke the quiet at last, and his voice had become even more raspy than usual, as if the words were being torn from deep within a raw throat. "Flaka,

I'll leave if you want me to, but you've got to let me tell my story first, before you decide."

"If you think it'll make a difference, perhaps you should've told it to me a long time ago, before some sheriff came to my home and told me the story instead."

"I hear what you're saying, but let me tell it to you now, please."

"I ain't stopping you."

He let out a faint little sigh, almost a moan, and there was true, deep despair in it, the kind of despair in the words of that poetry book we had read together. More than anything in the world I wanted to fold him to my breast, to kiss his face and forgive him, to go with him into the night when he went out through that door. The last low glow of the oil lamp fizzled and died, and Oliver began the story he should have told me months before.

"Some of this you already know, but there's a great deal you don't. I was born in Boston, to a working woman, a prostitute, if you will. My mother was Olivia Kedar, and she named me after herself. All my life she would work at night, but I never met any of her clients. There was only one man that kept coming back, and sending letters, and money, and buying fine things for Olivia. That was Ian Marcus. He would come on business to Boston time and time again. He always had a toy for me. He would play with me, too. I didn't think much about it until I was maybe ten, then I thought maybe this kind, stern Mr. Marcus might be my father. It didn't seem like I could ask about that, though. Mother didn't take kindly to prying questions, so I didn't ask. I just wondered. And the more times he came, the more I became convinced that my theory was correct.

"The last time Ian Marcus came to our home was when I was twelve. He brought me a pistol, this one here." He set the revolver on the table with a thunk. "He gave it to me when I was twelve and taught me how to shoot it, too. After that he still sent money, lots of money to Olivia, but he stopped coming back. He sent enough money for Olivia to get out of whoring, but I think she liked it, honestly. She wasn't a good-looking woman by then, and no one would take an ex-whore for a wife. Whoring gave her company, made her feel less alone. I finished school with high marks and started at university with the money Ian Marcus had sent, studying literature, of all the useless things. By then I had learned to shoot really well. I fired that pistol every day, spending every extra penny I had on bullets. I was fast, and I was accurate, incredibly accurate.

"After a while I found a showplace in town that would pay for a trick shooter, so I took to doing that, on the side, for money and . . . well, for girls. Mother didn't know about what I was doing. It . . . well it got me a lot of girls, if you want me to be honest. Women love a cowboy out there in the civilized parts of the country. They get tired of their stuffy old dandies."

I snorted. "So you've probably got your own little Oliver Kedar, or forty of them, out there in Boston."

"None that I know of, but your point is well taken. I was being stupid and foolish, but I was young and naive. I was squandering my education. I still got high marks in university, but I had lost interest in it all. My mother fell sick my last year at school. So I dropped out and took care of her until she died. I still had money left over, not a ton, mind you, but enough to travel. I had one person that I knew out West, and I knew my skills with a pistol might just get me somewhere out here, where might maketh right. So I packed up my belongings and headed west. That was less than two years ago. Imagine Ian Marcus' surprise when I showed up on his outfit, asking for a job."

"Did he give you one?"

"He did. I showed him what I could do with that gun he'd given me, and he asked me straight away to break Grant

Marcus, his only legitimate son and heir, out of a prison up near Dallas."

I drew in a slow breath at that. I had not expected this part of the story.

"Grant was in prison for raping a girl and murdering her, and he was liable to be hanged if ever the circuit judge made it to those parts. For some reason this sheriff couldn't be bought off, like most of the others Ian had dealt with over the years with regard to his son's wild antics and crimes. So I broke my brother out of prison and joined his gang of killers and thieves. I won't say that I didn't enjoy a lot of it, Flaka. I did enjoy it. I loved what I could do with a pistol. I loved the wild freedom and excitement of it. I loved that men were afraid of me just from hearing my name. It felt . . . it felt like power, crazy power, the kind that only great deeds can get you, power born of renown and abilities, not born of family money, which was the only other kind of power I knew about back East. But this—it felt different—like real power. People knew of me, and they were afraid of me, and for a little while, I liked that a lot. I'm not proud to say that, but it's the truth.

"I kept reading, like I told you, poems that would burst your heart asunder. Grant's men found it funny, but as much as they derided me, they would shut up and listen around a campfire at night when I read or recited. It was in the poems that I found solace and began to see the error of what I was doing. I watched Grant and his father kill men in the most brutal, horrific ways imaginable, and I was fast losing the taste for their way of life. I should have been proud to be the son of such a powerful man, but I wasn't. I was ashamed to be in that bloodline, a line of coldhearted killers.

"A year ago we were in these parts, doing some nefarious work, cattle thieving and running the animals across the border, I may as well tell you. We stopped here for one night and camped on this land. I remember in the morning when I woke up and saw what this was, that I was determined to have it, to settle down and raise a family and put up the pistol that Ian Marcus had given me. So I laid down some security for the plot of land overlooking the river and the little, dilapidated house, and I started saving every dollar I could scrounge from our jobs."

He was quiet again, as if mulling in the darkness over all that he was about to lose, and all that it had cost him, and how much it meant to him. Finally he continued, "We robbed a stage the day I met you, Flaka, and I watched Grant torture the stage driver for hours before he killed him. Then I took that strongbox and I fled, and they followed. I knew there was far more than enough money in there to buy this plot of land, far more than enough to make a real start out West, to be more than a gunslinger, always on the run. I honestly thought they would kill me, but I was better with a pistol than any of them. I had a fair chance." He trailed off again for a few moments, then he chuckled. "Chance. It was just pure chance that led me to your doorstep that day in August, seeking a place to make a stand on that desolate plain. But when I saw you and had all the money in hand to buy this place, it didn't seem like chance, it seemed like fate."

We waited, neither of us sure what to say next. At last I broke the silence, because my mind was set. For more than two months, my husband had been lying to me, not about something small, but about everything that he was. He had told me a little—in Tombstone when we bought our land— but he had been vague. He had avoided telling me the true depths of his crimes. He had led us across the desert, fleeing from his own nightmare of a father. He had been lying to me, and his lies had put us in danger. Everything he had done had put us in danger.

"I packed your saddlebags, Oliver. I don't want to see you again." Saying those words aloud felt like I was being gutted alive. Like someone took a machete and cut me in two, spilling my insides out in our tiny house. But I jutted out my jaw and tried to still the trembling of my fists, clenched at my sides.

Oliver drew in a breath sharply, waited, and then he asked, "You're sure, Flaka? If Ian Marcus is near here you will need my help to protect you."

"The current acting sheriff of Tombstone is my brother, Ephraim Garcia Hasani. He'll protect me," I answered quickly. Reaching up, I brushed away an involuntary tear. "I want you gone, Oliver. And I don't want you to come back."

"I hear you, Flaka, I hear you," he returned, and never in my life had I heard such anguish in a man's voice as that, as if someone was crumbling his heart into a thousand pieces. He didn't say another word, he didn't check the bags I had packed, he just took them and left. It was only a few minutes later I heard the sound of his mare's hooves clattering away, and Butterball nickering for his friend from our rebuilt little stable. I wanted to nicker as well, for the loss of my love, for the loss of everything that made life worth living. But I was firm. I could not be married to a liar, I could not be married to a bank robber and a horse and cattle thief, I could not be married to a murderer, and I could not be married into the family of Ian Marcus. It was like being married to the gallows themselves, as they held ultimate sway over my husband's life or death. I stewed in my anger that night, until I became dull and numb again and fell asleep alone in our bed.

XVII

Three days went by, more slow and terrible than I could ever have imagined. I felt like a shell of a woman. Susanna came on Sunday after church, which I didn't attend. She was all smiles. She must've sensed I was in a foul mood, but she didn't press me much about it. I didn't tell her that I had sent Oliver packing, and I don't think it was obvious looking around the place. He was often out building fences or in town when she came by. Despite my gloominess, her visit was like a soothing balm on the raw, aching wound in my heart. I wasn't fully alone if I still had friends out there in Susanna and her husband. Perhaps there was some hope for me. Perhaps life could go on there without Oliver. Perhaps I could make a new, bright future without my husband.

After that, I set to work on fixing up the last few projects inside the house. With Oliver gone, the farm was my responsibility. I hadn't given much thought to the deed that was made out to him, or divorce papers, or any of that. Things I probably should've taken into account. But when I did think of it, I figured it would work itself out at some point. For now there was cleaning and gardening to do, and carpentry, and clearing land.

There was a terrible dullness to me, as if life itself had gone out of me and I had become a mindless machine, like the piston pumping on a train. Just going through the motions, but without any spirit. A few more days went by in this haze, and I remember waking up on Wednesday, a week since Oliver had left, and finding myself alone again, in that empty house where once I had lived with a husband I had adored. I got up, still in my nightgown, and went to the door and threw it wide, taking in a deep draft of the thick, foggy morning air, trying to find something in it, something that would animate the lifeless corpse that I had become. Some purpose or meaning as to why my heart was still beating when all joy had left me.

A gunshot blasted through the air, disturbing the perfect quiet of that misty morning. I heard the wood beside my head splinter. I slammed the door and ran to the rifle hanging above the hearth, tearing it down as another shot rang out and a bullet buried itself in the side of my home. I crept to the window and peered out. It was still gloomy and dark outside. I wished then that Oliver was there, but only for a second. There was another part of me that wanted to die in a gunfight today, to have it done, and not wake up to this empty, pointless existence tomorrow.

Another bullet sang through the air, and another, embedding themselves into the wooden walls of my house. One crashed through the window above me and I shielded my eyes from the spray of glass shards. In my mind I was already dully calculating how much these repairs would cost against the remaining money that Oliver had not even touched when he left, stowed under a floorboard in a ceramic pot.

"Flaka Garcia Hasani Kedar!" called a voice, a familiar voice, seeming to mock me with the formal use of my full name. The voice used all the parts of that long string of names, my first name—the part that was fully me—my ma's Mexican part, my pa's Balkan part, and my husband's part, the part that I had lost. "Come out of there, girl. With your hands up."

"Fuck you!" I cried into the dim light, squinting through the window, trying to find where the voice had come from. My ma would've washed my mouth out with soap for using language like that. There was no movement in the fog as I waited, staring at the hazy world around me, the clouds come down to earth to suffocate me and hide my enemies from my bullets.

"Wrong answer, Flaka," said the voice again, low and amused, and terribly threatening. A shiver ran through me, and then I saw a dim shape looming in the fog, moving toward me haltingly, almost seeming to struggle. I trained my gun on that form, but something made me hesitate, and then the mist cleared just enough to make out the face of the approaching person. I gasped and lowered my rifle. It was Oliver. He had his arms twisted tight behind him, his bonds wrenching painfully at his shoulders. There was a bandana gagging his mouth, and his face was all scuffed and bloody, bruises purpling his skin, and a half-wet, half-dry stream of scarlet along the side of his cheek from a cut on his brow.

The voice chuckled again, cruelly. "Now, perhaps you'll put that gun down and come out with your hands up before I put a bullet through your husband's skull."

I swallowed hard, debating what I should do. I had kicked Oliver out, but I didn't want anyone to hurt him. I still loved him, with every part of my being. I wanted him free. His eyes were fixed on the window where I was hiding, peering out from behind the flowery, bright curtains that Susanna and I had sewn. Oliver had seen the flash of the gunbarrel and he knew I was there. He was shaking his head a little as the man using him as a shield continued to push him forward. Oliver looked as if he had been beaten badly, all over. He moved with halting, slow steps and there was something irregular in the way he breathed, as if there was some catch in it, a broken rib driving into his lung with every intake of air.

"You wouldn't kill your only son!" I called.

"Wouldn't I?" asked the menacing voice again, and then I saw him, Ian Marcus, taking shape out of the mist, holding Oliver's neck from behind, shoving him forward, his other hand training a pistol to the base of Oliver's skull. He was an enormous man, a head taller than Oliver and broader of shoulder and abdomen. I don't know if I had ever realized before just how big he was, even when he had me as a prisoner. He almost seemed to dwarf my husband. My husband.

I swallowed hard. The gunshots would hopefully have aroused Susanna and Edmund, unless . . . the thought flashed through my head that Susanna had said they were going into town on Wednesday. If they had left already, then there was no hope for me and Oliver. My racing thoughts screeched to a halt as Ian Marcus paused and pressed his pistol hard into Oliver's nostril and cocked the gun.

"Stop! Stop!" I cried, practically hurling the gun from me. Oliver was still staring at me, wide-eyed, and trying to shake his head. I paid him no mind, racing to the door and stepping out into the dim light to stand in my nightgown on our rickety porch, my hands held high. "Let him go! I'm the one you want. Leave him alone!"

"So affectionate. You know Oliver told me you didn't care about him, that you had sent him packing and that you had run off to Mexico with some other bloke. He tried to convince me that bringing him back as leverage was a foolish notion, and useless. That you wouldn't be here, and even if you were, you wouldn't care about him. But I guess that ain't the truth, after all. I thought he was lying."

"Let him go! Please. Just leave him alone. I'm the one you want, and you can have me. Just . . . just let him go." I was nearly crying as I spoke. It didn't matter what happened to me. The only thing that mattered was that Ian Marcus didn't hurt my Oliver.

Out of the darkness two cowboys loomed up, rushing onto the porch and taking my arms. I recognized them as the same two men that had come through my parents' window with Grant Marcus on that fateful day when all this hell had started. How appropriate for them to be here now, on the day my cursed story ended. It was so fitting. So right. So perfect.

Oliver was struggling madly in his bonds, writhing and fighting until Ian cracked his pistol against his head and he sank to his knees, stunned, though his eyes were still open, looking at me with fear and desperation. Ian Marcus glanced around, finding the beautiful sycamore tree that overhung the high bluff above the river. He grinned cruelly and nodded toward his men, leaving Oliver on the ground. I did not fight the men holding me. One of them went inside, returning with a rope that he quickly began to fashion into a noose.

"Please, I . . . can I speak to my husband before you hang me?" I pleaded, looking at Ian Marcus.

He nodded, and the man holding me shoved me across the yard. I hurried to him and dropped to my knees in the dirt beside Oliver. I felt everything within me crumbling, remembering how I had hurt this man, who looked at me with those adoring, fearful eyes. How could I have treated someone who loved me so much in such a beastly way? Together and both armed, Ian Marcus would have been no match for Mr. and Mrs. Kedar. We wouldn't be in this position. But I had sent him away in my stubborn pride, and now we were incapacitated, and at the mercy of a man we had spent weeks fleeing from, across two countries. Reaching to Oliver's face, I yanked the bandana from his mouth, and his words came tumbling out, telling me to run, that the fog would hide me, telling me he was sorry, telling me I had to get away. I shushed him with a finger to his lips, my other hand running along his cheek, over his brow, through his hair, tenderly touching the new cuts and bruises that littered that perfect face.

"It's alright, Oliver, it's alright, my love," I whispered. "I'm sorry, I'm so sorry." Then I leaned in and let my lips rest upon his swollen and bloody mouth. Even as battered as he was, his kiss was the same beautiful one I remembered. It was a kiss of passion, a kiss of wild, hopeless desperation. *El beso al final de un sueño.* The kiss at the end of a dream. A perfect dream that never could have lasted.

I stood up, my shoulders back, my head held high and proud, and the men began yanking me toward the tree. Ian Marcus had taken the rope and looped it over a high branch of the sycamore, one end tied to the trunk, the other dangling loose, waiting for my neck. I was going to die. In that moment, the thoughts that kept flying through my head were all jumbled phrases and stanzas from the poem, the first and only book I had ever read. The men tied my wrists tight behind me, and then Ian Marcus thrust the loop of rope over my neck, yanking it taut, and I tasted death, just a few seconds away. He would push me out over the riverbank and I would swing there until I passed on into whatever punishment or reward awaited me.

"She didn't kill Grant!" came Oliver's clear voice suddenly, tearing through the grim silence around the hangmen.

The three men stopped and turned back toward him, and I twisted my head around, a sense of panic rising inside me. I was willing to accept death for what had happened to Grant Marcus. I didn't know what Oliver was going to say, but I feared what it might be.

"Flaka didn't kill Grant. You think that slip of a girl who couldn't hit a barn door if it was right in front of her face could kill Grant Marcus? Why would she kill Grant anyway? She had no motive to shoot him. I killed Grant. Your men were wrong. Ask them who they saw coming in through the kitchen just as Grant went down. Just ask them."

Ian Marcus stood like a man riveted in place, his eyes darting between me, the two men at my side, and then back to Oliver, still on his knees, but with his head held high and proud. Finally Ian spoke to the men flanking him. His voice was gravelly, and, for the first time, uncertain. "Is this true?"

They both nodded, their stupid faces solemn. "Aye, he was there. He was coming through the kitchen door into the room where we was when Grant went down."

"Yessir, he's the one what shot me, he was."

"Why are you only just now telling me this?" asked Ian.

"It seemed plain 'twas the girl that done it. Her gun was smoking, we saw that. But we fled when we saw Grant go down and Oliver coming. You know how well Oliver Kedar can shoot, sir."

Ian Marcus let out an exasperated sigh, and then, quick as lightning, three shots rang out. Something hit me hard in the head, hurling me back against the sycamore tree trunk. For a second there was blackness, and I heard Ian Marcus say, "Useless bastards." Not exactly a poetic phrase to fade from life on, I thought and almost chuckled, but then the blackness receded and the world began to return.

Everything was a blur. There was blood streaming down my face, onto my nightshirt, and a high-pitched screaming sound filled my ears. I had been hit somewhere on the head, I thought, but I was still alive. I was stunned, but not so stunned that I couldn't feel a new fear, much more terrible than the one before, much more terrible than any fear for my own death could ever be, rising up to choke me. The blurring cleared and the high-pitched whistling sound faded, and I watched in unspeakable terror as Ian Marcus stalked toward Oliver, leaving me helpless on the end of my tether. I backed up to the trunk of the tree, facing toward Ian and Oliver, while my tied hands sought the knot binding the rope to the sycamore.

"Is it true?" Ian Marcus asked again, his voice a menacing growl.

"Of course it's true. I killed Grant, and that bastard son of yours had it coming. You think I'm the bastard because I was the son of a whore, but Grant was the real piece of work. He killed just for the sport of it, helpless people, women, children. He tortured people, I watched him do it. That son of Satan that you raised deserved to die, Ian, and I'm glad I finally put an end to him. I should have killed him the first time I met him, locked up in that prison. I never felt happier about killing anyone than the day I put a bullet in my brother."

Marcus was getting closer and closer to Oliver, still on his knees, but with his shoulders thrown back, defiant, handsome, brave, and in terrible, unspeakable danger. I kept scrabbling at that knot on the tree and yanking at my neck madly, trying to set myself free, to get to Oliver's side before Ian Marcus did. Each time I managed to loosen the noose a tiny bit, I would make the wrong move and the rope would pull taut again. I felt like a fly caught in a spider's web. The knot around the tree trunk wasn't coming undone at all, no matter how wildly I scratched at it. I barely felt the burning of my head wound, but a horrible, twisting pain was blossoming in my gut, radiating into my chest, as if someone had shot me through the belly.

"It's not true!" I screamed. "Oliver didn't kill him, I did! It was me. It was me! Are you listening? He didn't do it! I fucking killed Grant Marcus! It was me!" I was practically sobbing, but Ian Marcus paid me no mind, intent on his son as he stalked threateningly closer. It was like he couldn't even hear me. Like he was a dog in a fight, bred and raised to kill, and nothing now could possibly deter him from his prey.

"She couldn't have killed Grant," Oliver continued, also

ignoring me. "Grant wasn't stupid, he wouldn't have let some girl with a gun kill him. The attack had to come as a surprise. So while he was distracted by the girl—and you know as well as I do how much Grant could be distracted by a girl—I plugged a hole in his heart and he died. Good riddance."

Ian Marcus stood over his son, with his hands on his hips. He had holstered his pistol, and that gave me a tiny sense of relief. By that point I had given up on the knot, but I was rubbing the noose against the rough bark of the tree with my head, smearing blood all over the trunk. This at least was working, opening the loop a little. I didn't know what I would do when I got free, all I knew was that I was going to fight like hell, arms tied or not. I had to save my husband, if it was the last thing I ever did.

Oliver's glance kept darting back and forth between me and his father. He was defiant—he was almost gleeful. I had never seen him look so childish, so excited, so . . . brave, so horribly brave in the face of death. It made me sick.

"When I was a boy I used to wish you would take me away, back to Texas, to raise me as your own, to claim me and be proud of me," Oliver continued, his voice getting a little higher in pitch, as high as that husky voice could go. "I used to think that being your son would have given me the chance I needed to succeed, to be a great man, a really great man. But then I met Grant, and I rode with that cowardly bully, that monster, all over the West, and now I know what being your son, your real, claimed son, would have done to me. It would have turned me into a monster just like him. Grant wasn't born the way he turned out, you made him into that filthy bastard. He was following the lead of the man who raised him. And now . . . now I thank God that I was raised by a whore in Boston, and I wouldn't trade that for anything in the world. I'm glad I killed Grant, and I'm glad you're going to kill me, and I'm so fucking glad that you'll have no grandchildren to carry on the evil that you are." With that last word he spat on his father and then he looked directly at me. I was still on a leash that pulled and yanked at my neck, rubbing it raw, making a new, angry mark where the scars still sat from the last time Ian Marcus had tried to hang me. I had never, in all our flight and all our battles, felt so helpless.

I don't know to this day if I really saw what happened next. I was nearly unconscious from tearing against the rope. I had quit my failing attempts at loosening the noose and started yanking against it like a dog in a collar, madly, hoping to just tear it free. But it was doing nothing except making my vision go spotty around the edges. Oliver was looking at me, with such love in his eyes, such unspeakable love and kindness, that I thought my whole body and soul would explode. As my vision started to dim, I saw him mouth the words, "Look away, Flaka, look away."

Ian Marcus drew his knife and stepped behind Oliver, taking my husband's chin in his hands and yanking his head up to look directly into his father's eyes, away from me, and then he cut my Oliver's throat. For a second there was blood everywhere, gushing scarlet, Oliver's lifeblood spilling out like a raging flood, spraying onto Ian Marcus' face and all over his garments. Then Ian Marcus released his grip and my husband dropped, a lifeless heap on the ground. I let out a bloodcurdling scream, so loud it must have echoed for miles. Ian Marcus didn't seem to hear me, didn't seem aware I even existed anymore. Like a man in a trance, he turned from the body of his son and stalked slowly away into the fading fog.

Sobbing, I went back to loosening the loop around my neck against the tree. At last it gave way and I ran to Oliver's side, dragging that rope behind me. I curled up in my husband's still-warm blood, pressing my lips into his shoulder, pressing my head into his chest as I sobbed and sobbed and sobbed into the emptiness that remained where once my husband had lived.

XVIII

My name is Flaka Garcia Hasani Kedar, and it's my fault my husband is dead.

Sure, folks say it weren't my fault, they say it was his own damn fault, but I know better. They tell me that just so as I feel better about that empty spot on the bed next to me, and so as I don't get crushed by that overwhelming guilt when I wake up to an empty house, on top of all the other struggles of running our little patch of land in this godforsaken stretch of desert all by my lonesome. But I ain't stupid. Oliver Kedar would still be alive today if it weren't for me.

When I was a little girl, after my brother and sisters had moved away, I remember sometimes I would have nightmares that my ma and pa had died in some terrible way, fallen down a well or into a ravine, or been shot by bandits. I would wake up to a cold, empty room, and the only way I could reassure myself that it was a dream, a nightmare and not reality, was to go to my parents' bedroom and crawl under the covers with them. They were real, I could hear them breathing and snoring, I could reach my hand out and touch them. But now I wake up to an empty room after having the nightmare over and over again where Ian Marcus cuts my husband's throat, and when I wake up, there is no breathing, sleeping form beside me to tell me it was just a dream. Because it wasn't just a dream. It was real, and Oliver Kedar, the one thing that made my life worth living, is gone, and gone forever.

It was Susanna that found me, I think, or maybe it was Ephraim. They were both there when I began to come back to my senses. I don't remember them prying me away from Oliver's body. I don't remember burying Oliver. I don't remember Susanna sponging the blood off of me in the river and dressing the wound that Ian Marcus' bullet made, a furrow in my scalp where no hair grows. I don't remember any of it. But I was told that's what happened. All I could see was Oliver's face, flushed with excitement, with defiance, and that goddamned beautiful smirk of his when he stood up against his father, and then I could see that last look of love he had given me, right before Ian Marcus slaughtered him.

I don't remember eating or drinking the weeks that followed, but I must have. I think Susanna took me in for a week until I began to function again. I use the word *function* loosely. I was just goin' through the motions of living: cooking, eating, sleeping. I gradually became more active, though. Ephraim was busy, and I think he was trying to get the men who had done this to me and my husband. But I didn't tell him what happened. Everytime he asked who did it I just cried. To relive that memory was hell itself. I couldn't say Ian Marcus' name. But I didn't have to neither, Ephraim knew. There weren't no one else that could have done this.

Weeks went by, and then, before I knew it, it had been two months since we'd buried my husband, and I was starting to show. It surprised me that I was pregnant. I really hadn't noticed it, and then one day I looked down and felt the hardness in my belly and knew I was carrying Oliver's child. I think that set me back even more. I was sobbing, sobbing that Oliver wouldn't be there to meet his child, sobbing that I was alone, a widow on a plot of land that held nothing but pain for me. Every night I cried myself to sleep and awakened feeling dull, listless, and slow. What kind of life was this for a child to be born into?

I remembered too the words that Oliver had spoken, how happy he was that Ian Marcus' line died with him, without an heir, and his triumph at that fact. For a while I hated the thing growing inside me. But that couldn't last, it just couldn't. This child was Oliver's, so I couldn't help but love it.

Somewhere in my fourth month of pregnancy, Ephraim came out to my place. He often visited, but this time felt different. He gave me a hug, and sat me down, and then he told me that he had exhausted every recourse against Ian Marcus, but without me as a witness and with my husband having been an outlaw, there was nothing more he could do to get justice for Oliver. Even if I did choose to testify, Oliver's criminal record would poison any lawman or jury against him. Ian Marcus had won, truly and fully. If I had died that day and not Oliver, he wouldn't have won. Hell, Oliver probably would have killed him. But he had managed to destroy me more than my own death could have, and there would be no justice for what I had lost.

I didn't cry at this revelation. I was all cried out by then. I just sat there at that little *mesa*, staring dully at Ephraim, and then beyond him, at the wall, my hands resting on my abdomen, feeling that child growing inside me, the grandchild of Ian Marcus. The grandchild of the man who killed my baby's father.

"I'm sorry, Flaka. I'm so sorry," whispered Ephraim. After a while he removed a worn, tattered book from his jacket, and my heart leaped at the sight of it, the first flash of real joy and life that I had felt since I sent Oliver away. I was transported back for a moment to the little campfires on the plains where Oliver taught me how to read and recited those verses into the beautiful, starlit nights. Ephraim reached out and handed the book to me, closing my fingers around it as he spoke. "I . . . I finished it. I forgot about it for a while, but now, *después de todo*, I figured you'd need it a lot more than I do."

I flipped it open, feeling the thick pages against my fingertips, feeling strangely alive, for the first time in months. It felt as if here, within these pages, perhaps Oliver still lived, the man who had recited all those poems to me a hundred times in the desert.

The first verses that my eyes fell upon stopped me dead. For a moment I didn't breathe, or move, or think. I ain't even sure my heart was beating as I read those words over and over again, faster and faster each time.

> "Something it is which thou hast lost,
> Some pleasure from thine early years.
> Break, thou deep vase of chilling tears,
> That grief hath shaken into frost
>
> Such clouds of nameless trouble cross
> All night below the darken'd eyes;
> With morning wakes the will, and cries,
> 'Thou shalt not be the fool of loss.'"

I snapped the book shut and looked up at the wall, at the revolver hanging there where Susanna must have put it. The pistol Ian Marcus had given his bastard son on his twelfth birthday. Then my gaze flitted back to Ephraim, and perhaps he read something in my eyes of what I had just realized I had to do, or die in the attempt.

"What is it?" he asked, darting a look toward the revolver on the wall, then back to me.

When I spoke my voice was gravelly, low, and ominous.

"If the law won't help me, Ephraim, I reckon I'll have to help myself."

Ephraim opened his mouth, and I could already hear the lecture he was about to give, but then he snapped his jaw shut again, looking down at my belly, at the book, and then into my eyes with his solemn brown ones. "You shouldn't travel alone, Flaka."

I felt a warmth spreading in my chest. *Mi hermano.*

He glanced at the home around us then and asked, "What do you mean to do with this place, when everything's done?"

"I aim to keep it, but . . . I'm going back to Ma and Pa's for a while, until after the baby is born," I replied.

"Flaka . . ."

I reached out and placed my hand on his wrist. "I know, Ephraim. Don't you think I know? But I have to do it. It's the only way. And if you want to string me up after it's done, be my guest. I don't have all that much to live for now. He took Oliver from me. The man's a bastard, Ephraim, a coldhearted bastard. There ain't nothing in him worth savin'."

"You think what you're thinking of doing is what Oliver would want?"

"He's dead, so there ain't no way to know. If he were still alive, then he'd have a say in this. But he can't protect his father now he's dead."

Ephraim didn't speak again for a few minutes, then he breathed out a slow sigh. "I'll ride with you, Flaka. I'm just a deputy again now, with the sheriff back on his feet. And I've earned a furlough."

"You're sure?" I asked, staring at him as serious as I'd ever looked at anyone. He was setting out to assist me in doing something that could not be more against the law, the law of man, and the law of God. But he nodded, never flinching, never an ounce of indecision crossing his face. I felt easier then, stronger with Ephraim to help me. But whether he had offered or not would not have changed the decision I had made in that moment. *"With morning woke the will, and cried, 'thou shalt not be the fool of loss.'"*

"I'm sure," replied Ephraim. "It's about time I paid a call on Ma and Pa anyway. It's been too long."

After three busy days of packing and putting everything in order, Ephraim and I headed east. I wore the same garments I'd worn on the road west, the dark pants and the leather jacket that fell past my knees. It was a lot colder then, being late in January, so I did need that jacket. I wore a black wide-brimmed hat on my head, and at my side, under the jacket, I carried the revolver Oliver had used, the pistol his father once gave him, when he was a boy. It felt like everything I wore, everything I saw, everything around me, was a constant, incessant reminder of Oliver.

Before we stepped outside I paused to survey the quiet little *casa* we had fixed up together, the dim early light creeping through the windows, illuminating our sparse furnishings. It felt like the door would burst open at any second and Oliver would be there. Like he had never left me. He had just stepped out. He'd be back any second. I picked up the little book of poetry from the table and stowed it in my jacket pocket.

Just as on our journey west, I rode Butterball, my stolid little pony, who didn't seem to mind the added weight of the child growing inside me. Ephraim rode a tall chestnut gelding, full of vigor and speed that Ephraim was forced to rein in to let Butterball's short legs keep up.

The first place on that journey that gave me pause was just a little way from my home, on the banks of the San Pedro. I stopped, recognizing the place where Oliver and I had consummated our marriage. I stared at the ground for a long time. Ephraim was already across the river when he realized I hadn't followed and stopped, watching me and waiting. There were flashes in my mind of overwhelming memories, of the smell of Oliver, the feel of his skin against mine, the beauty of the moonlight and stars on that perfect night, rolling and writhing in pleasure on the stoney bank of the river.

At last I drew in a shaking breath and turned Butterball across the river, letting the cold water shock me back into wakefulness, into the grim reality where Oliver no longer existed. Ephraim didn't say anything when I joined him on the other side, and I wondered how much he understood.

In about a week we reached Ciudad Juarez. Martha had done alright with the money Oliver had sent. She had set up a new home, a little adobe house just outside the city. The children were in school, and she had finally kicked Javier out. In her new neighborhood she had found employment cooking at a little restaurant. In only a few months her whole life had changed for the better, indeed, it couldn't have changed more, all thanks to my Oliver. When she saw us riding up, her eyes immediately went to my face, and she seemed to understand what had happened without me saying a single word.

Ephraim told her the story. I hadn't the heart to. After hearing it, she came to me and wrapped me in her arms and kissed my face. I couldn't cry anymore, like I said. There weren't no more tears left inside me. I appreciated her love, I felt the warmth of it, but it was a warmth I couldn't understand, a warmth that couldn't enter me. My soul had a shell around it like the plating on a crawdad, and it seemed like nothing could pierce through that armor. I just had to go on. I had to do what needed to be done, and then . . . I hadn't given much thought to what would happen after that. Perhaps I didn't need to. More than likely I'd be dead, along with the baby inside me. I hoped heaven was real, and Oliver would be waiting for me beyond those pearly gates, with that big, easy grin on his face.

The third night after leaving Juarez, Ephraim suggested I play him a tune on my harmonica, and I obliged. After the first few bars of "Beautiful Dreamer," a distant howling began to sound, carried on the wind, the dirgelike moans of coyotes wailing along with the hollow, lonesome tune of my mouth organ. I felt a misting to my eyes, and I tried so hard to conjure up the sound of Oliver's husky voice, the way he had sung months ago. But his voice wasn't there, only the coyotes, and I thought the piercing cry of *un lobo* as well. When at last I stopped and began to pat the harmonica on my thigh, getting the spit out, Ephraim was in tears.

"It always made no sense to me how you could make music so well like that but couldn't read worth a damn," he said, sniffling and smearing his sleeve over his eyes and nose. "We all tried so hard to teach you to read. I know you don't think that, but we did. And it went nowhere. 'Twere like trying to teach a rock to dance."

"Oliver managed to do it where you all failed," I snapped back. "So mayhap you shouldn't have given up on me so quick. He taught me in a few weeks."

"Or perhaps we all laid the groundwork that helped Oliver succeed."

I shook my head and glowered a bit, sinking back onto my bedroll. "You can't take credit for it, Ephraim, none of you can. You gave up on me, everyone in my family, and that piss-poor teacher I had for those two years that I even bothered with goin' to school. You all gave up on me, but Oliver didn't."

He sighed. "Fair, Flaka. We did give up on you. And then some gunslinger from Boston succeeded where we all failed. I don't know why it goes that way. Sometimes people give up too easy, you know." He waited in the quiet, and I took his words as an apology. After a long time he continued, "Flaka, what are you going to do when this is over?"

I lay down, staring up at the sky, an endless black wool blanket spangled with a million tiny lights. A sky I should have enjoyed gazing up at alongside the man I loved. "It won't never be over, Ephraim," I replied. "Never." Then I rolled over and drifted off to a sleep of endless nightmares, the only dreams I ever had anymore.

Nothing had changed in the scant collection of buildings that made up Acantilados since I had left. I had never been one for fooling around in town, preferring the desert and hardworking country folk to all the stuck-up townsfolk with their high-falutin' ways. When we rode in, I got more than a couple surprised stares, with my pants and men's clothes.

We hadn't talked about this part. Ephraim and I had just let it sit between us. We both knew why I was going to Acantilados. We both knew what I had to do, and we both knew it was the right thing to do, no matter how wrong it might look. But now we had made it, and folks were calling out greetings to Ephraim, recognizing him despite all the years that had passed since he last rode through that little town—though no one seemed to recognize me. I didn't know I had changed so much, but I think I had hardened in a way that made me difficult to recognize.

I weren't little Flaka Garcia Hasani no more. She had been a naive child compared to what I had become. She had been open-faced, foolish, trusting, stupid. I was Flaka Garcia Hasani Kedar, and Ian Marcus was about to learn what exactly that meant. I had become something else, something new, driven to become a monster by that hateful man's actions. I would do what I had to do, and go into hiding afterward if I had to. It didn't really matter what happened afterward, as long as the man that killed Oliver no longer drew breath.

"Not to cast doubt on your foresight, little sister," said Ephraim as we completed our ride through the tiny but bustling town and paused on the other end, turning back to survey the twenty-odd buildings that made up Acantilados. "But what exactly is your plan here? We've come, we've made everyone aware of us, and now . . . what?"

"First, I need you to find out if Marcus is in town."

"He is. You must be mighty distracted, Flaka. I asked Mr. Delaney. He said Ian Marcus has been drinking hard at the saloons for the past few months. He's there right now."

I grinned, maybe the first time I'd smiled since Oliver died. "We wait till dark. He'll be leaving town tonight and heading home."

"We're going to ambush him?" Ephraim's face twisted a little as he spoke. I could almost feel the churning of indecision in him. He had come this far, but would he take that final path down that darkest of roads with his little sister?

I smiled at him again, and, though I couldn't see my own face, I felt it was a sad, broken sort of smile. "You don't have to come with me for this, Ephraim. Go visit Ma and Pa."

He shook his head hard. "No, Flaka. This man done slit your husband's throat. And it was my fault he ended up at your home. I'm sure he had his men follow me out there, and then staged that trouble up at Turpenny Mine to draw me away so he could get to you. Then he killed Oliver right in front of you, in the most brutal way imaginable. I've exhausted the reach of the law trying to get justice for what he did. It's like you said, when the law fails us, we've got to take it into our own hands. That's the only real law of the West. I'd die for you, Flaka, and on any given day, I would most assuredly kill for you."

"Thank you," I whispered and turned my gaze to the rocky hills in the distance, where we would find a place to ambush Ian Marcus.

We left our horses stabled in town. Horses on the trail would only draw attention to us, or risk the animals nickering to Marcus' horses and alerting them to our location. The place I had in mind was two miles east of the city where low hills covered by enormous boulders stretched for miles. There was a place along the trail that led to Ian Marcu's spread where high boulders formed a narrow pass. The easiest way home for him was to go through. The pass was too tight for wagons, but horses could make it in single file. The only other option to get around those rocks was to go about six miles out of the way.

We had let ourselves be seen in town that day, but we would go to Ma and Pa's after everything was over and make it seem like we were just visiting. Like we had nothing to do with what happened tonight to Ian Marcus. It did bother me that folks would know Ephraim had been in town, and they would know that Ian Marcus died the day Ephraim showed up. Ephraim had tried to bring legal action against Marcus for months, and perhaps questions would arise. Ephraim was risking everything for me. He was an outlaw right now, same as me, same as my husband had been.

"You really think you should do this, Flaka?" asked Ephraim again as we hiked out toward the stretch of boulders rising from the desert. "Bringing vengeance down on Ian Marcus is just going to make you the same as him, in a way. He chased you across the country to try to kill you, now you're doing the same thing."

"You said earlier that taking justice into your own hands was sometimes the only way you could find justice out here."

"I know, but . . . killing a man is a big thing, a heavy thing. Not something you walk away from. You know that, you killed Grant Marcus. But this here is different. We've ridden all this way hunting a man to kill him. It's premeditated. That's another level. And once it's done, there's a good chance people will eventually figure it out, and you'll become a hunted, wanted woman, all over the West."

I shrugged. "I've already been a hunted, wanted woman. I'm sure, Ephraim, I'm sure. This really ain't the right thing to do. It's not . . ." I swallowed hard and stared down at my trudging feet for a minute before I could continue. "It's not what Oliver would have wanted me to do, but I ain't Oliver, and he's not the one left here mourning his spouse, just a husk of a person without the one they loved. It ain't the right thing, but I have to do it, Ephraim. He has to pay for what he did, for what he took from me."

We waited on a rock that jutted out just a few yards above the path, at the place where the pass was most narrow, as the glowing sun turned fiery red, casting long shadows across the earth. We waited for hours, watching as men who weren't our quarry passed through, not many, but a few. The night ground by, and every minute that passed I felt my gut twisting and tightening till I thought it might explode. After a long while I took out the little book of poetry, the book that felt like a letter left for me by Oliver. I flipped through the pages, looking in the bright moonlight for a passage that would leap out at me, as if Oliver's voice were reading it. Sure enough, there was one. There always was. I remembered him reading this verse as I knitted his skin back together from that terrible wound.

> "A man upon a stall may find,
> And, passing, turn the page that tells
> A grief, then changed to something else,
> Sung by a long-forgotten mind.
> But what of that? My darken'd ways
> Shall ring with music all the same;
> To breathe my loss is more than fame,
> To utter love more sweet than praise."

I thought of the wailing cries of my harmonica in the desert, and the answering mournful *canciones* of the coyotes. Almost it had seemed as if they knew what I was saying in those plaintive wails from that little mouth organ. They too understood loss, they too understood how final it was, and how inescapable. I had said it to Ephraim, that Oliver wouldn't want me to do this. I had spoken aloud that nagging thought that had been flitting on the edges of my mind ever since I'd made the decision to kill Ian Marcus. I thrust those misgivings back down, remembering the child growing within me that would never have the chance to know its father.

I startled from my reverie at the sound of clattering hoofbeats on stone below us. Three men were passing along the path. A cloud had dimmed the moonlight some, but I recognized the careless, hefty slouch of Ian Marcus, and thought my heart stopped for a second.

Ephraim caught my eye, holding a finger to his lips. I slid forward on the rock, careful to move so slowly that no quick change in position would startle the horses below us, or the men. Until that moment I think Ephraim just thought we were going to shoot the men from atop the rocks, that there would be no close fighting. I hadn't really told him my plan; perhaps I hadn't really known my plan until I saw my prey below me. I waited, holding my breath, Oliver's gun loose in my holster, but not drawn. I barely drew breath, watching, my entire body taut and tense, like a guitar string tuned too sharp. Then Ian Marcus, the man who killed my husband, rode below me, and I hurled myself on him.

There were shouts, and shots rang out, the shots of Ephraim dropping the other two men that rode with Ian Marcus, but I barely heard that, lost in a scuffle against a man twice my size. The element of surprise had served me well. Marcus had fallen hard off his horse, with me atop him. The horse reared, squealed and a moment later was just a plume of dust disappearing into the gathering darkness. I heard the thump of Ephraim's feet hitting the ground behind me, and then the thud of fists as he was stopped by one of Marcus' bloody men who hadn't died yet, though he was wounded.

I punched hard and fast, my fists flying, but Marcus quickly overpowered me, rolling over and straddling me, taking my wrists in his massive hands and pinning me to the ground. I wriggled to free myself, fighting for all I was worth, realizing that I might not win this battle. But at least then I'd be dead and joined with my Oliver. Marcus released one of my hands to reach for a weapon, and that was my opportunity. I lunged upward, punching at his groin with my one free hand and biting at his face like a wild animal. He startled and recoiled in pain from the blow to his nethers, and that gave me the second I needed to struggle out from under him and begin to scramble to my feet. He grabbed my leg, yanking me back down, striking me repeatedly as I kicked at his face and hands.

Then he let go and I saw him reach for his pistol again, and I grabbed for mine, but Ephraim was there, slamming into Marcus, punching him with hard, quick thrusts, sending his revolver flying. I jumped to my feet as my brother beat the living daylights out of the man. Marcus' men lay dead, and it was now almost fully dark, *la luna* obscured by clouds, only the glittering of the stars illuminating the night around us. At last Marcus lay still beneath Ephraim's fists, stunned into motionlessness, though still semiconscious.

"Tie his hands with his belt," I said, my own voice startling me in the darkness. Ephraim, his face streaming with blood from a wound somewhere under his scalp, looked at me for a second in surprise, but then he obliged.

Then Ian Marcus was on his knees before me, sweating and covered in blood, blood dripping from the corner of his mouth where his lips were swelling and turning dark from bruising. I stepped forward, holding my revolver, and Ephraim drew back a little, his eyes darting around nervously. I stalked slowly around Ian in a circle, like a mountain lion toying with a disabled deer.

"You," Marcus spat out. "Filthy little Mexican whore. All this is your fault, Grant's death, and Oliver's. All your fault. Their deaths weren't enough? You want to kill the entire family now?"

"I never wanted to kill anyone, Ian, until you murdered

my husband. You slit his throat in cold blood. Lost any sleep over that?"

Marcus' lip curled in contempt. I struck him across the face with the pistol, feeling a rush of pleasure with that blow, a tingling in my hand and a spinning, buzzy sensation in my head. "Oliver lied to you, to protect me," I said. "I killed Grant Marcus, because your son was threatening me in my own home. I killed him in self-defense. And you chased me all across two damn countries, and when you finally had me, you killed your own son instead of me. You are a ruthless, worthless, cruel, spiteful old man."

"I don't think you'll do it," sneered Marcus. "You kill me and the entire territory will come looking for you. Ephraim will lose his position as deputy. Yes, Ephraim, I know it's you, the man who was *so* helpful when I was in Tombstone. Not only will he lose his job, but he'll go to jail, most likely hang, for being an accomplice to murder. But you're not the type to kill, Flaka. You're a preacher's daughter. A good, stupid girl who made a mistake and married a wicked gunslinger."

Again I struck him hard across the face, and this time the warm tingle of pleasure ran all the way up my arm, into my neck, into the base of my skull. It felt good, like life coursing through me, like power. Power over someone who had once had complete power over me, power over someone who would kill me without a second thought. I stepped forward and grabbed a hunk of that old man's thinning, graying red hair, yanking his head back and bringing my pistol to his nose, stabbing the barrel into his nostril the way he had done to my Oliver. Still he sneered at me, his lip curling up, mocking me, daring me to do more, daring me to go all the way.

Ephraim spoke then, his voice soft and soothing. "Flaka, are you sure you want to do this?"

I looked up at my brother, but I didn't see him there. I saw Oliver, standing in the darkness, looking at me. My husband wasn't wearing his habitual smile, his face was sad, his eyes were sad. I saw him and I wanted him more than I ever had before, more than anything in the world. I wanted my husband back. I felt a sob rising in my throat, but I squelched it into nothingness, a boggy heaviness settled in my chest and my eyes misted with unshed tears.

I could hear his voice too, his husky, low voice, the way he had spoken to me so many weeks ago in the desert. "So, what I'm saying is, I've made my peace with killing to defend myself and to defend the ones I love. I haven't made peace with killing the way Ian Marcus does, hunting a man or a woman for weeks or months for revenge. Brutalizing them when the opportunity arises, losing all sight of everything, losing all sense, living for murder. There's no justification for that, and there's no peace that can be made with that sort of killing. Nor, despite what Marcus thinks, is there any peace to be found in vengeance."

They were all looking at me, the taunting face of Ian Marcus, Ephraim's serious, calm expression, and my husband's mournful countenance. They were all looking at me, to see what I would do, what choice the gunslinger's widow would make, the woman whose fault it was that Oliver Kedar was dead. Even the cloud moved from in front of the moon to let its pale gray face peer down at me, and the stars seemed to grow brighter, all waiting for me.

Then Ian Marcus began to laugh as my hold on him relaxed a little. A cruel, mad laugh. I took a step back, releasing his head.

"Flaka," he said, his voice mocking. He spat blood and a tooth out of his mouth as he said my name again. "Flaka. What the hell kind of name is Flaka anyway?"

I drew myself up, as tall as I could stand, silhouetted above him against the black velvet sky, and I replied, "Flaka means fire, you son of a bitch," and then I blew Ian Marcus' brains out.

EPILOGUE

"Fuck," said Ephraim softly in the darkness. The narrow pass still seemed to echo with the sound of my pistol shot, though several minutes had already gone by. Ephraim dabbed at the blood on his face drizzling from his scalp. He was staring down at the mess that remained of Ian Marcus, blood and brains and fragments of skull spewed all around us. "You alright?"

"I surely am," I replied, my voice hoarse and dry. I glanced around, looking for Oliver, who I had seen so clearly a few moments before, but he was gone. I sighed. Perhaps I would have preferred to die than to kill Ian Marcus, to die and be with my Oliver. But this was the best I could do. Ian Marcus was dead, my husband was avenged, and now . . . the part of the *la historia* I hadn't spent any time thinking about, the part where I didn't know what was going to happen, had begun.

"Should we try to hide the bodies?" asked Ephraim.

"Just take whatever money they have. People will think it was robbers," I replied, feeling dull and numb and sick, like a person who wasn't supposed to be on this side of eternity but through some stupid mix-up had ended up here.

Ephraim nodded and I heard him rifling about in Ian's pockets before moving to the other men. The horses were long gone. Whatever had been in their saddlebags would be of no use to us. After a while he left the bodies and returned to me. I was still standing over Ian Marcus, fighting the urge to shoot him again and again and again. I had felt such a rush of life when I blew his brains out, a feeling of absolute triumph, and I wondered if putting more holes in his corpse would make me feel it again. Probably not. Once that thrilling second had passed I was left drained and empty. I had had only one purpose since I had awoken again to life after the loss of my husband, and now that purpose was gone.

"Ephraim," I whispered.

"What is it?"

"You were right. Oliver wouldn't have wanted me to do that. It really wasn't the right thing to do, despite what I said. But . . . I didn't do it for Oliver. I did it for me. For me." My voice broke, and then I felt my brother's arms around me, embracing me as I sobbed into his shoulder. I sobbed until I couldn't anymore, until there were no more tears to shed. There was nothing left, just the broken shell of what had once been a woman.

"It's alright, Flaka. The world's a better place without Ian Marcus in it. You've done a service for all of Texas, though it don't feel that way yet," said Ephraim, his voice low and soothing. He rubbed my back as I trembled.

"But I . . . I killed a man, another man, and now . . . I don't know what else to do. These past few weeks, that need to kill him was the only thing that I was stayin' alive for, waking up for, drinking water for, eating for, breathing for. The only reason I was going on. What now, Ephraim? I don't know what I should do."

Ephraim took my face in his hands, peering deep into my eyes. "Flaka, listen to me, listen. You're expecting, and you've still got a family, Ma and Pa, and me, and Martha, and Rachel, and you've got your dear friend Susanna. You've still got a lot of reasons to go on livin'. After all this, after everything, you have to keep going. Someday, maybe, I can't promise it, but someday, I do think that all this will hurt less than it does now. Your baby will need you to raise it, to tell it what kind of a man its father was."

But I wasn't listening. I sank down to my knees in that narrow pass between the boulders, sobbing again, and nothing Ephraim said could pull me from my agony. I put my head on the ground, squelching in the still-wet gore of Ian Marcus' mind, and I wept and called the name of my beloved. I didn't know how to go on. I didn't know why to go on. I think I had the vaguest notion of turning my pistol on my own head, but that passed after a while, and after a while Ephraim helped me to my feet, still whispering dull but hollow words of comfort as we walked together back toward Acantilados.

Hours later, cleaned up in the little hotel in town where we had stabled our horses, Ephraim opened my book and I heard him reading as I lay numb upon my bed. And as he read I thought it was Oliver's voice that began to speak. I held still, listening to that little book, the book that I had thought before was just a tale of someone else's sorrow but now I knew had always been a prophecy of my own.

> "Thy voice is on the rolling air;
> I hear thee where the waters run;
> Thou standest in the rising sun,
> And in the setting thou art fair.
> What art thou then? I cannot guess;
> But tho' I seem in star and flower
> To feel thee some diffusive power,
> I do not therefore love thee less:
> My love involves the love before;
> My love is vaster passion now;

> Tho' mix'd with God and Nature thou,
> I seem to love thee more and more.
> Far off thou art, but ever nigh;
> I have thee still, and I rejoice;
> I prosper, circled with thy voice;
> I shall not lose thee tho' I die."

Time moves on relentlessly, no matter how heavy the grief of those it marches past. I rose the next morning and was dressed before Ephraim awoke. I saw myself in the room's mirror as I waited for my brother. The face in that looking glass wasn't the face of Flaka Garcia Hasani but of Flaka Garcia Hasani Kedar. I saw what I had become, and who I was, a strong, fierce, proud woman. A woman who could read and write. A woman who could shoot straight as any gunslinger or trick shooter. A woman with a child growing inside her, a child who would be just as strong as its mother was and just as brave as its father had been.

Ephraim awakened with a start, looking at me in bewilderment, like he didn't recognize me for a second. I must've changed overnight, I think, growing up from that foolish, stupid girl that had been sitting slack-jawed on her parents' porch in August when a fine-looking specimen of a man walked into her life. I wasn't that girl anymore. I was someone else, and I was ready.

"We'll go visit Ma and Pa, like we said. I think I'll stay there until I have the baby, as I planned before, so Ma can help me. But then I'm going home," I said.

"Back to Arizona?"

I nodded. "That's my home, the home Oliver bought for us, the home where we meant to raise our family."

"You know, we might be found out, and people might come after us still, even years from now."

"I know, Ephraim. I know."

He dressed and packed up our few belongings and we set

out across the desert, toward the place our parents waited. The dimness of the world had lessened in the night, and I felt the first tinge of movement in my abdomen as we rode, the first real sign that something alive was growing within me. The words from the little book, the love letter that Oliver had left behind with me, along with the love letter he had left in my womb, flickered into my mind.

> "I hold it true, whate'er befall;
> I feel it when I sorrow most;
> 'Tis better to have loved and lost
> Than never to have loved at all."

THE END

A NOTE FROM THE AUTHOR

Dear reader,

Thank you so much for taking the time to read Flake's story. I cannot express how grateful I am for your attention and support. If you have time, please consider leaving a review on Amazon, Goodreads, or Storygraph, or wherever you purchased this book. For an independent author, your honest reviews make an immense difference in reaching other readers that might enjoy this work.

In gratitude and solidarity,
A.M. Vergara

ACKNOWLEDGMENTS

I would not have been able to write this book without the love and support of my husband, Eric. Furthermore I owe a great debt to my parents, who instilled in me from my earliest days a love of the great outdoors, old westerns, and reading. I am also deeply grateful to my many siblings for all their support in my writing journey.

I must specially recognize my beta readers who identified many places where Flaka's story could be improved and brought them to my attention. Special thanks as well to the members of my Wednesday writing group, particularly Natalie and Anne-Sophie, as well as Sarah and Anna. They are an inspiration to keep going every week. PurpleEggHead, who also served as a beta reader for this work and has been my long-time writing buddy, provided an incredible amount of encouragement and I cannot thank her enough for that.

The historical sources for this book were legion, including many online resources, primary documents from the time period, as well as the work of Candy Moulton, *Everyday Life in the Wild West*. Inspiration came from many incredible works including books like *True Grit*, *Lonesome Dove*, *Shane*, and many others.

I must also acknowledge the quotes of some of the greatest masters of prose in history, Alfred Lord Tennyson, Dante Alighieri, Stephen Foster, and William Shakespeare. The works of these giants—authors whose skill with words I could never aspire to—serve as such immense inspiration to me.

This work would be riddled with extraneous commas, misspellings, and grammatical errors without the assistance of Eliza Dee, my incredible editor. I must also thank Ergi Pasho who provided meticulous Albanian translation of the phrases spoken by Jozef Hasani. Special thanks to the designer of my cover S. J. Hosken, and to Matthew Buchanan and Ravven who created the stock images used for it. As always, I deeply appreciate Casey White for her typography. For my author portrait I would like to give a huge thanks to Erika Saguran.

Thank you all for believing in me, supporting me, encouraging me, and making it possible for me to tell this story.

ALSO BY A. M. VERGARA

Legend tells of a city of gold on a phantom island. The wealth of that city could end the American Revolution. But the only person who knows the island's location is the world's deadliest assassin. And he's not giving up that secret without a fight . . .

"Original, deftly crafted, riveting, and a fun read from start to finish." ~Midwest Book Review

———

As the British and French fight over the Great Lakes Territory, three reluctant allies must join forces in a desperate attempt to save all that they hold dear.

"A delightful read, telling of great courage, immense fortitude, and familial love that crosses warring factions." ~Readers' Favorite.

ABOUT THE AUTHOR

A.M. Vergara is a physician associate and paramedic. When not writing and reading voraciously, she can be found working her day jobs in the hospital or on the ambulance, or out in the woods, camping, hiking, foraging for edible mushrooms, field herping, riding her mule, or playing her banjo.